The Kindred

Rachel James

CRIMSON
ROMANCE
Avon, Massachusetts

This edition published by
Crimson Romance
an imprint of F+W Media, Inc.
10151 Carver Road, Suite 200
Blue Ash, Ohio 45242

www.crimsonromance.com

Dedication

This book is dedicated to Sheila, Fran, Ellie, Lois and M.J. Our friendships have stood the test of time. Romance, adventure, successes and setbacks. We've shared it all and we're still here. And best of all, our story's not over yet. There are still many more pages to turn.

Acknowledgments

My heartfelt thanks go to Jennifer Lawler, Imprint Manager, Crimson Press. Her unwavering dedication to publishing the best of the best when it comes to love and romance is awe-inspiring; and thanks for all the kind words you sent my way during the course of getting this book published.

My undying gratitude goes to Julie Sturgeon for her keen editing eye and savvy insights. She has proved that when the time is right, kindred spirits always find and connect with each other. Thanks, Julie, this book is a thousand times better because of you!

Special thanks to the Tuesday Night Writing Workshop, especially Michael, Mary Kay, Sheila, Sherry and Bob. Your never-ending enthusiasm for this book (and my writing) has enriched my life in more ways that I can count.

A special shout-out goes to Dan and Carole Duckworth who made theater come alive in my heart six nights a week, plus two matinees on the weekends.

Lastly, to the detectives at the Jupiter Police Department (you know who you are), thank you for showing me for fifteen years that heroes and heroines *do* exist outside the printed page. Your commitment, integrity, and willingness to put your life on the line day in and day out for total strangers, is a shining example of what every hero should be.

Chapter 1

A shadow of alarm touched Janice Kelly's face, and she stepped back from the three-legged easel, tossing her paintbrush into a jar of cloudy water. The painting before her had changed background colors again. On its own. No, she brought herself up sharply. Paintings did not change colors by themselves. She had done it. She had changed the colors. She let her gaze travel across the now bright yellow background, struggling with the uncertainty it aroused. Had her divorce from Jimmy finally sent her mind over the edge? If so, this mind-fugue was dangerous. She might hurt someone. She might hurt Sarah. Horrified, she raised a hand to her temple. Damn! If she weren't careful, she'd work herself into a full-blown migraine.

Unaware of the streaks of brightly colored paint she was dabbing into her flaming red hair, she rubbed the sore spot vigorously. This was no regular headache she was battling. That's why the pills she'd taken this morning had done nothing to quiet it. No, she'd experienced this kind of pain before, and she knew what it meant. Now, more than ever, she could not put off her trip to Maine tomorrow. She had to go and not just for the debt she owed to her mentor.

Fingers trailing down her temples, she strode back to the easel and began to pack up her paints. She needed sleep desperately—the dead-to-the-world kind. She had been on a five-state gallery tour for months, skipping meals, signing autographs and hopping trains. And now, just when she got home, she was leaving again. No wonder her face had looked pale and pinched when she woke this morning. She was so tired her nerves throbbed. "Mama, what's a Si-Pip?"

Janice jumped at the sound of the high-pitched voice and quickly brought her gaze from the paints to the open doorway. Her eyes lit with pleasure as she spied her daughter, Sarah, bouncing from foot to foot in the middle of the alcove.

"Sarah, sweetie, I don't think I know that word. Where did you hear it?"

"From Aunt Bibi." She bounded through the doorway and sailed onto a cushioned workbench beside Janice. Once there, she eyed the huge canvas. "Is that my Daddy, Mama?"

Janice grinned, amused.

"No, sweetie, I don't know who the man is."

"Aunt Bibi told Uncle Roddy he's your dream lover."

Janice's grin vanished, replaced by a quick frown.

"I've asked you not to spy on your aunt and uncle, Sarah, remember?"

"Uh-huh." She tucked her feet beneath her rump and tipped her face to Janice. "Who is he, Mama?"

Her persistence brought Janice's focus back to the painting, and she let her gaze sweep the dove gray breeches and matching topcoat. An absolutely gorgeous rake. And her sister was right. She was becoming enamored with the handsome figure she had painted, seemed inexplicably drawn to him.

"Mama?"

"He's just a man I've been seeing in a dream, sweetie."

"He's handsome."

"Yes, he is. Devilishly handsome."

"Is he as devilish as me?"

The question was cheeky, and Janice chuckled, tweaking one of Sarah's bright red curls. Sarah was an adorable poppet, no doubt about it. She took a moment to study the snow-blasted cheeks as Sarah began to riffle through her paints.

"Aunt Bibi says you're a Si-Pip, Mama."

Janice lightly smacked the prying fingers and gave a sarcastic laugh.

"Little pitchers have big ears."

"What's that mean, Mama?"

"Nothing, sweetie. C'mere."

Dropping to the workbench, Janice opened her arms and wiggled her fingers. She must divert Sarah's attention from the tubes of paint. Sarah toppled forward and sprawled across her legs eagerly. One hand flew beneath her cheek to wait patiently for an answer to her earlier question. But which question? Janice wondered. A contented sigh singed her ears, and Janice gave another bright laugh, tickling the round belly peeping between the folds of the yellow flannel jogging suit. Sarah squirmed and giggled, their hands entwining.

"Stop, Mama . . . you know that tickles."

"But you have such a yummy laugh, I can't help myself." Janice cooed. She slid her fingers along Sarah's tummy again, eliciting more spontaneous giggles.

"Stop . . . Mama . . . please!"

Hearing a serious hiccup, Janice stilled her fingers and, with a swift tug, righted Sarah to a sitting position in her lap. She dropped a quick kiss on her warm cheek and gave her a light bear-hug. Sarah's face sobered, and Janice knew her attention was back again on getting answers to her questions.

"What *is* a Si-Pip?"

"Psychic. The word is psychic. I'm a psychic."

She saw the flash of alertness in the eyes studying her face.

"What's a Si-Kick?"

"It's a person who can see things before they happen, see things that are way off in the future."

"Like the gip . . . gip-sies who look into the ball? "

Janice craned her head thoughtfully.

"Umm . . . more like a television set. I see pictures in my head, sweetie, kinda like our television set downstairs. The pictures can be funny, sad, scary . . . "

"Mon-sters?"

Janice smiled, once again brushing back a stray curl along Sarah's temple.

"No, no monsters. At least not the kind you mean."

"Does the television set hurt your head?"

"Why no, sweetie, what makes you think it does?"

"Aunt Bibi's gettin' you some ass . . . ass-prin from the drawer. She says your head aches."

Janice rolled her eyes.

"Bless your Aunt Bibi."

She gave Sarah's cheek another brief kiss then slid her back onto the padded bench. Rising, Janice returned to the portrait and picked up her paintbrush. Why did she feel compelled to embellish on the yellow hue when the painting was already quite perfect? She didn't know, but found herself less than a minute later ignoring the mocking voice inside and dressing up the background with a few flourishes of her brush. Beside her, she heard a light humming and joined in. It was marvelous the way she could tune into Sarah's boundless energy. Recharge from it. Without warning, the sound of spit bubbles began to mingle with their humming.

"Pa-tew . . . pa-tew."

Janice looked over in amusement.

"Whatever are you doing, you silly bear?"

"I'm spittin'."

"I can see that. But why?"

"Aunt Bibi says I'm the spittin' image of you, Mama."

A choking laugh bubbled out before Janice could stop it. What a delightful ragamuffin she and Jimmy had produced. And so infinitely precious. Yet her sister's comment was true. She and Sarah were unmistakably related. She swished her paintbrush into the water jar, stealing a peek at the appealing face now displaying Janice's own familiar signs of thoughtfulness. Their faces were identical delicately carved facial bones, both blessed with the Mignon family trait of a full-bodied lower lip.

Scanning the young features, Janice sensed the face so pink with eagerness at the moment would eventually showcase high, exotic cheekbones like her own. As for their hair, Sarah's was bright red, too, but not quite so crackling red as her own. She decided they were as alike as two peas in a pod—except for the eyes. Sarah had extraordinary blue eyes, as blue as the Aspen summer sky, while her own eyes gleamed emerald, like deep green ice.

There was another difference between them. But as of yet Janice couldn't bring herself to discuss it with anyone, not even her sister. She knew without question Sarah did not possess second sight. She would hold no psychic tremors in the coming years. And that relieved Janice immensely. Not that she would have changed things for herself. But she was glad Sarah's carefree nature would not be hindered, her eyes lose their sparkle when carrying the weight of the gift.

She looked at those eyes now, twinkling with untold mischief, and she heard the giggle, unmistakably Sarah's own. Responding, Janice made a sudden dive for the workbench. Sarah screeched in delight and vaulted from the bench. She hit the floor running, and Janice marveled at her fleet-footedness. Was she raising a future track and field star? Perhaps not, since in the next instant Sarah collided with a pair of long, tanned legs. Janice's sister, Bibi, glass in hand, reared back to absorb the unexpected impact, and Janice heard her call out sharply.

"Hey, slow down! I'm carrying a full glass."

Sarah's giggles echoed louder as she grabbed Bibi's knees, using the tall, sturdy body as a shield.

"Mama's gonna tickle me, Aunt Bibi. Don't let her."

"Have you been teasing her while she's painting, you naughty munchkin?" She attempted to shake Sarah loose of her leg, but the motion only managed to slosh water over the rim of the glass. Seeing the juggling act, Janice sank onto the workbench in convulsive laughter. Across the space, Bibi prodded Sarah more sternly.

"Sarah Anne Kelly, you let go of my leg this instant! Your

mother and I need to talk. Go help Peter out of his snowsuit this minute." She gave a last shake of her leg, and Janice heard her say even more sharply, "Go!"

Janice caught a brief flash of yellow as Sarah bounded out on the landing and tripped down the hallway. Her sing-song call to Peter echoed back gaily.

"Come out, come out, wherever you are."

Bibi entered the loft, her face finally turning up in the smile she'd fought from showing.

"She's a sunny little thing, Jan. She reminds me a lot of Anna sometimes."

Janice propped herself on the bench, swiping at her eyes.

"Anna?"

Her sister came forward, offering Janice the glass of water plus two aspirin tablets in her palm.

"Oh, she's you through and through, but she has a tiny little imp inside her that jumps out every now and again. Like Anna."

Janice took the tablets and glass with a nod and tossing the tablets to the back of her tongue, she swallowed them down quickly. Wiping her mouth, she handed the glass back with a sigh.

"Her temperament resembles Anna's, too. She accepts things so easily. She pouts but never frets."

"Or throws a nasty temper tantrum like you know who."

A bemused smile trembled on Janice's lips.

"Peter has his good qualities, Bibi."

"Yes, he does." Her voice became tender, almost a murmur. "I'm lucky to have him, aren't I? Dr. Walsh said I wouldn't carry to term, being the old broad I am. But I proved him wrong."

"Dr. Walsh meant well, Bibi. Truly. Having your first baby in your forties is risky. Of course, he didn't know you as well as I do. There was never any doubt of miscarriage."

At her words, Bibi spun around and plunked the half-empty glass onto the worktable behind her.

"I hate it when you go all psychic on me, Jan. You know I have no defense against your damn second sight."

"Does my being a psychic bother you after all these years?"

"Hell, no. I'd love you if you had two heads and fourteen arms. And as for your psychic powers, they awe me." She broke off abruptly, and Janice saw her lift a photo frame from the worktable. "Lord, Jan, I didn't know you still had this photo."

Janice dipped her head.

"Ummm, next to Sarah, it's my most treasured possession."

Bibi caressed the glass, and Janice heard a wistful sigh.

"God, we were a trio back then, weren't we? How old was Anna?"

"Thirteen."

"That's right. I remember now." She raised her chin, and Janice saw a faraway glaze cloud her eyes. "You were a funny little twit then, Jan. You'd stand in the corner of your crib and stare and stare at Anna, who couldn't help crying out in pain while Mama forced her lifeless legs to exercise. You'd stare as if sending her some kind of healing thought. And she'd be better. No one could see it outwardly, but I could. I knew you were gifted and special even back then."

Janice crinkled up her face, determined not to cry. She hated that she always got teary-eyed when reminiscing about Anna.

"I don't seem to remember that time clearly, Bibi." she remarked. "Sometimes it seems so important that I do."

Bibi replaced the photo quickly and moved away from the table.

"Hell, you were only Sarah's age at the time—three or four—how could you? But you'd stand by her bed. And she'd be better . . . no, I swear it! Mama didn't believe it, of course. She never believed anything she couldn't taste, touch, or see."

"Now, that I DO remember. " Janice replied, sliding to the edge of the bench and hoisting herself up. Moving back to the easel, she ran a finger across the canvas. Was there now a hint of red streaks clogging the pores? She felt a warm presence beside her.

"You've changed the painting again, Jan. I like what you've done."

"Do you?"

"Yes, don't you?"

"I don't know. I don't remember repainting it."

Distressed, Janice turned from the canvas. She wasn't going to breakdown and blubber. Not over a stupid painting.

"You're scaring me, Jan."

She whirled back at the sound of her sister's stricken tones.

"I'm being stupid. I'm sure I made the changes to the painting. I just don't remember doing it."

"That's exactly why you should cancel this trip to Maine tomorrow. You're burned out, and this memory lapse proves it. Why don't you let me call Lloyd and tell him you're too exhausted to attend this seminar?"

"Because I gave Lloyd my word I'd be there. I can't renege now. I'll be back in four days and rest then. Besides, Sarah and I have plans."

"That's why she's a giggling idiot."

"She's the dearest, most precious thing in the world and don't you dare criticize her!" Bibi grinned broadly at her, causing Janice to let out a long, audible breath. "When I come back, I'm going to stay put for a very long time. Enjoy Sarah's company." She reached out her hand to Bibi, who took it readily. "I don't know what I would have done if you hadn't been there after Jimmy walked out on us."

Bibi flushed, and for once Janice realized she had caught her sister completely off-guard.

"Hell, Jan, I'd walk through fire for you and Sarah."

She would too, Janice knew, through hell and back again. They exchanged warm smiles.

"Hearing her constant giggles thrills me, Bibi. She's such a silly little bear, happy and alive."

"And she teases you on purpose. She certainly knows which buttons to push on you." Bibi's face sobered again. "Anyone interesting going to be at this big seminar in Maine?"

Janice crinkled her nose.

"Well, let's see . . . there's Lloyd."

"I said interesting. Not stuffy."

"Lloyd's not stuffy . . . he's . . ." She gave a smart ass little grin. " . . . intellectually stimulating."

"Forget the intellectual stimulation." Bibi responded. "You need a red-blooded male with active sperm to stimulate you physically."

"Bibi!"

"Don't sound so shocked! I know you didn't find Sarah in a cabbage patch. You've had your share of blissful nights beneath a man."

Janice felt a warm rush steal across her cheeks and knew she was blushing.

"What's got into you today, Bibi? Have you been reading those naughty romantic novels again for pointers?"

"Nope. I got Roddy. He's all the outside stimulation I need. You want to get rid of your headache, Jan? Make love. Does the trick every time."

Janice gave a hearty laugh, amused by her sister's foolish banter.

"Sex with a stranger is dangerous these days."

"Damn! You're right. Guess your only hope *is* aspirin." They broke into shared laughter again until Bibi prodded. "Go on. Who else will be at the seminar?"

"Jasper and Muriel Grisomb. She did the television series *Dream Robbers* a few seasons back. Her husband is a Lutheran minister."

"Ummm . . . go on."

"Adrian Magus . . . "

"Aaahhh!" Bibi's squeal was ear-splitting as she bolted upright on the bench. "You can't mean that gorgeous hunk Roddy and I saw perform in Las Vegas last year?"

"Yep." Janice dropped alongside her, gesturing for her to scoot over. "Was he as good as you said he was . . . as the papers say he is?"

Bibi shifted on the bench, and Janice saw her expression

grow wistful.

"Are you kidding? He was incredible. And lord, what a bod! "

Janice took a swipe at Bibi who ducked.

"Will you stop already! If anyone's hormones need adjusting, it's yours!"

Laughing, Bibi hoisted herself up from the bench and struck a dramatic pose. Grinding her hips, she ran her fingers suggestively over her body.

"Well, if you don't *ska-rew* that gorgeous hunk, danger or no danger . . . " Janice snickered loudly. Bibi would never change. She would always be outrageously outrageous. At her snicker, Bibi dropped her pose. "Don't think he won't ask. That red hair of yours is like a magnetic flame. One look and they burn!"

"Burn out, you mean."

Disgusted, Bibi took a swat at her arm.

"Don't joke. I mean it. You need a man, Jan. Sarah needs a father."

"She has a father."

"Balderdash! I mean a father, not an asshole."

"Bibi!" Janice's voice turned brittle.

"All right, alright! I won't harp on Jimmy."

"Thank you."

"Peter's ready, Aunt Bibi."

The shrill voice held a rasp of excitement, and both women turned simultaneously. An astonished shriek rent the air as Bibi bolted to her feet. Janice's hand flew to her mouth, attempting to stem a ripple of laughter as she spotted her near-naked nephew poised in the doorway, clinging to Sarah's hand.

"Sarah Anne Kelly!" Her sister flew across the space, and with a swift tug, scooped Peter up from the carpet and rubbed his goose-caked arms. "Stop laughing, Jan. It's not funny. You know how delicate Peter is."

Janice made an effort to contain her laughter by sitting upright. She knew Bibi was right. Peter's health was fragile. However, one look at Sarah's impish face, and she found herself dissolving into laughter again. Sarah joined in, all girlish giggle. Swiftly, she sailed in through the doorway and pounced onto the bench into Janice's arms. Together, they studied Bibi, who Janice saw was alternating between keeping a straight face and trying to look outraged. Finally, she tore into the dimpling pair.

"You are naughty, Sarah Anne Kelly. Just like your mother." She caught Janice's eye. "And I hope you get snowed in at Carrington House with no one to make love to!" Janice's laughter pealed again, and she began tickling the flesh wrapped in her arms. "Jan?" She looked up quickly. "Seriously, Jan, have you remembered to pack everything? Anna's compass?"

Janice tilted Sarah and reached into her slack pocket. Withdrawing the small object, she held it up for Bibi's inspection.

"Never leave home without it."

Bibi nodded, clucked to the bundle in her arms once, and disappeared into the hall landing. Watching her go, Janice felt a tremendous surge of pride well within her. Bibi was right. She had been blessed. Only Bibi didn't realize that she, Roddy, and Peter were the blessing. Feeling grasping fingers on hers, Janice released the compass into Sarah's tiny palm.

"What's this for, Mama?"

She peered down at the small face intently studying the arrow wheel pointing to a big red "N."

"It helps people who go away to come back safe and sound."

Sarah mulled that thought over for a few seconds, and then to Janice's surprise, she bent her tousled head and kissed the plastic face. Janice reached out and brushed through a stray curl, touched by the gesture. Sarah had such an innocent abandon about her. She envied her that innocence. Cradling her closer, she placed her cheek atop Sarah's head.

"I'll be back in four days, sweetie. And then we'll go to Hollow Lake."

"And you'll teach me to skate, Mama, right?"

"That's right."

"When I grow up I'm gonna be the bestest skater in the ekopades."

"Escapades."

"Ess-ca-pades." Sarah mimicked, snuggling closer. A moment later, Janice heard a warm sigh and craned her head to view Sarah's face. She was dozing already, eyes closed, her lips tilted at the corners. Janice began to rock her gently. Four days and she'd be back. Four days and she'd teach Sarah to skate. She gave a long, exhausted sigh and began to hum one of Sarah's favorite ditties lightly. Four days. Not so long.

She felt a ripple along her left temple and lifted her gaze to the painting. Was there another change of colors? No, not this time. The breeches and topcoat were still surrounded by a yellow flecked background. She looked away hastily. She was tired and distracted and had repainted the background without thinking. That was all there was to it. Nothing mysterious, nothing abnormal. Still . . . her gaze swept back to the easel and she chewed on her lower lip thoughtfully. If there was nothing mysterious going on, why hadn't her gift of premonition set off in its usual way? Why all of a sudden had her gift chosen to be secretive, leaving her to feel as if she were the proverbial Alice about to tumble headfirst into the looking glass? She didn't know, and not knowing could mean only one thing. She wasn't going to like what was coming one little bit.

Chapter 2

THURSDAY—10 AM—LAS VEGAS, NEVADA

Sensually attired in pure white, his skin-tight pants and shirt fringed with colorful light-catching spangles, Adrian Magus lost his concentration and stepped from the glare of a center stage spotlight. His movement brought the ongoing rehearsal to a grinding halt. The orchestra continued for a few more bars then labored to a stilted halt as they finally noticed the motionless group on stage. The house lights drifted up slowly and there was a silence as the crew waited for a sign.

Center stage, Adrian lifted long tapered fingers to his forehead and rubbed vigorously. Blasted headache! Down in the theater seating area, he heard his best friend and daily tennis partner, Todd Landis, call out loudly.

"Take ten, everyone."

The crew scattered, spilling off the stage in half-groups, obviously thankful for the break. Grateful himself, Adrian waved his thanks to Todd. He stood a moment more, running his hands through his jet-black hair, massaging his scalp from crown to nape. The act of juggling reality and illusion twenty-four hours a day was exacting a toll, he could see. Lately, like just then, and in odd moments of his performance, he was besieged with an uncanny sense of displacement. As if his on stage life were the reality, and his offstage life were the illusion.

Disturbed by that thought, he gave a sardonic grin and lowered his tall, athletic frame onto a bulky set piece. He dropped his face into his hands and sighed deeply. What was happening to him? Was he about to split in two, giving birth to some new and preposterous schizoid personality? He heard the quiet thud of shoe heels across the stage floor and soon saw the tip of white penny loafers. He raised his head to see Todd's craggy face wreathed in smiles.

"You've got to learn to pace yourself better, Adrian, old buddy. You can't keep living life as if you're white-water rafting and you'll never have to face the white water. Lay back some. Rest on your laurels."

"I can't. The hype is what makes my act a sell-out each and every performance."

"Man, oh man, who do you think you're talking to? What makes you so great is your ability to hide from anyone and everyone that you have extraordinary psychic powers."

"If I'm so good at it, how do you know it?"

"Elementary, old buddy. I've worked this strip for twenty years. Seen magicians good and bad come and go. Now, granted Siegfried and Roy had an illusion with a tiger I couldn't fathom—never will, I daresay. But you? I can't fathom *any* of your illusions, nary a one. And you know what? Neither can those who participate in it with you."

"It's just a case of the hand is quicker than the eye."

"Don't give me that rot. We've been friends too long for you to pull the old pea under the shell routine on me like some back street carney. You're different. Special. And I know it." He reached out and shoved a dangling spangle on Adrian's shirtsleeve. "And hiding behind all this tinsel crap don't mean that what you got ain't there."

"It's there. I just have to channel it properly."

"And lately it's getter harder to channel?"

"Something like that. Some days it's hard to separate the illusions from the reality."

"It's all in the perception. You taught me that. One man's fantasy is another man's reality. Follow your own advice or you'll space out, or burn up, or do whatever it is you gifted people do when you're in trouble."

That was easier said than done, Adrian knew, since Todd didn't know about the dream. Only Captain Jesuit knew, and Captain Jesuit was long dead. Yet nightly, more and more, Adrian felt his quick-silver mind insist on reverting back to when life was less complicated and his only worry was learning the identity of the red-headed woman whose face danced in his head. He felt a bump as Todd lowered his beefy frame down and Adrian shifted to make room for him on the block. He heard a wistful wheeze.

"How long we been friends, Adrian?"

Adrian shrugged.

"Fourteen years."

"That long?"

"We're pushing forty," Adrian mocked him.

Todd grunted.

"Next you'll be spouting I'm older than you."

Adrian laughed in spite of the thin hammering in his head.

"Feeling a little long in the tooth today, are we?" he teased.

"No, just waxing philosophic."

"You need more filler in your diet." Adrian retorted.

Todd snapped his head around, chuckling.

"I thought I was supposed to be the comedian here."

Adrian rubbed his forehead vigorously again. Todd noticed the motion and bumped his knee against Adrian's.

"Perhaps you should call off this performance in Maine, Adrian. It can't be that important. Besides, the weather is damn dismal this time of year up there, and your audience sounds like something out of fruitcake land."

For the first time that day, Adrian felt himself fire up, a welcome response. He couldn't be losing his mind if the blood in his veins could pulse with hot anger. His eyes, black as volcanic rock, impaled Todd.

"Before they make *you* a saint . . . "

"Geez!" Todd interrupted, throwing up a hand. "Don't start using that viperous tongue of yours on me. This is Todd you're talking to. I know you don't give a rat's ass what I think of a group of psychics holing up in a research center in the dead of winter, but why do you have to subject nice Ginger to the indignity?"

"I can't take the whole show and she's willing to go."

"Can't the other guests fill in? By the way, who are the other guests?"

Adrian couldn't help his grin.

"The list is about as interesting as a washing machine manual, so I won't bore you."

"That must mean you're sorry you agreed to go."

"Not sorry. Bitter. But I have a debt to repay Lloyd Marks from Iraq."

They both fell silent and Adrian enjoyed the moment. The pain in his head was finally lessening. If only there were soothing fingers to massage the rest of his aches away. If only he could hear the sound of a certain woman's laugh, smell her freshness, feel a rounded belly . . . he felt a sharp bump against his shoulder and forced himself back to reality.

"You ever sorry you and Katie didn't have kids?"

Adrian snapped his head around. That was uncanny. Yes, he had been thinking of children just then, but not with Katie. His eyes met Todd's and then dropped. He heard Todd's soulful sigh.

"Yeah, me, too. " He looked away, out over the row of tables, to the back of the theater and Adrian sensed his next thoughts. "I go into the lounge there sometimes and purposely stand next to a woman——any woman. Just to revel in the smell of her. Dammit, Adrian, I want a home, family, a woman to slap fondly on the buttocks. I want to press every inch of her body to mine. Not these teeny boppers who cram the stage doors, their tits . . . by the way, I like Ginger's tits."

"Good. I'll tell them."

Todd snorted, his chest heaving.

"You're as screwed up as a Chinese fire drill, Adrian, old buddy. I bet if I asked you to describe Ginger's breasts this minute, you couldn't do it." Adrian flushed. "I thought so. She's just a front to keep those teenage nymphos from slipping their fingers into those skin-tight pants you pour yourself into every performance."

"Are we attempting one of our rare excursions into humor now?" Adrian sarcastically countered.

Placing a hand on Adrian's shoulder, Todd hauled himself up. "We all have headaches, old buddy."

"Those of us who have heads," Adrian remarked.

Todd snickered this time, slipping his hands inside his pants pockets. "You 'bout ready to go again?"

Adrian stood, nodding. His headache had all but evaporated. "Tell Andy we'll take it from Sylvia's entrance."

Todd left him then, hurrying toward the orchestra pit. Once there, he leaned over and Adrian saw him tap Andy's shoulder and then dust off his hands. Seconds later, he was vaulting the stage steps two at a time. Passing the lounging theater crew, he gestured impatiently. They scrambled up at once, resuming their former positions before the break.

Center stage once again, Adrian waited for the house lights to dim. He started to readjust his pants, then caught himself, remembering Todd's earlier taunt. He muttered a fierce curse under his breath then reversed his thoughts just as quickly. Dammit, but he did enjoy being called a sexy hunk. He enjoyed being the current darling of the circuit immensely. And dammit, he was even enjoying his brief fling as Ginger O'Toole's current lover. It didn't matter they had never slept together and never would. They shared satisfying kisses and enjoyed heavy petting sessions. Their arrangement worked. If it ain't broke . . . yet, Todd was right. He was screwed up, but he had reason to be, didn't he? The dream had resurfaced again, and he couldn't push it away. Couldn't push *her* image away.

He heard the tap of Andy's baton tap in the pit and the spotlight snapped on. Wincing under the blinding ray, Adrian forced his mind to shift gears. The music tapered in and he set his shoulders confidently, raised his hands, and watched as the house lights dimmed to black.

Standing in the bright white light, his mind slipping away from reality, Adrian tried to imagine the shape and feel of Ginger's breasts. Were they round? Firm? Supple? Todd was right. He didn't know.

Chapter 3

THURSDAY—10 AM—MADSEN, OHIO

The fiery, red Subaru ground its gears, rounded one curve of the church parking lot, and barreled out the driveway and down the steep incline of Chrysler Hill. Reaching the bottom of the incline, it sailed through the intersection, ignoring the blaring horns and the four-way stop signs posted.

Hearing the squeal of brakes, Reverend Jasper Grisomb eased his rangy-rugged frame back into the cool church interior. He shut the church doors firmly. Agatha Pryor was the devil incarnate when seated behind a steering wheel. Shortly, there would be no less than five irate phone calls to the parish house, imploring him to convince Agatha to give up driving once and for all and hire a chauffeur. He shook his head in amusement. He'd talk to her of course. Like always. And she'd listen attentively. Like always. And then? A slight smile tinged the corners of his mouth. Like always, out of sight, out of mind—she'd revert to driving any way she damn well pleased. God help him, he hoped when he reached senility, someone would have the good sense to chain him to his rocker. His mouth broke into a broad grin, and he chuckled for the first time that morning. Muriel. Muriel would chain him down—with barbed wire, most likely. Muriel. Her name seemed to dance in his head.

Turning slowly, he let his eyes adjust to the dimly lit alcove and the surrounding pews. Instinctively, he knew she was there, though as yet he couldn't perceive her through the dim shadows. And then, like a room suddenly flooded with light, his mind connected with hers. Just as quickly, he jerked his mind away. As he always did— would always do. It had been an unspoken vow between them from the first, when as teens they had discovered they both possessed uncanny psychic ability. Only in his case, he carried the heavier burden of the gift. He was a master of mental telepathy and excelled in precognition. It was an ability that sky-rocketed his mind almost daily through myriad abrupt mood swings. He could read minds, easily, effortlessly, as a gentle breeze stirs a blade of grass. But it was refraining from it that constantly sapped his energy and strained his nerves. It was tricky to stay out of people's minds, but in the last years, he had forced himself to do so out of self-preservation.

Flinching, he rubbed his forehead vigorously. Of course, since the headache had come, his precognition had been blocked in all ways. He didn't understand why, or what caused it, but a small part of him felt immense relief. For the first time since he was ten, he had absolutely no idea what tomorrow would bring. For him. For Muriel. For the children. He enjoyed the emptiness a moment longer, then heard a discreet cough and glanced up.

Halfway down the aisle, Muriel sat decked out in her Sunday paisley dress with matching brimmed hat. She was staring his way, a burst of sunlight outlining her gentle face. God, he loved that face. Small, oval, moderately wrinkled, with sparkling blue eyes and genial mouth. Even if now at the age of seventy her once trim shape had meta-morphasized into overly plump, he didn't care. She was his Muree, and he loved her. With a devotion so fierce it scared and overwhelmed him at times.

Jasper strode down the aisle with a light whistle. She was the lighthouse beacon in the worst of his storms—a home away from lashing wind and rain. Reaching her side, he bent and planted a brief kiss on her lips. She gave a delightful laugh and made room for him in the pew.

"Was that Agatha I heard leaving skid marks on our parking lot pavement again?"

"Who else?"

They both laughed in unison. Jasper pulled his collar free and stole a peek at Muriel's face.

"How's the headache?" he asked.

"Subsided about an hour ago." She returned his stare. "Yours?"

"Finally subsiding." His gaze found the pulpit stand. "Funny, though, I'm still having trouble concentrating. My energy is diffused and unfocused. It's an odd feeling." He swung his gaze back to Muriel. "I don't ever remember feeling this way before."

Jasper heard her sigh as she turned her gaze to the colored windows opposite them.

"We've shared a lot of things the last thirty-five years, Jasper, but I don't remember us ever sharing a headache." Her gaze found him again. "Strange as it is, I don't sense any negative vibrations, do you?"

Jasper shook his head.

"No, I don't sense fear of any kind."

Muriel took his hand and squeezed it lightly.

"I called Dr. Wharton. Asked if it was possible the headache is an unexpected side effect of my stroke. He was adamant in his denial."

Jasper grasped the fingers entwined over his.

"Called you a damn fool, no doubt. Probably even told you to take two aspirins and call him in the morning."

Her bright laugh reverberated through the stillness, pleasing him. He loved the sound of Muree's laughter. It was warm and enchanting.

"Indeed. Exactly so," she bantered. They broke into another bout of laughter and then fell silent. Jasper was the first to share his thoughts.

"We can cancel the trip, Muree, if you're not up to it."

She swung around, her gaze challenging his.

"Cancel? Whatever for? You know we've both been anxiously awaiting this trip."

Jasper swung his gaze away and, like her before him, studied the full stained glass etching of the Virgin Mary.

"Perhaps it's too soon for you to travel after your illness. Sometimes headaches are warning signs."

"Jasper Grisomb!" He heard the censure in her voice and flushed.

"I have spent the last six months climbing up and down Chrysler Hill. You never once objected to that. Almost shoved me out the church door yourself. And now you're worrying that I'm not well enough to ride for a couple of hours in an airplane?" She gave a sharp sniff. "This is really too aggravating of you! You know how I hate being coddled and fussed over. I wouldn't let the children do it in the hospital, and I certainly won't let you do it to me now!"

"Hold on, Muree, no need to get so lathered up." Jasper cautioned, "I only meant it's your first big trip since the stroke . . ." He broke off, touching his forehead again. "Actually, it isn't you I'm worried about at all. It's not being able to see whether we should go. I've always been able to tap in and get some sense of what might happen. I'm totally baffled. And if the truth be known, it unhinges me not to be in control."

He felt a gentle touch on his brow, felt warm fingers probing gently, brushing through his scruffy locks.

"That smacks of vainglorious pride, my dear."

"Indeed, it certainly does. Right up my alley, to my way of thinking."

They laughed simultaneously and then, patting his hand, Muriel signaled for him to rise. He stood, extricating himself from the pew, and then turning, helped Muriel to slip from the long bench. Once out in the aisle, he shrugged out of his long robe and handed it over to Muriel.

"I understand Adrian Magus is quite a showman, Muree."

"Extremely handsome too, from the picture I've seen in the trade papers."

"Well, if it comes to that, Janice Kelly is quite a knock-out in that department."

"Indeed? And how would you know? I don't remember seeing her picture on the front page of the New York papers."

"Caught a fragment of her once."

"You never said so before."

"Didn't seem important before. Besides, my head was

aching at the time."

Muriel reached out and plucked at his shirt collar.

"If the headaches don't subside, we'll call Dr. Wharton when we return."

"Good idea."

"Now, how about we go straighten up the vestibule?" Muriel urged. She offered him his robe. "Though Sam has promised to look in while we're away, I don't want to overburden him with responsibilities."

Jasper took the robe and bent over, giving Muriel a feathery nuzzle on her neck.

"I love you, Muree. Did I tell you that today?"

"Not even once." she scolded lightly. "And, indeed, I think it pretty shabby of you to forget."

Jasper dipped his head in a mock salute, then stretching his arm across the back of Muriel's left shoulder, he prodded her forward. As one, they made their way up the aisle and into vestibule, slamming the door behind them. A second later, a swirl of lights hit the closing door and bounced upward. A second after that, the stained glass window of the Virgin Mary rattled loudly and drained of all its color.

Chapter 4

THURSDAY—10 AM—MACEDONIA, MAINE

It took only a moment for the smell of jasmine to penetrate Lloyd's nose. He looked up from the check he was writing and surveyed the room behind him. There it was again. That sickly sweet smell of jasmine. He twisted further in his chair, his eyes casing the dimly lit shadows at the base of the ceiling. For three days straight, the smell had come and gone, sending the house staff through an annoying game of hide and seek. His housekeeper had tried to remain nonplussed by the search, but now she was nervous and crabby, and who could blame her? He was on edge himself. Houseguests were arriving in a matter of hours and tempers were flaring in the kitchens at the smallest of inconveniences.

Pushing back his chair, Lloyd arched his back. He was tired. So tired that he had given himself a headache again. He slammed shut the ledger in front of him and pulled his six-foot frame to its full height. No more pencil pushing tonight. He arched his shoulders, eliciting small cracks along the tired joints, and then sighing, he removed his reading glasses from his nose and flipped them to the desk. Jesus! He was learning to hate the smell of jasmine! He sniffed the air again and almost gagged. It was all around him, seeping into his pores, making him want to puke.

Forcing down the rising bile, Lloyd turned from the desk, urgently needing a fresh spot of air. He found it in the warmth of the blazing fireplace. Taking a deep breath, he inhaled the aroma of burning wood chips and was grateful to have a different tang of air invading his lungs. Exhaling, he caught sight of himself in the mantle-piece mirror, and his mind tripped ahead one day. How would his houseguests find him? Handsome? Time-worn? A bright mockery invaded his smile as he listened to his own thoughts. The others be damned! How would Janice find him? Would she still think of him as only a tried-and-true mentor? Or could he make her see him differently just for once?

Lloyd's eyes sought the framed photo displayed with special prominence on the otherwise barren mantle-piece. Janice Kelly had blossomed considerably since her university days. He smiled at the current photograph. It profiled a woman of extraordinary beauty—high cheekbones, red hair, green eyes, a tempting full bodied lower lip—just right for kissing.

Lloyd pushed that disturbing thought away with a growl, deeming himself an old fart trying to hold on too long to his vanished youth. He let his gaze rest again on his own reflection. Was he still attractive at sixty-two? He tried to assess himself through a feminine eye. His massive shoulders still filled the coats he wore. There were age lines around his mouth and eyes, but he thought they added strength to his character. His hair still held its bulk, texture, and color. An Iowa cornfield, Janice had deemed it once during one of their late night sessions. His jaw line was strong, forehead broad, mouth generous. He didn't smile enough, of course. But then, the weight of running a seven-acre retreat nine months of the year didn't leave him much time for smiling.

Lloyd bent to stoke the glowing embers, and again, the smell of jasmine invaded his nose. Damn! He shooed the air around him and straightened, feeling the first stirring of real pain along his temples. This goddamn smell was nauseating! He'd stress to his housekeeper the importance of using a strong air freshener before she left for the weekend.

Above him, lights snapped on, and Lloyd winced in surprise. Spinning, he saw the object of his thoughts scowling at him from the doorway. Standing in repose, Dora always reminded him of a cartoon character lost in folds of fat and fabric. He saw she was wearing the pink and white frilled apron that housed gigantic, bottomless pockets. Lloyd could already see her unspoken censure forming so he threw up a hand in protest and moved toward her.

"No need to look so disapproving, Dora. I haven't been standing in the dark for long."

He heard her tell-tale snuffle.

"I should hope not!" She met him half way, offering a glass and two aspirin tablets. "Here, take these!"

Grateful, Lloyd took the glass and tossed the tablets down.

"Have you become a mind reader in the last weeks, Dora? Perhaps I should have you tested along with the others."

She sniffed disdainfully. A sniff that sounded to Lloyd like some large, aberrant animal wheezing.

"As if I'd let you poke around inside my head with all that magic drivel! Don't care to know what's rattling around in my head. Don't care to have other folks knowing it either!"

Lloyd handed the glass back, marveling at its skillful disappearance into the folds of one large pocket. He pushed by her, settling in his desk chair once more.

"You're eminently sensible, Dora. It's far and away your best quality."

She took a chair beside him, a noticeable creak emanating as she sat.

"Waste not, want not. That's my motto." She pulled a notepad from her other miraculous pocket and grinned at him.

"You're a terrible snob, Dora," he stated.

"Yes, sir. Proud of it."

Lloyd let the remark slide and turned to retrieve his own typewritten sheet.

"Everything ready downstairs?"

"All taken care of and the solarium's been arranged as Mr. Magus requested. His boxes arrived this morning."

"Good." Lloyd brushed at his temple. "I expect one hell of a show here next week, Dora. We spare no expense. No shortchanging the bed sheets." At the half-censure, Lloyd expected to hear one of her haughty sniffs but it never came. He stole a peek at her out of the corner of his eye. Her face was relaxed; she was listening to him attentively. "Have we a final guest tally?" he asked.

"Five for the weekend, twenty-two starting Tuesday. I'll return with the staff Sunday afternoon to finish up the room arrangements." Dora stiffened suddenly. "There's that obnoxious smell again." She lumbered from her chair and approached the terrace doorway. Once there, she flung the latch back and began to fan the air repeatedly. "This room reeks of lilac and dead frogs."

Lloyd scanned the room, his gaze coming to rest on Dora's rigid figure.

"It's jasmine, Dora, remember? We've been smelling the stench for three days."

"Well, it's obnoxious nevertheless." She fanned the air again. "Shall I send Giles up to investigate?"

"Don't bother. By the time he comes, the smell will have evaporated."

"But suppose the guests should smell it?"

"Suppose they should." Lloyd commented. He rose, seizing her elbow and propelling her to the doorway. "It's not so bad. I'm actually becoming used to it." He saw her look of repugnance and groaned. He never could tell a lie well. She was seeing right through him and he detested her for it. "Will you stop being a scaly prig and make one last check of the bed sheets?"

Taken back by his attack on her person, Dora pulled her elbow from his grasp and barreled out the doorway with a final sniff. Lloyd cringed inwardly again. That sniff said it all. He was dead meat. Well, at last he knew what that infantile phrase meant. He heard the door slam and released a long drawn-out sigh. Yes sir, he was dead meat. And all because of a damn sickly sweet smell and an overworked nasal passage.

Whirling about, he caught a whiff of clean, fresh air. No jasmine! Gone! Vanished, just as he predicted. He sought his pipe on the desk. And if the smell returned? Let it! He'd not be here to endure it. He had guests arriving over the next four days and all of his time would be spent getting them settled and seeing to their needs.

Stoking his pipe, Lloyd dropped into a turquoise recliner and shifted its angle more in line with the blazing fireplace. Leaning forward, he lit his pipe from a glowing remnant of ash and then settled back. At last his nose was clearing and the room was livable again. His eyes gravitated to the top of the mantle-piece and he laid his head back, studying the photograph. She was still there, smiling at him. He felt the hammering in his head begin to ease. He closed his eyes and let his mind drift. A vivid image of words began to dance in his head. He transported himself to an alpha state and once there, he could almost hear Janice's lyrical voice offering inspiration.

Cherish yesterday. Dream tomorrow. Embrace today.

Chapter 5

FRIDAY—3:30 PM

Squaring her shoulders, Janice inhaled deeply. The cold ocean spray splashing against her skin was invigorating—just what her tired, screaming muscles craved after a long day of traveling. She clutched the handrail, jostling her feet along the wooden deck and smothering a groan. If she didn't erase the numbness that threatened to invade her lower limbs soon, she'd reach Carrington House curled into a tiny ball fast asleep atop the orange crates stacked nearby.

Pensively, she shifted her gaze to an orange life jacket hanging along the forward rail. ANNIE B. The words were bold, but fading. Her glance skimmed left. The ANNIE B seemed a sturdy vessel, trim and seaworthy as her bow coasted through the crested waves with a graceful rhythm. To the out-islanders cut off from the mainland, Janice surmised, the ferry would be a welcome lifeline, serving as postal, passenger and delivery ferry.

Jamming her hands into her pockets to ward off a blast of icy wind, Janice let her gaze drift to the horizon ahead. In the distance, the rooftop turrets of Carrington House were no longer mere silhouettes on the horizon. They were now towering peaks, inching closer by the minute. Studying them, Janice gave an unexpected shudder. Now, what was that for? she wondered. Her brain signaled a primitive warning. *Déjà vu.* Stuff and nonsense, she chided her inner voice, but the nagging refused to be stilled. *Déjà vu, Janice, déjà vu.* She glanced ahead again. Was there a vague familiarity about the twin peaks?

Overhead, the sky let loose with a somber rumble and Janice's gaze shot upward. Now, what was that all about? Patches of light scurried in a series of alternating patterns through the clouds and she felt her breath catch in her lungs. Lightning storms in winter? She studied the light patterns more closely, enjoying the sporadic activity until a sudden rush of perplexing emotions sent her pulses racing.

Gripping the handrail for support, she fought to control the swirling emotions. For a brief instance, the world around her darkened, faded, then came back. Instincts kicking in, she stepped back from the rail and sought cover. She had almost tapped in. What had prevented her from doing so? Damn! She hated storms. They played havoc with her brainwaves, overloading and confusing her thoughts.

Seeking cover beneath a canvas roofing, Janice perched atop a packing crate filled with the zesty smell of lemons and oranges. She folded her arms across her chest and decided not to budge until the storm had run its course. Not even for Lloyd would she defy her intuition and stay out in the open. Her intuition was always right. And right now, it was warning her to be on the alert.

Smoke assailed her nostrils and Janice turned to find the ANNIE B's captain studying the skyline with the same odd wariness in his eyes.

"It be powerful strange to see lightning in winter, lass."

"Powerful strange." Janice agreed, her gaze gravitating to the skyline with renewed interest. Seeing no ominous flutters, she brought her attention back to the man who had stopped alongside her. She had liked Captain Bowers on sight. Calloused hands, massive oarsman shoulders, thick sandy hair, fulsome red beard, he was the very picture of a ferryboat captain. She especially liked his deep, tobacco-roughened voice flavored with a light Scottish brogue. Obviously feeling her stare, he turned from his contemplation of the sky.

"Would'na thought you'd be part of the party going to Spook House, lass."

"Spook House?"

"Aye." He gestured with a firm, direct nod that Janice felt told a lot about him. "Leastways, that's what folks 'round here calls her."

Janice's lips snaked to a smile.

"Is the chateau haunted, Captain?"

"Some say she be, back when she were Witchwood."

"Witchwood?"

"Aye, lass. She be fancy Carrington House today, but she wasn't always so respectable." A merry twinkle appeared in his eye and his laughter was a full, hearty sound. His broad wink at her was mischievous. "The waters hereabouts used to be filled with pirates, lass. Cutthroats they was. Luring ships to their doom. Ramming them up against shoreline reefs."

Janice's eyes widened in astonishment, yet in spite of herself, she chuckled. She was sure Captain Bowers relished telling this tale to strangers. She was also sure if one searched his family tree, they'd uncover a pirate of their own.

A sharp bolt of lightning sprayed the sky, causing both of them to wince at the ripple.

"That no be pirates, lass." Captain Bowers commented. "That be spirits. They be signaling from the sky to leave them alone. They no want to be disturbed."

Janice managed to hide a choking laugh.

"Are you trying to frighten me, Captain?"

"Sure thing, lass. Them that spooks the spirits pays, don't ye know. One way or t'other."

Janice met his gaze and her response was heartfelt.

"I promise I won't spook any spirits while I'm here, Captain."

"I believe you, lass." His thoughtful gaze scoured her face. "You be pretty to look at with that red hair—if'n you don't mind my sayin' so."

"I don't mind, Captain."

"They say them that has bright red hair has the temper to match, but I think it no be true in your case, lass. You be comfortin'—if'n you don't mind my sayin' so."

Janice still didn't mind and found herself telling him so. A deep chuckle greeted her.

"Ye be different from the other ones, lass."

"Other ones?"

"Brought them over a whiles back, I did. Four of 'em. They be powerful different from each other. The tall one, he be fierce handsome—some s'lebrity, he is. Stood where you be sittin'. Watches the sky, he does. Don't say nothin', mind ye, just watches. Fairly gave me the creeps it did. The pretty one with 'im, she tries to chat 'im up, but he no be listenin'. Leastways, he no be listening to outside folks. I think he be listenin' to inside his head. It be an eerie crossing, 'im speaking to spooks and all."

Janice offered no comment. She wondered what Captain Bowers would say if she revealed she herself had almost "spaced out" moments ago. Was it a trait common to most psychics? She must remember to ask one of the others if they had had a similar occurrence on the crossing.

"Now, the other ones be right pleasant," Captain Bowers continued. "T'were a couple, him big, her small. Like a China doll he treats her, fussin' over her, worryin' whether she be warm or not. She laughs at 'im. Prettiest sound I heered in a long time. 'Minded me of Hattie—she be my missus—fore'n she died that is. They be right ones all right." he concluded. "Tipped me plenty, they did. Didn't have to—no sir—but they did. They no be snobbish like some others I could name." He gave a distinctive snort Janice could only conclude was meant to single out the master of the chateau that now lay only yards away.

A last ripple of lightning showered the sky, outlining the mansion atop the cliffs as well as the human shape pacing the landing dock below with long, purposeful strides. Even at a distance and after the long, passing years, Janice recognized Lloyd's lithe form. Tall, straight and supple, his long legs resembled a vibrant engine in motion. From her perch beneath the overhang, she could just make out the outline of smoke rings drifting around his head, intermingling with his cold intakes of breath. She gave a faint smile. Lloyd still hadn't managed to kick his cigarette addiction after all these years.

"I'll say goodbye to ye now, lass, and wish ye luck." Captain Bowers tipped his cap respectfully and shot her one last admiring glance. "Don't envy ye stayin', though. Me scalp fairly prickles with electricity. Somethin's up."

Janice nodded sympathetically, watching as he traversed the companionway and disappeared down the stairwell. She knew exactly how he was feeling. Her own arms were caked with goose bumps beneath the warm, plain leather coat she wore. And it wasn't from the winter cold. Her senses fairly sang with electricity. The spirits *were* spooked. She gave a wide smile. It had been a long time since she imagined the spirit world as a living thing. Not since Anna.

Soon, the creak of rope against wood echoed and the ferry made a faint lurch. Slipping from the crate, Janice headed for the stairwell. Once on the lower level, she zig-zagged her way between two cars, then stopped alongside Captain Bowers who was unfastening the latch of a chain link gate. She quickly slipped him a tip and then her gaze met Lloyd's across the space. He greeted her with a brief lift of his hand. She called out playfully to him.

"What an entrance, Lloyd! Did you arrange the fireworks especially for me?"

His rumbling laugh came floating back and he pitched his cigarette tip into the churning water beneath the bow. Stepping forward, he reached out and grabbed her hand.

"Quite a display, huh?"

Squeezing his fingers, Janice jumped across the tiny chasm to his side. As she landed, he spun her around for a careful inspection.

"You look terrific, Jan. But I knew you would."

She executed a graceful curtsy at his compliment.

"You haven't changed a bit either, Lloyd. You're still telling lies to young women."

"Well, you certainly fit that bill. You've hardly aged since the university."

A deep foghorn blast belched loudly, claiming their attention and showering the air above their heads with cinder smoke. Diving away, both waved, catching sight of Captain Bowers' massive frame outlined in the pillbox window of the wheelhouse. Another short blast bellowed and the ANNIE B slipped from the dock, churning sand, water, and sludge.

Lloyd bent and retrieved her standing suitcase and signaled her forward. He called above the engine whine.

"Stairway is just ahead."

She nodded, falling into an easy stride alongside him, and tucking her hands deep into her coat pockets to ward off the icy breeze still kicking up. Lloyd's stride increased alongside her.

"Saw your *Stellar* painting in the New York gallery last week, Jan. Super stuff."

"Sales are strong."

"That doesn't please you?"

"Oh, the timing's bad, nothing more. I've been on the road for months with the collection. Now it seems it's going to start again. I don't want to go. I've been away from Sarah too long. I miss her."

"How is the little tyke? Watch your step. These first steps up are tricky."

Janice gave him her hand and soon they were ascending a short spiky stairway. Rounding a sharp incline, the stairway finally widened and they fell into matching strides again. Janice picked up the threads of conversation.

"Sarah's fine, Lloyd, a happy little thing. Never seems to let things get her down. Physically, she's my mirror-image."

"And psychically?"

"No. She doesn't possess the gift."

"Does that disappoint you?"

"Heavens, no. I'm thrilled for her. She won't have to . . . My God, Lloyd!" The soft gasp had escaped Janice's lips before she could contain it. They had reached the top of the stairway and were now staring at an ocean front masterpiece clinging to the rise of cliff walls. "You can't mean all this is yours?"

Her gaze swept the main edifice before her. The house was a

masterful blend of Old World architectural craftsmanship. Hearing Lloyd's chuckle, Janice gave a gargled croak. Never in her wildest dreams had she imagined such grandeur. Carrington House was simply magnificent. So versatile and dramatic in design. She craned her head upward and blinked. The walls, made of light pink stucco, seemed to be endless. Up and up, they stretched. Five stories? Janice tried to count and found her body swaying. She brought her gaze back to ground level. Beside her, Lloyd's soft voice urged.

"It is overwhelming at first, isn't it?"

Janice threw him a sharp glance. Who was he kidding? It was cataclysmic. She had never expected such wealth and splendor. Again, her gaze scanned the numerous windows and skylights dominating the architecture. How could one describe a corner of heaven? No words were adequate. Luckily, she managed a foolish stammer.

"It's fabulous."

Lloyd's features became animated.

"I can't wait for you to see its true grandeur though, Jan." He pointed to their right and Janice saw more walls and skylights. "The old wing," he offered, "was built by a young French baron in the 1700s." Taking her elbow lightly, Lloyd prodded her forward. "Though I've refurbished the chateau completely over the last years, I've never been able to bring myself to touch the old wing. It carries too much history, I guess. Too many priceless antiques."

"Witchwood?" Janice said, half-to-herself.

Lloyd's head whipped around.

"Now, where in the hell did you hear that name?"

"Captain Bowers. He told me some lurid tale of pirates and sunken ships. Is it true?"

"Ghosts and goblins, you mean? Spook House?"

Janice nodded.

"Conjecture only. None of us here have ever felt a presence or been given a sign."

Janice transferred her gaze from Lloyd to the cobblestone

walkway they were now traversing. Ahead, she could hear the sound of tinkling chimes.

"But as psychics, Lloyd, we can't discount the existence of the other side. Too many of us have experienced unexplainable visions throughout our lives. Speaking for myself, I know there is a spirit world. I have tapped into it on odd occasions. I know you have, too." She slanted a peek at Lloyd's thoughtful features.

"Believe me, Jan, we'd know if a ghost were haunting our halls," he finally stated. "There's too much psychic energy channeled here for a spirit to go unnoticed."

"You'll get no argument from me on that, Lloyd. Still, sometimes, we really can't see the forest for the trees, can we?"

Lloyd's face broke into a wolfish grin as they reached the main door and he switched her suitcase to his other hand. Turning the doorknob, he pulled open the door and signaled her inside.

"We're entering the house through the lower atrium." His hand arced upward as she stepped inside. "The atrium is the place to be for the teens. Pool, music. Lots of those techy gadgets they love."

"Nothing for techy adults?" Janice teased, glancing around.

"No, I have something better." He picked up their stride, crossing the rec room to an outer hallway and heading toward an elaborate staircase housed in the middle of the house. He paused for a moment at the bottom of the steps. "First floor holds dining rooms, sitting rooms, parlors of all kinds. Second floor has ballrooms, music rooms, an art gallery, and solarium. That's where Adrian is scheduled to perform, by the way. I think you will find him highly entertaining."

"So I hear. My sister saw him perform in Vegas last year. She talked about nothing else for weeks."

"The trade papers have dubbed him the darling of Las Vegas, but I think heavy is the head that wears that crown," Lloyd stated.

"Amen." Janice said, giving a sudden shiver. Seeing it, Lloyd commented.

"You'll get used to the chill in the hallways, Jan. We all did.

Trust me, your sleeping quarters are comfy and warm."

Janice gave a grateful nod. She was feeling a strange chill all of a sudden, but she didn't think it was from the cold air in the halls. Something . . . someone . . . damn! Why did she keep thinking that someone was involved in shaking up her senses?

Fifteen steps later, they had reached the new landing and entered a mammoth art gallery filled with elegant but understated paintings and furnishings. Lloyd set down her suitcase and signaled to the far side of the room.

"Over there, Jan. I've saved the best for last." He pointed to a wall painting a few yards from where they stood and Janice found her curiosity bubbling over. It was sweet of Lloyd to remember she was partial to historical paintings. And by the look of things, he had inherited a magnificent set of portraits when he had purchased the chateau. Stopping at the second portrait she came to, she could almost feel the artist's brush strokes saturating the canvas.

"Do you know who they all are, Lloyd?" she asked, scanning the masculine face outlined. He came to stand alongside her, studying the painting as well.

"They are the past masters of Witchwood and their families." He pointed to a painting down the way again. "Come meet Baron Aubert Dumas."

Janice found herself following eagerly. It had been a long time since enjoying a painting just for the sake of art, and if the paintings in front of her were any indication of the ones to come, she was in for a treat. A moment later, standing in front of a gorgeous oil painting, her heart did a gigantic flip-flop. Good Lord, it was him! The rake from her oil painting! He stood looking out at her, an exquisitely handsome man with the same dark eyes and devastating smile, yet in this painting, his dress was richer. Janice immediately sensed he had a monopoly on virility, knew it, and enjoyed flaunting it. She could feel his masculine charm clear to the tips of her toes.

"My God, Lloyd, I know this man. I have been painting his portrait for weeks. He's Baron Dumas?"

"Yes. He built the chateau as a wedding present for his bride, the Princess Lisette Fantine."

Janice's gaze scoured the surrounding paintings. Which lady had captured such an exquisite man's heart? She scanned the female faces assembled and couldn't imagine the handsome baron drawn to any of them. They were overstuffed, overdressed, pampered dowagers, not one under the age of forty. All too quickly, she let her imagination run wild. The baron had lost his heart to a wild, sultry vixen who had kissed him hungrily and welcomed him into her body. A sharp nudge to her ribcage brought Janice back to earth.

"She's over there." Lloyd pointed to a section of wall further down the gallery. Janice sped away, eager to have her imaginings confirmed. When she laid eyes on the face and figure captured in oil, she gave an enraptured sigh. Now, this was a woman made to lie beneath a naked male torso. *Janice Kelly, whatever possessed you to think such a starkly sexual thought?* It must be the damn lightning, she silently answered. It had short-circuited her brain waves, shoring up her libido. Or was it the sight of the woman with flaming red hair to equal her own that made her senses tingle? Janice studied the hair. Shade for shade, they were a match. But there the similarity ended. Lisette had a slim wild beauty, with jutting breasts and narrow waist. Her wedgewood blue eyes glowed with an inner excitement, as if she had recently been thoroughly and magnificently kissed. *Brother, Janice,* she admonished herself, *you've got sex on the brain and it's all Bibi's fault!* She started it with her infernal teasing about making love with perfectly total strangers.

Janice turned away from the portrait annoyed that her senses could be shaken so readily by a mere look at an oil painting. She found Lloyd studying her face. They shared a smile.

"Quite a beauty, eh?"

"Ravishing," Janice agreed.

She saw Lloyd cast a wistful glance at the portrait.

"Wish I knew more about her. I can't seem to find any reference to her in the old wing library. She reminds me a little of you, Janice."

"Balderdash, as Bibi would say. We're as different as night and day——except for the hair."

"I don't know." Lloyd shook his head. "She has something I can't put a name to."

"I can. It's called chemistry, the sexual kind." Lloyd's laugh was buoyant and seeing his honest enjoyment of her remark, Janice wondered why he didn't laugh more. When he did, the lines in his face vanished, making him appear years younger. Responding with a wicked smile of her own, Janice linked her arm through his and, together, they retrieved her suitcase and exited the gallery door to the next staircase.

"Tell me about the other guests, Lloyd. What made you decide to bring us all together?"

He shrugged and Janice thought he didn't intend to give her an answer, but as they climbed, he seemed to think better of his silence.

"Actually, I wanted to do it several years ago but couldn't work out the scheduling."

"Just as well. I couldn't have come."

"Neither could Adrian or Muriel. He was knee deep in ugly divorce headlines and her television series was in the top ten . . . here we are." He broke off, taking the last two steps at a leap. As before, Janice found herself in a newly decorated floor of the chateau, this one more contemporary in design. Beneath the overhang of the double arcing staircase, two doors beckoned.

"Your suites are here to the left, Jan. Adrian's there on the right, and Ginger is in the middle."

"Ginger?"

"Adrian's assistant. Although, between us, I think she's more his girlfriend than assistant. Pretty thing."

Janice gave another wicked smile. She ignored the distinctive click that sounded in her head. A torrid love affair going on right beneath their very noses! Just like olden times, wives, husbands, mistresses . . . light questing kisses, rough aggressive kisses . . . bodies surrendering to overheated senses . . . her thoughts derailed to find Lloyd staring at her with a questioning glance. She came back to reality immediately.

"Sorry, I spaced out, didn't I?"

"It's okay," he nodded "This place is a psychic's dream. Stimulates the senses and the libido."

Janice had the grace to blush.

"I suddenly felt a strong sense of yin and yang."

"We've all felt it at one time, Jan."

"And you said there were no ghosts here, Lloyd?"

"There aren't. Just strands of time to tap into and relive. But only in our heads. So don't go having any foolish, romantic notions and start searching for secret passageways."

"I'll be discretion itself, I promise. Where are the Grisombs staying?"

Lloyd swung around, gesturing to a pair of twin stairways down the corridor.

"The West wing is a half floor up. My suite of rooms is there as well."

"And above that?" Janice craned her head, able to view the decorative ceiling at last. It appeared to end within another two floors.

"More sitting rooms, a bona-fide chapel, an indoor palatial roof garden. This way, Jan." She felt a tug on her arm and followed.

Janice gave a squeal of delight at the sight of the bright yellow room. Lloyd had remembered her favorite color after all these years. She surprised him with an enthusiastic hug as he set down her suitcase.

"Thank you for remembering I'm partial to yellow, Lloyd. And the crackling fire is heavenly." She slipped her coat from her shoulders, reveling in the warmth emanating from the burning wood.

Lloyd gave a hoarse laugh, clearly amused by her sudden, contented sigh.

"Well, I see you've done all the exploring you're going to do for the moment. Dinner will be served at six thirty, cocktails at six. We'll be using the dining room at the left of the first floor staircase."

Janice dropped into the plush settee in front of the fireplace. That was an hour away—plenty of time for a nap. Her head dropped to the sofa arm with a will of its own and she stared into the glowing embers.

"Watch the time, Jan. Can't have you missing dinner."

"You won't. I'm ravenous." Her eyelids drifted downward. Ummm, the room was marshmallow toasty. She was totally exhausted as well as sensually disturbed. Lloyd's chuckle reverberated around her head.

"I mean it, Jan, don't be late."

She gave a leisurely wave and heard the door close softly a moment later. The click became the second-to-last thing she remembered as she nestled deeper into the cushions. The last thing she remembered was a fan of air along her right cheekbone. Contented, she gave a sigh and drifted off to sleep.

Chapter 6

FRIDAY—6:00 PM

Tuning out the lively conversation around him, Adrian leaned back and let his gaze scour the room's speckled wallpaper. Why in the name of Holy Vegas had he allowed himself to be lured to this blasted seminar? He loathed reunions. He'd rather try to win a dog-sled race with a team of Chihuahuas than be part of a new-age seminar. He despised no-win scenarios even more, detested those who got caught up in them. And yet here he was—caught in one of his own making. For more than twenty minutes, he had been spouting all the polite words to his companions and hating himself for doing it. To make matters even more intolerable, he was cold. Why didn't Marks turn up the heat?

Switching his focus to the blazing candelabra ensconced in the furthest corner of the room, Adrian realized it was more than the chateau's coldness he detested. It was the vastness. It made him feel inferior. Threw up in his face how little in life he had accomplished in his thirty-five years. Sitting here made him ask vast questions of himself that he didn't give a rat's ass about the answer.

He let his eyes sweep the frescoed ceiling and gilt furniture. Marks had become a wealthy giant over the years. Everything in the room spoke of money and class. His taste was excellent, hundred proof. Returning his gaze to the whiskey glass in his hand, Adrian gave a tight smile. Marks' whiskey was hundred-proof, too, and extremely enjoyable. He tossed the last shot down, savoring the burning fire as it scorched his throat and lungs. And then dropping the glass to the table, he tugged his pullover down. He was underdressed for dinner but at least he was warm.

Slowly, he turned his attention to the sideboard table filled with steaming dishes of hot food. Would they ever get around to eating? He was starved. The gurgles in the pit of his stomach had been churning for at least fifteen minutes. He took a quick peek at his watch. How much longer would their host keep them waiting? He glanced a second time and caught himself. Jesus, he was on edge! He was becoming a god-damned shit-ass clock watcher!

Angered by his own foul mood, he took a deep breath. His jaded sarcasm was working double time, his obscenities worse than usual. Why did he feel compelled to know the time? He didn't care a rat's ass for time. Why should anyone? Time was merely a manmade word that catalogued man's physical realm within limited parameters. Physical parameters that stung and hurt and fed on the soul like hungry piranha.

Not liking the slant of his dark thoughts, Adrian turned to find something more pleasant in the room. Ginger seated beside him was a pleasing eyeful in her red wool gabardine pantsuit. The material hugged her ample curves in all the right places.

He liked her blond hair piled on top of her head in lacy ringlets. He wondered if she had done it to please him. He banished the thought immediately as absurd. Ginger had no need to stroke his ego. He had been the one to pursue their relationship, not her.

Catching a whiff of her special brand of peach perfume, Adrian knew he had gotten the best part of their bargain. She was gregarious by nature; he tended to dark mood shifts. Her honest, open friendliness combated and, most times, quelled his jaded sarcasm. She was truly Beauty to his Beast.

Ginger was overly animated now as she and the spry woman across the table argued over favorite smoky cafes along Bourbon Street. Twirling his glass, he listened to their cheerful banter. He had never seen his assistant so relaxed or talkative. Did being around him and his increasingly sour moods dampen her natural, lively exuberance? He frowned thoughtfully. When they returned to Vegas, he would have a talk with her. Clear the air. Perhaps, finally offer a commitment.

It was time to let the past go, cut the umbilical cord of dreams that chained and kept him from moving forward into the future.

At the thought of the future, Adrian found his gaze slipping to the couple across the table. Muriel and Jasper Grisomb were perfect together. As content with each other as field mice in a harvest bin. She was small and plump; he was big and compact. He liked their obvious respect for each other and he especially liked the way they shared secret threads of communication. The lift of her hand to his to gain attention, his return smile holding an emotional resonance that lingered long after she had found something new to draw his attention to. It had taken a lifetime of growing together to build those kinds of threads. He felt a slight ache above his ribcage and knew that he was envious of their happiness.

He set his glass down abruptly, ice clinking. He should never drink when he was feeling melancholy. It unleashed too many unpleasant memories. He felt a sharp jab in his side and slanted his gaze to his right. Ginger sat looking at him, a suggestion of annoyance hovering around the edges of her mouth.

"For heaven's sake, Adrian, where are you? Muriel has asked you a question."

Adrian's mercurial black eyes narrowed, and tilting his head back, he peered at the older woman who sat with a sweet smile, patiently awaiting a reply.

"Sorry, Muriel, what were you asking?"

"I wondered how long you had known Lloyd."

Adrian's lips twisted into a cynical smile.

"We met once—in the psychiatric ward of an Army hospital."

"You were the patient, of course."

Adrian's mouth twisted into a sneer.

"Of course."

"My God, Adrian, you never told me that."

The shock in Ginger's voice was semi-accusatory, and Adrian suppressed a sigh. Where were the secret threads of communication when he needed them? Her shock had siphoned the blood from her face.

"It was a long time ago, love," he teased. "I barely remember it." Her slender fingers twisted together and Adrian knew she was dying to hear the whole sordid story. He returned his gaze to Muriel. "And you, Muriel? What's your history with Marks?"

"Like you, Lloyd and I were friends for a short period of time. I interned at Duke University with him in the mid-eighties. As part of his Dream Laboratory Team."

"And you, Jasper?"

The man who had been sitting quietly came to life. He removed his pipe stem from between his teeth and gave a conspiratorial wink.

"Never met the man until today. Like him, though."

He returned his pipe to his mouth and the room fell suddenly quiet. Adrian realized they had now exhausted all the topics of conversation polite strangers could indulge in. He cupped the empty whiskey glass in his hand and gave it a twirl. Probing fingers touched the warmth of his outstretched hand and stilled the glass.

"I've often wondered, Muriel, why Adrian is so reluctant to discuss his second sight with me. He admits to it but he won't let me inside to understand it. Are all psychics so reticent about their gift? I would like to understand, for Adrian's sake. It makes him so black some days."

"Get your hand off my behind, Ginger."

"See, that's what I mean. All I have to do is mention the gift and his sharp fangs appear."

"Make your point, love. No need for Muriel to wait as long as an elephant's pregnancy for the point."

Adrian saw Muriel's lips twitch in amusement.

"Are you really as jaded as you sound, Adrian? You'll be the first psychic I've met who is."

Adrian shrugged, not about to confirm or deny her statement. She didn't seem to mind, though as he saw her swing her attention once more to Ginger.

"I myself am not so jaded about psychic gifts, my dear. I've had nothing but good luck attached to mine. But then, I am a trance channeler. I can pick and choose and turn the channel off when I want to. However, others, like Jasper and perhaps Adrian, are not so fortunate." Adrian saw her transfer her clear gaze to him. "They suffer unwanted visions—visions that intrude and sap their energy. Visions that have haunted them since childhood in many cases."

Adrian didn't even pretend to hide his discomfort. She was picking up some strand of time associated with him, he knew. Could sense it in his head. Her probing could be costly. Already, she had Ginger staring at him as if he was dirt-under-the-fingernails poor and it was her job to haul him up from the gutter. He shut his mind down from Muriel's probing and stifled Ginger's curiosity with a curt command.

"Don't ask about my childhood, O'Toole. Save your questions for our host . . . by the way, where the hell is our host?"

His question produced a scornful laugh from Jasper, who swiveled in his chair. His pipe stabbed the air.

"Meeting Miss Kelly. She was late in arriving."

"I hate modern women who enjoy being fashionably late." Adrian leaned over and refilled his whisky glass. His gaze met Muriel's smile across the table. She was probing his mind again, trying to make him feel less surly.

"You're really too unkind, Adrian. Janice's flight was delayed. You can't blame her for that. It's the weather."

A door slam echoed in the outside corridor and Adrian gave a heartfelt sigh.

"Well, it's about time."

Fingers clasped his wrist and Ginger's voice was low and throaty in his ear.

"Behave please, Adrian. Stow that viperous tongue of yours. For me?"

Adrian suppressed another sigh, raised his glass, and saluted her wryly. Hearing approaching footsteps, he turned and saluted the doorway with a smug taunt.

"To late arrivals . . . may they . . . "

The words froze on his lips at the sight of the red-headed woman crossing the threshold with Lloyd. For a fraction of a second, he heard a pop in his head and his pulse did a rapid nosedive. In its wake, an icy chill swept into the pit of his stomach and crawled upward to constrict his lungs. Holy Christ! It was *her*!

The glass in his hand began to tremble as his black eyes met her green ones across the crystal. A light, friendly smile greeted him. And then in the next instant, the glass in his hand exploded and the smile vanished. Shards of glass sprayed the air and Adrian shot to his feet with a painful yelp. His dinner companions bolted from their chairs as well.

"Sweet Jesus!" The curse was out before Adrian could stop it—and hurled directly at the woman before him. For a brief instant, the group stood paralyzed before Ginger took control, snatching up a napkin and grabbing his bleeding thumb, which caused another muttered curse to fly from his lips. "For Christ's sake, woman, there's glass in there. Why don't you just rip my thumb off while you're at it?"

She mopped at his thumb with her napkin.

"I ought to. What the hell happened?"

"The glass shattered; what the hell do you think happened?"

"But you weren't even clutching the glass tight. It shattered by itself."

"Give me a break, O'Toole. Magicians have been known to break things every now and then."

Adrian cupped his thumb with his free hand in an attempt to stem the heavy throbbing that was now part of the digit. Beside him, Lloyd picked up the remnants of the shattered glass and held it up to the light. Adrian saw his unspoken confusion and bit down on a rising curse. No, he'd not say it. Instead, he stared at the woman across the table from him. He let his gaze rake every inch of her as she stood anxiously watching Ginger's busy fingers. Adrian didn't leave his eyes on her face long. No, he didn't need to study her face. It was ingrained in his memory. Had been since he was ten years old, and she had come to taunt him in youthful dreams. It was the body he now looked at, his mind dislocating itself from the pain in his thumb. Holy Vegas! She was beautiful. With a body more rounded than ever he created for her in any of his wet dreams.

A sharp stinging pain assailed him and he snarled under the abuse.

"Jesus, Ginger!"

"Sorry, Adrian, I can see the sliver. If you just hold your hand still a little longer . . . "

Her voice tapered off and Adrian smothered a second growl. He transferred his gaze to the group, and while he gave a tight-lipped smile for their benefit, inside he cursed the flesh that felt as if it were a raging ball of fire. Ginger's finger tweaked the sliver at last and he inhaled with a sharp jerk as she muttered "got it." Feeling the pain dwindling, Adrian signaled to his companions.

"Sit down, everybody. No use continuing to steal Miss Kelly's limelight. She obviously needs to be the center of attention."

Adrian knew from her quick intake that his viperous remark had stunned Janice. So much for making good first impressions, he thought. But what the hell? It didn't matter. Nothing mattered except to stop the aching in his hand. And of course, the one closer to his rib cage.

"Adrian's right." Jasper echoed. "The scare seems to be over." He sat himself quickly and Adrian saw him motion to the others, who dropped back to their places with less speed. Adrian didn't miss the bewildered glance Janice tossed his way as she settled into a vacant chair. Holy Christ! He wanted nothing more than to offend her—to goad her into despising him. That way he could end his personal torture. Lloyd's voice cut through the sudden silence and Adrian watched his attention return to the glass he still held in his hand.

"Can't imagine how the glass came to break. These crystal glasses are hundreds of years old." His gaze lifted to Adrian's face. "Are you sure you're alright, Adrian?"

"I will be if I can get Florence Nightingale here to wrap my thumb with a clean bandage."

Ginger came to life beside him, snatching up a clean napkin and twirling the fabric into a make-shift bandage. She then tied it around Adrian's thumb, giving him a tremulous smile when she finished.

"Too tight?"

He heard the tears in her voice and reached up and stroked her cheek.

"Buck up. You know what a clumsy lot we magicians are."

Muriel's lilting tones crossed the table.

"I don't think you broke that glass, Adrian. I felt a strong electrical current just before it shattered. You felt it, I know, and I know Miss Kelly did. Her face gave her away."

Adrian's mind froze. Her face? What about his? What had he given away? His mind-rambling came to a screeching halt as Janice picked up the conversation.

"You're right, Muriel. I did sense something just as the glass exploded."

Adrian felt his throat constrict and closed his eyes. What had she sensed? His fear? His rising body heat? For no reason he could think of, he felt his heart beat begin to race in his ears. Across his mind, vivid images formed, invading his senses. His hands spanning Janice's waist, drawing her to him . . . the whisper of his breath on her cheek . . . his mouth moving over hers in sensuous exploration . . . the piston-driving strength of his body possessing hers.

"Adrian?" Ginger's concerned voice cut through his thoughts like a knife, severing the images. "You've gone completely white."

"It comes from bleeding all over the tablecloth and having to endure Miss Kelly's inane comments about shattering crystal."

Adrian shot each of them a withering scowl in emphasis, saving Janice for last. Every curve of her body stiffened as she read his intense dislike and Adrian knew he was being a surly son-of-a-bitch. But what else could he do?

"Have I offended you in some way, Mr. Magus?" she asked politely.

"Of course you haven't," Ginger cut in. "Don't pay Adrian any mind. He's been in a black mood ever since the headache started."

"Headache?" Her look was startled as she leaned in to him, her confusion seeming to evaporate with the news. "Have you been experiencing headaches?"

"One or two." Adrian evaded. It wasn't evasion enough, however. She turned toward the woman on her right.

"And you, Muriel?"

Adrian saw her brief nod.

"Jasper, too."

"Lloyd?"

Adrian swung his gaze in time to catch their host's reluctant nod.

"Psychics experiencing headaches is serious business," Janice commented. "But for the five of us at the same time?" She let the sentence hang and Adrian heard the unspoken concern in her voice. What was she driving at? He drilled a probing stare her way.

"Make your point, Miss Kelly."

She angled her head more toward him, her eyes boring back into his. Her tone was terse as she spoke.

"Do you still have your headache?"

Adrian wondered what she'd say if he told her he had an ache, but much lower down. Could he make her blush to the roots of her being? He had an urge to try.

"Do you?" she prodded.

He chickened out with a growl.

"No."

She swung her gaze back to Muriel who shook her head and tossed a questioning glance to her right. Jasper shook his head and Adrian had the impression nothing much perturbed his even demeanor. Certainly not inane talk of linked headaches, which was what Janice was implying. Turning to the man seated at the head of the table, Adrian heard him verify their unspoken question.

"Gone. "

At that the simple word, Adrian found himself the target of ice green eyes daring him to make a scathing retort. He refrained, listening to her sultry tones instead as she addressed Muriel.

"I felt a distinct ripple while coming over on the ferry. I thought for sure I was going to tap in but something—someone—kept me from doing it."

"Someone?" Muriel asked, startled.

Jasper's pipe tapped the table.

"Winter storms are often electrical in nature," he advised. "Especially when it's dismal like it is now." He swirled his pipe in front of his face. "Don't forget, as psychics, we run on electrical impulses."

Adrian pondered that thought.

"All right, for laughter's sake, let's say we've all shared the same headache. So what?"

"Strangers, living hundreds of miles apart, linked to the same headache?" Janice responded. "All of us about to meet each other for the first time? What are the odds of that?"

"We're all telepathically linked whether we know each other or not," Jasper replied. "Given the right set of variables, I could tap into your thoughts from hundreds of miles away."

Beside him, Ginger stirred in her chair and Adrian knew she was unnerved by the talk of sizzling heads and tapping in. Feeling for her, Adrian placed a reassuring hand on hers, surprised to find it trembling.

"Relax. Nothing more than shop-talk. If Miss Kelly were less free with her mouth and more inclined to stuff something edible into it, we could all face the next few minutes in a much better frame of mind. I'm starved."

His sarcasm roused Lloyd from his chair immediately. Reaching out, he uncovered the steam trays on the sideboard behind him and called "dig in" over his shoulder. Adrian was the first to bolt to his feet. Finally, some food to counteract the alcohol buzz in his head. Behind him, he heard chairs scrape and knew the others were following his lead. As he dumped a heaping portion of roast beef onto his plate, he heard Muriel remark softly to Janice.

"Adrian's rather hard to take at first, my dear. But once the shock of the first set down wears off, his barbs are highly entertaining. You'll find it so."

"I doubt it," she responded. "I don't hold a black belt in mouth karate the way he does."

"All men are little boys and all little boys misbehave, my dear. Some more than others. Rather than losing your patience, it's best to just search out the reason for their naughtiness and act on that."

Adrian thought that a truly revealing statement and wondered what Janice would do if she learned outright why he was being so naughty. He forestalled further thoughts on the subject as slim fingers reached out and around him in search of a plate. Her light touch on his shirt back sent his pulses skittering again. When she straightened from him, the smell of her fruity perfume remained, mingling with the smell of roast beef.

Adrian felt his knees start to buckle and quelled the tremor by moving back to the table. Once there, he attacked his mashed potatoes with grim ferocity. Who was she? A sorceress out to rend him apart? First in his dreams, now in the flesh. He loathed her. For smelling good, for looking good, for touching him and not seeing the result of that touch.

He speared a broccoli stalk and stole a peek at Janice through lowered lashes as she rejoined the group at the table. He'd make her pay! Pay for all the torturous wet dreams he had suffered through as a teen. He tossed the spear into his mouth, and then tasting its blandness, he reached for the saltshaker only to have his fingers collide with Janice's slender ones.

At the collision, their minds linked to an erotic image of wet-soaked thighs, rounded buttocks, and orgasmic rhythms. Caught off-guard by the unexpected mind meld, Adrian shut off the image, severing the shared link. He felt Janice's guard go up and knew she had been as disturbed by the vision as he had. Well, he didn't give a rat's ass. Let her stew. And as for his thoughts . . . so what if she had tapped into his mind at the link? He had tapped into hers as well. And he liked what he had discovered. She had come to Carrington House prepared to like him, but after his earlier rudeness, she had changed her mind. Now, she wished they had never met.

Delighted to be the cause of her discomfort, Adrian tossed down a slice of roast beef. If she thought she had seen him at his worst, she was mistaken. He could be much, much worse. And he would be. She didn't know it yet but her fortune cookie had just come up empty. His ribcage suddenly hitch-kicked and a staggering, sobering thought flashed through his brain. What if his fortune cookie had just come up empty, instead of hers?

Chapter 7

FRIDAY—7:00 PM

Janice took a last swallow of cheesecake and forced the creamy wedge to slide down her throat. Now, if only she could make it stay there. Sometime during the last ten minutes, her stomach had turned sour and she wished she had remembered to pack a box of Di-Gel tablets in her purse. How quickly things could change, she mused. Only a few hours ago she had been looking forward to this trip. Now, she wished she had never agreed to come. Damn Lloyd for putting her in this uncomfortable situation. And damn Bibi for not putting her foot down more forcefully about coming.

Irritated, she laid her fork down and opted for a sip of ice water. She savored the refreshing wetness as it cooled her parched throat. Along with her churning stomach, she had managed to develop a mouth as dry as dust. Was it her body's way of defending itself against the ego-bashing it was taking? Nothing had gone right since she entered the dining room. Now here she was, wishing more than anything she could cram a grocery bag over her head. Perhaps then Adrian Magus would leave her alone and find someone else to vent his acerbic wit on.

Janice listened for a moment as Muriel's melodic voice to her left regaled Lloyd with a new procedure in dream work discovered by a former college mate of theirs.

Listening to the cheerful give and take, Janice decided she was glad she had come to Carrington House after all. If she hadn't, she'd've never met the Grisombs. They were darlings, both of them. All during dinner, they had ordained themselves her guardian angels, one on either side of her. Their cheerful commentary served as a constant buffer to Adrian's caustic tongue. He insulted; they parried with a droll story or change of subject. Finally, seeing through their subterfuge—or growing tired, Janice couldn't be sure which—Adrian had given up his insults, leaving her to feel as if she been sucked into the eye of a hurricane and spewed out minus part of her senses.

Stealing a peek at the man across the table from her, Janice felt a pang of regret. Adrian was remarkably handsome, just as Bibi predicted she'd find him. She thought in another space and time, they might've been friends, perhaps even dated. But in this time and space, they were enemies. And she didn't know why. They had never met or corresponded. What had she done to make him hate her so?

"Penny for your thoughts, my dear."

A warm hand descended upon hers and Janice turned to find herself under Muriel's interested scrutiny. Smiling, she squeezed Muriel's fingers and lowered her voice.

"I was thinking how well some people go together. You and Jasper. Ginger and Adrian."

Muriel glanced down the table for a second and then back to her.

"Fate does indeed pair strange bedfellows. Perhaps we've misjudged Adrian, my dear. Cutting his thumb like that must've hurt like hell. Such an odd happening. It would make any of us a bear, I dare say."

"Can't understand it," Lloyd stated, joining their conversation. "He wasn't holding it tight. All of us could see that."

"Perhaps there's a mischievous ghost in the chateau you've forgotten to tell us about," Muriel commented cheerfully.

"I was telling Janice only a few hours ago, Carrington House has no ghosts," Lloyd playfully chided. "And then this damn odd occurrence has to spring up. I don't suppose she'll believe anything I say about the house now."

"Nonsense," Muriel scoffed. "She's a perfectly rational young woman. I can't imagine her being ruffled by a ghost. Besides, if there are ghosts here, you really need to rout them out."

"Better to leave them unknown," Janice interjected, remembering her earlier conversation with Captain Bowers. She suppressed a shiver. She wanted to keep the conversation far away from talk of breaking glasses and restless ghosts. When the glass shattered, she had seen a vivid image of legs intertwined and two bodies consumed with naked desire. And when her fingers collided with Adrian's minutes later, the unexpected happened. She had tapped into his mind, sharing the same, mysterious, disturbing, erotic image with him, only hers seemed to be in more detail. He had shoved her prying mind from his, like a door slammed shut by a howling wind, and her guard went up instantly. Why was he afraid of the image?

Hearing her name spoken, Janice returned her thoughts to the present, realizing Ginger had just asked if she had any children.

"Yes, one. She's four. Her name's Sarah Anne."

"And your husband? Is he psychic, too?"

"No, he wasn't. We're divorced now."

"Does your daughter resemble you, Miss Kelly?" Adrian cut in abruptly, a bemused smile staining his lips.

"My sister says we're mirror images."

"Lucky mirrors."

Janice blushed at the unexpected compliment. Now, why had he said that? She had finally come to terms with his stinging wit and here he was saying something nice to her. She felt tears and turned away. *Get a grip, Janice.* Next, she'd be thinking his dislike is all an act—a continuation of his show. Ginger's voice came again, still curious.

"Does your daughter share your gift, Janice?"

"I'm afraid not."

"You're sure?"

Amused chuckles emanated around the table and Adrian placed his hand on Ginger's forearm affectionately.

"She's sure, O'Toole."

Ginger fiddled with her fork, and sensing her embarrassment, Janice sought to comfort her.

"I'm thrilled Sarah has no psychic abilities. Truly."

"But why? It must be wonderful to know the future and your place in it."

Muriel's hands glided through the air.

"Psychic gifts often ride the rails of opposites, my dear. Extreme pleasure or extreme pain."

"Pain?"

"Psychic overload," Jasper clarified. He removed his pipe for a moment. "The mental pain can be extraordinary."

Lloyd nodded, dipping his head in Adrian's direction.

"Just ask Adrian there. He'll tell you about pain."

All eyes swung to Adrian and Janice saw a tell-tale flush steal across his features. What had caused him to overload? A woman? He swiveled in his chair and Janice knew he wasn't going to answer. But then, to her amazement, he did.

"Iraq. Early days there."

Shock flew through Janice. He had joined the service? She had heard of an occasional psychic doing so, but thought them daft to put themselves in such a vulnerable mental and emotional state. Somehow, she hadn't imagined Adrian would make a mistake as critical as that. She saw Ginger's fingers wrap around the plaid fabric of Adrian's sweater.

"That must've been hell, Adrian."

He didn't answer and Janice was certain this time he wouldn't. Lloyd took up his tale.

"The best way to describe Adrian's suffering is to have you imagine a nightmare-filled sleep but you're awake. By the way, Adrian, did you ever meet that red-headed woman from your dreams?"

Adrian stiffened and his face shut down. Janice wondered why Lloyd's question should disturb him so. His shoulders lifted in a shrug of mock resignation.

"No, never did." His voice trailed away and Janice knew he was lying. There was a long, brittle silence and then he sprang to his feet, pulling Ginger up and fastening his arm around her midriff.

"Would you mind, Lloyd, if Ginger and I took a peek at the solarium for a half hour or so?"

"Not at all. I'll show you." Lloyd shot to his feet, pushing his chair back. He signaled to Janice and the Grisombs to stay put. "I'll get Adrian settled, then join you three for coffee."

Janice nodded her agreement, along with the Grisombs. As the trio exited, she sighed at the sound of footsteps tapping on the wood oak floor, a great weight lifted from her shoulders. Her sigh was followed by a sudden drain of energy and she admitted to herself that the vibrations in the room had been more intense than she realized. Next to her, Muriel poured coffee into her cup from a colorful beaker.

"You're holding up very well, my dear," she complimented.

Janice was surprised by her acute insight.

"Am I? I wanted nothing more than to find one of the bed sheets and cover my head. I've never been disliked on sight before. It's an unpleasant feeling. Very ego-deflating."

Jasper's chair scraped closer to her and she heard his appreciative chuckle.

"Adrian doesn't dislike you, my dear. Quite the opposite."

Janice felt Muriel peer around her shoulders as taken back as she by such a bald statement.

"Have you sensed something, Jasper?"

"Eavesdropping, I'm afraid, Muree. Been reading Adrian's mind quite clearly for the last ten minutes. He's confused, doesn't know what to do about Janice."

"Do about me? Good Lord, what have I done to him? Have we met before?"

His denial was swift.

"Never. You've never met in person but he's seen you many times in his dreams." Jasper leaned in closer and Janice found his voice alluring. "My dear, you are the red-headed woman Lloyd mentioned to him a few moments ago."

"But he said he hadn't met her. You heard him."

"Did you expect him to admit it in front of you? He's got more pride than that."

Janice cradled her head in her palm for a moment. She let one fingernail draw empty circles on the tablecloth. What a mess! Jasper was actually making her feel sorry for Adrian, and he didn't deserve it. Not after the tongue-lashing he had bashed her with during dinner. Warm fingers closed over hers and stilled her lazy drawing on the tablecloth.

"I don't see how you can continue to dislike a man whose only desire at the moment is to make mad, passionate love to you," Jasper said calmly.

"What!" The squeak was out before she could stop it. In her ears, Janice reheard Bibi's last whispered words as she boarded the plane: "Live a little, Jan, screw the gorgeous hunk." She had bashed Bibi's arm hard then, and now she felt like doing the same to Jasper. Instead, she curled her hands into tight fists in her lap and wondered what excuse she could use to leave the room and seek sanctuary somewhere else in the house. To stay meant hearing more disturbing nonsense. She was hallucinating and the sooner she went to her room and pulled herself together the better. Popping up from her chair, she offered a weak apology.

"I need to find a restroom . . . "

Alarmed, Muriel rose from her chair, her hand floating to Janice's arm.

"I'm sorry, my dear. I should've warned you that Jasper's telepathy is exceptional. Obviously, he has upset you. He'll stop now."

Janice's fingers fluttered to her neck. Why was she being such a killjoy? She knew in her heart Jasper hadn't meant any harm. He couldn't help being a telepath any more than she could stop her own visions. Sighing, she sent Jasper an apologetic glance. He rose quickly, offering his own apology.

"My dear, I had no idea I'd upset you. I only thought if you knew that Adrian's as confused as you about the glass incident, you'd feel better. Like him better."

"What does the glass shattering have to do with it? It was just an accident, wasn't it?"

His eyebrows creased to a frown and when he spoke again, his voice was almost a murmur.

"Keep asking myself that very question and can't get an answer. Keep getting blocked out." He leaned toward Janice and in a level voice asked politely. "How good of a psychic are you, Janice? Can you mind link with another person easily?"

"I've never really tried," Janice remarked in surprise. "My gift has always revolved around sudden tap-ins instigated by the other side."

"I wish it was the other way around," Jasper stated.

"Have you sensed some danger we should know about, Jasper?" Muriel asked anxiously. "You know that ninety-nine times out of a hundred when you sense a thing, it occurs."

"Not this time, I'm afraid. I'm at a loss. However, I do have some good news for Janice. Her sister, Bibi, is pregnant again."

"What!" Janice re-sat herself eagerly, her voice flushed with excitement. "Bibi's pregnant? How did you pick up on that without touching me?"

He gave her a mischievous wink.

"Secrets of the trade, my dear." He pressed a gentle kiss along Muriel's rouged cheek. "Another cup of coffee, luv?" he queried.

Muriel nodded and Janice returned her attention to her own cup. Twirling it in circles, her mood suddenly buoyed. So Bibi was pregnant again. Tonight there'd be no shadows across her heart. No way. She had a striking thought and turned to Jasper eagerly.

"Is it a boy or girl?"

Jasper threw back his head and roared with laughter.

"I forgot to check."

Janice's laughter bubbled up, joining his. Beside her, Muriel's sweet laugh chimed in.

"Psychic dolt!"

Laughter pealed again and the trio settled down, rewarming their coffee and waiting for Lloyd's return. Janice was relieved to find her thoughts were a million miles away from erotic images, shattered crystal, and Adrian Magus.

Chapter 8

Outside the solarium window, lightning specks arced wildly through a scribble of clouds, lighting up the ebony sky. Witnessing the spectacle from the window seat where he lounged, Adrian marveled at such brutal beauty. He had no clear view of the tall cliffs covered in ice and snow, but the snowflakes sticking to the glass pane inches from his face were undeniable clues that the weather outside had not changed since their arrival. It was still January, dreary trench-coat weather, accompanied by a bone-numbing cold. Yet as he watched another pitchfork of light fan and hang to the earth, he felt a familiar fear resurge within him. Which part of his life was reality and which part was the illusion? For so many years, he had been able to tell the difference and keep them separate. Now his life was as strange and mysterious as the lightning storm showering the winter sky.

Why did none of the others suspect the lightning overhead might be linked to their headaches in some way? Adrian put a sudden brake on the thought. Janice suspected. She had hinted as much at the dinner table earlier. To her credit, she had been born with brains as well as beauty. His mind braked down hard on that thought, too. He couldn't allow himself to think of Janice's beauty. When their minds had collided earlier, had they simultaneously tapped into some long ago memory, his wishful thinking, or an experience about to occur between them?

Hearing a soft creak, Adrian turned to find Ginger curling onto the window seat inches from his toes. Her eyes scanned the night sky with as much concern as his first had. His mouth curved upward and he reached out and brushed her cheek lightly.

"What's the matter, O'Toole? Ain't ya never seen a lightning concert before?"

She turned to him with a worried look and Adrian saw her usual exuberance had fled. It was obvious she was frightened and her stilted words confirmed it.

"I'm scared, Adrian."

Adrian gave her cheek another light tap and chuckled.

"Scared of what?"

"This place . . . the glass exploding in your hand . . . " She nailed him with a curious stare. "It wasn't an accident, was it?" Her tinge of panic urged Adrian to cover her hands with his.

"I'd be lying if I said I was holding the glass tight. I wasn't."

"Did she do it?"

"Who?"

"Miss Kelly. The glass exploded just as she entered the room."

Adrian countered hastily, squeezing Ginger's slim fingers.

"No. Miss Kelly didn't do it."

"How can you be so sure? What do you really know about these people? You're strangers meeting for the first time."

Strangers! Could he explain to Ginger that only two of them were strangers? That he knew one of them intimately, better than she knew herself? Adrian looked away, his gaze resettling on the outside darkness. For the moment, the night sky was quiet, devoid of any telltale patterns of light. Observing the inky blackness, Adrian realized it matched the dark foreboding in his own mind. Could he tell Ginger the unvarnished truth about his recurring boyhood dreams of Janice and expect her to understand? Could he add their recent mind collision to the story and expect her to understand what he himself didn't yet? No, he couldn't reveal the truth to anyone. Not while he remained in his present state of confusion. Maybe later— when he was more in control and had deciphered what it all meant.

"Adrian?"

Ginger's voice pricked his thoughts and he lifted a hand. Slowly, he began to trace a figure eight on the moist windowpane in front of them and drew Ginger's attention to it.

"Can you imagine your life following the pattern of this figure eight?" He saw her quick nod and continued on. "You flow round and round, ever-circling, never-ending. Behind you, another life traces the pattern, ever-circling, never-ending, different speed. And behind that life, another life doing the same. And another. And when there are hundreds of lives circling the pattern?" Adrian left the question hanging in mid-sentence.

"Eventually some of them will collide . . . here." Ginger placed her finger eagerly over the point where the two circles conjoined.

"Exactly. They'll be strangers meeting for the first time."

"But they aren't really strangers, are they?" Ginger piped up, satisfaction showing in her eyes. "They've passed each other numerous times before while circling the pattern. They've just never collided before."

Adrian nodded, pleased by her astuteness, and then he saw one of her smiles emerge.

"Why do they collide, Adrian? What is the purpose behind it? I don't think I'm spiritual enough to grasp it."

"Of course you are. You sing about it every night in the third act of our show."

She wrinkled her nose and Adrian soon saw her flash of understanding.

"Kismet, do you mean? Destinies tied to each other?"

Adrian nodded, wiping the figure eight from the glass pane and then drying his fingers along his pants leg. Ginger still wore a troubled frown. Lifting her chin, he mocked her fear with a grin.

"What now, O'Toole? There's nothing to be scared of. You are perfectly safe. I'm here to chase away any pesky ghosts hiding in your bedroom closet."

He heard her shaky laugh.

"Who's gonna chase away the ones hiding in your closet?"

Adrian started to laugh then felt his heartbeat lurch as once again outside the window, lightning ripped across the blackness. Ginger's fingers sought his for comfort and he clutched them firmly.

At the touch, a brief image of a lace-frosted white silk peignoir, shimmering with tiny pearls, floated across his mind. The image faded quickly, leaving Adrian no time to ponder its meaning. Instead, he attempted to make his body shut down the strange excitement mounting within him by gathering Ginger closer to him, clinging to her familiar curves the way a drowning man clings to a solitary lifeline. Above their heads, the ceiling lights dipped and quickly resurged. Ginger attempted to hide a feeble shiver.

"There'll be no dress rehearsal if this keeps up," she remarked.

"Nonsense, O'Toole. Where's your sense of tradition? Don't you know the show must go on? We'll perform by candlelight if we have to."

"Not me."

Adrian smiled at the denial, knowing she had no intention of reneging on the performance. She was a trooper, a showbiz junkie. No one had ever been able to keep her from *not* performing.

Settling her more comfortably in the crook of his arm, they both were content to watch the snow flurries assaulting the windowpane for a few moments. However, Ginger soon began fidgeting.

"Settle down, O'Toole," he scoffed, "Have I ever locked you in a box and left your there?"

"No, but there's always a first time. You're not yourself tonight. You're distracted." She lifted his fingers and caressed his injured thumb pad thoughtfully. "Your hands tell all your secrets, Adrian. I bet you didn't know I knew that. Your face never gives anything away, but your hands? They tell volumes. Tonight, I watched them shake, and I don't believe it was from the glass embedded in your thumb. You were afraid." Adrian's breath caught at her words, though she didn't seem to notice as she continued stroking his right palm, giving a tiny sigh. When she spoke, Adrian heard the resignation in her voice.

"I always knew this day would come, Adrian."

Adrian clenched his arms tighter around her waist.

"What? Consorting with psychics? Or having to nursemaid my injured thumb?" She broke his embrace, and Adrian let her go, watching as she tucked herself into the corner of the window seat and stared morosely at the darkness outside the window.

"Be serious, Adrian. I'm talking about us. We're over."

"What! Because of a stupid broken glass? I thought you were made of sterner stuff than that, O'Toole."

"I am. But suddenly, my hair color is all wrong."

Adrian held his breath for a second. Talk about slicing right to the heart of things. No appetizers here, just right to the main course.

"Get to the point, O'Toole. I gather you're referring to Miss Kelly's red hair?" he chided outwardly.

"You were mean and ugly to her on purpose, Adrian."

Adrian shifted his legs, flexing the kinks out of his knees and pretending as much indifference as he could muster.

"I'm mean and ugly to everyone, you know that."

"Yes, and you never spare a thought to the havoc you create. You couldn't care less about anyone's feelings in the matter. But you did care tonight. You shredded Janice's self-esteem in front of us all and on purpose. You wanted her to despise you. Why?"

"Surely I wasn't as bad as all that?" Adrian parried. He knew he had gone out of his way to goad Janice into disliking him. But what else could he do? She had stirred up old longings he had spent more than twenty years burying.

The window seat creaked and Adrian found himself impaled by Ginger's piercing gaze. For someone not possessed of second sight, her stare was remarkably penetrating.

"You saw something when the glass shattered, Adrian. What was it?"

He hedged with a shrug.

"An image."

"Of you and Janice?"

"No!" The syllable exploded from Adrian's lips, startling both of them with its vehemence. He felt himself flush at once and cautioned, "Dammit, Ginger, let it lie! I don't know *what* I saw. I had only a grasp of the image for a moment. The woman could have been anyone."

Ginger's face split into a wide smile and Adrian growled at his own stupidity. She had tricked him into admitting that to her. Her laugh echoed around the solarium wall and through his head. He studied her grinning features, and gave a second thunderous growl.

"What's so funny?"

"I've never seen you naked before, Adrian. It's a truly amazing sight."

She had cleverly manipulated him on all fronts. She had sensed, without being told, that the image he saw was an erotic one. She wanted nothing less than the truth from him and she had gotten it.

Angry with himself for not seeing the guise, Adrian could only stare pointedly out the window. He wished he could see a ripple of lightning crack the night skies apart in the way he had just been cracked apart. He waited but no flash came. Beyond the window, darkness reigned supreme. But for how long?

Outside, a snow-chilled wind had sprung up and was gathering force. Somewhere nearby, he could hear a tree branch slashing against wood. Above them, the ceiling lights continued to flicker and dip and Ginger stirred. When she started to speak, Adrian lifted his hand.

"Shut up, O'Toole. We're not canceling the dress rehearsal."

"I know," she stated, settling back with a sigh. She stroked the back of his right palm affectionately. "I don't mind if it's over between us, Adrian, really. I like Janice and you two look good together."

"Shut up, O'Toole. Curtain in fifteen minutes."

Chapter 9

FRIDAY—9:30 PM

Janice uttered a cry of delight as she peered through the solarium doors to find the room totally transformed into a stage setting of a Victorian drawing room. Good Lord, how had Adrian managed to create all this in just an hour? Her glance slid right. She supposed the room wasn't as real as it looked since magicians used the real as illusionary tools to fool their audience. If that were true, Adrian had certainly outdone himself. The set was impressive and she found the room's transformation so delightful, she was almost willing to forgive and forget his earlier rudeness. He couldn't be all bad if he could create such delicate beauty as this.

Hoping she had time to give the stage setting a closer inspection before the others arrived, Janice crossed the room and climbed the proscenium stage ramp. Once on stage, she perched on the arm of the sofa, surveying the rest of the set pieces. For illusionary tools, they were remarkably accurate. There was even a stuffed bird in a golden cage and Janice felt sure Adrian would bring the bird to life sometime during the performance. Her gaze skimmed the decorated boxes on the floor. They stood empty now, but no doubt Ginger would disappear and reappear within them throughout the performance. Janice closed her eyes for a moment. To be whisked away, only to reappear seconds later elsewhere. Mmmmm, she could almost imagine the joy of such a time slip.

With a contented sigh, Janice hiked her knees over the arm of the sofa and dropped her bottom into the belly of the cushions to continue viewing the set. To her left stood a fantasy bedroom, decorated with lace, ribbons, and roses. The main occupant, a four-poster brass bed, was straight out of an erotic novel and Janice's pulse quickened at the thought of two bodies making heated love beneath the silken sheets. *Dispatch that disturbing image to the back of your mind, Janice, and make it stay there.*

Obeying the command, her gaze swung to the mini-fireplace and the oil painting housed above it. The vitality of the young woman in the portrait struck her at once. So who was the woman and what did she mean to Adrian? Janice let her imagination run wild. She was a long ago lover. No, that was too simple. She was the woman Adrian wanted but couldn't have. Yes, she liked that idea. Adrian brought to his knees by a beauty who had twisted him around her little finger and then callously dumped him. No wonder he hated women.

"What a perfectly adorable set." Janice jumped at the sound of the lilting tones and then hid a smile as Muriel dropped onto the cushions alongside her. "One can well imagine the grandeur of being part of Queen Elizabeth's royal court," she stated with a sigh.

"Or a love-sick debutante, courted by impetuous dandies," Janice added.

"Exactly, my dear. We seem to be on the same wavelength again." They shared another smile, and then Muriel was studying the room on her own, her eyes, too, finally coming to rest on the oil painting above the fireplace. Janice sensed Muriel was as moved by the portrait as she.

"I would never have suspected that beneath Adrian's cranky exterior there lurked a sensitive, romantic side," Muriel commented. "His jaded wit is so overwhelming, it quite takes your breath away. I think I have done him a grave injustice."

"Do you believe the concept of the set is his?"

"I do. Don't you?"

Janice gave a quick nod, realizing she did. Furthermore, as much as she hated to admit it, Adrian seemed to be loaded with artistic talent. Blast the rotten swine! Why did he have to have an eye for arranging beautiful things in a most sensual, romantic way?

"Never judge a book by its cover," she quoted softly. "We all could learn from that lesson, don't you agree?"

When no response came to her question, Janice swung about, expecting to find Muriel's attention still riveted on the oil painting. Instead, she found her studying the entranceway, her lips tilted in delight. Janice followed her gaze to the door, and spying the star-spangled figure poised there, murmured a breathless "wow."

Arms resting on the doorframe, Ginger stood in a dramatic pose, smiling at them provocatively. To say that she looked sensational was an understatement, Janice realized. She was quite literally a page out of a Victorian novel, and her gown, if it could be called a gown, sparkled and shimmered under the tray of overhead lights. As she walked toward them, the dress showcased her tiny waist and ample breasts. With a pang of envy, Janice tugged uncomfortably at her oversized, baggy sweater.

Reaching the sofa, Ginger made a small pirouette before them. "Is this a sensational costume or what!?"

"You look absolutely ravishing," Muriel complimented.

Ginger attempted a small curtsey in thanks, but ended the bow with a quick clutch to her bosom. She gave a bright laugh to cover her embarrassment.

"As you can tell, I'm an overendowed substitute for Adrian's sexy stage sirens. They rarely stay clothed long enough to worry about popping out of their costumes."

"Can we look forward to some Vegas nudity, Ginger?" Janice teased lightly.

"God, no. This performance is strictly PG-rated."

"What can we expect?" Muriel asked quickly. "I must confess I've never seen a magician at work before."

"We'll be doing three of Adrian's most popular illusions. He thought since Carrington House has such a rich historical background, he'd set the scenes Victorian style."

"Is it his concept and design?"

"Every bit."

"It's magnificent."

Janice saw Ginger's lips curve upward.

"Trust me, it's not nearly as magnificent as Adrian under the spotlight. His first illusion will astound you. It's called the Vanishing Lady and I do mean vanishing. It segues immediately into the Artist's Dream, my personal favorite." She pointed directly at the oil painting nearby. "How Adrian accomplishes the illusion still baffles me every time I perform it with him."

Janice's gaze followed her pointing finger.

"Who is the girl in the painting, Ginger?"

Ginger's look at the painting was brief.

"Sylvia Parker. Adrian's number one assistant. Beautiful, no?"

"Beautiful, yes," Janice replied, emphatically.

"Well, I better find Adrian," Ginger said. "He always has last minute instructions before a performance."

Muriel's hand arced through the air.

"No need to go far—there he is now. And he looks as breathtaking as you do."

Janice's head whipped around, eager for a glimpse of Adrian in costume.

Muriel was right. He was breathtaking in his frills and satin, and like Ginger, he was a page out of a Victorian novel. Only he resembled no impetuous dandy. In his skintight breeches—and they were skin tight—he was every Victorian mother's nightmare. A man who radiated a vitality that drew women to him like magnets.

Deep in conversation with Lloyd and Jasper, he didn't seem to notice the hot looks in his direction. Janice wondered if he knew the effect he created wearing those breeches. Lord, he had to, she decided. There was a maddening air of arrogance that lived about him. Out of nowhere, she sensed he liked turning women on, perhaps even counted on his ability to do it. Disturbed by where her thoughts were heading, Janice realized forming an attraction for Adrian Magus would be fatal for a woman, a complete loss of her peace of mind.

He seemed in no hurry to join them, even seemed to ignore them. And then in the next second, his gaze was riveted on Janice's face. He gave a slight bow in greeting and Janice wondered why she should feel so strangely flattered by that steady gaze. And then he was all business again, whistling for Ginger who hurried to his side and was catapulted out the door. In seconds, Jasper was jumping the stage ramp and skidding to a halt in front of them.

"We're minutes away from the start, ladies," he remarked. "Time to find our front row seats."

He held out his hand to Muriel, who slid forward and allowed him to pull her up. Janice popped up and swiftly traced her way down the sloped ramp to the back of the solarium where Lloyd was finishing the final chair arrangement. He held a seat out for her, nodding.

"For you, mademoiselle."

Janice dropped down with a cheeky grin, settling herself in for a comfortable stay. She felt a shadow by her side almost immediately and looked up to find Jasper hovering close. A smile tugged at the corner of his mouth and she responded by raising her eyebrow. He bent down to her ear level.

"I have been dispatched by Adrian to take your compass, Janice."

"My compass!" Good Lord, how did Adrian know she carried a compass? She slid her hand into her slacks pocket and withdrew the oblong cylinder. "How did Adrian know?"

"I told him. He needed some personal effects for his illusion. He took my pipe. He wants Muree's wedding band. And since you brought no purse, he'll take your compass."

Janice dropped the compass into the middle of his outstretched palm.

"I'm not sure I like it that you can read minds so effectively, Jasper. It makes it hard to keep a secret from you."

He grinned affably, wrapping his palm around the compass,

and then retrieving the ring Muriel held out to him.

"Harmless hobby, really. I never intrude where I'm not wanted."

Janice laughed cheerfully, waving him away. Whirling, he sped out the door, but was back in seconds, pausing only long enough to switch the room lights off before slipping into his chair alongside Muriel.

In less than two minutes, music cut through the dark, streaming about their heads and bouncing off the walls. Center stage, a spotlight snapped on and Adrian stepped out of the dark into the light.

"Oh, my."

The words were out before Janice could stop them. *Gorgeous, he really is absolutely gorgeous.* His smile broke then, warm and spontaneous, and his gaze penetrated the darkness between them. Janice had the uncanny feeling that he had been able to read her thoughts just then. She stifled a shiver; however, in the next instant, the shiver fled, cut off by Bette Midler's rich, velvety tones and Ginger's sudden appearance from between the parted curtains. Adrian held out his arms and she stepped into his embrace, pressed her open lips to his and immediately vanished from his arms and their sight.

In the same instant, Janice felt a sizzle along her temple, her mind suddenly colliding with another's. In her mind's eye, a vision erupted, drowning out the room around her and sending a faint buzzing along the rim of her eardrums. Caught off guard, she gripped the chair arms in preparation for the phantom pain she knew would soon begin skittering along her pulse point. She hated unexpected tap-ins. They were painfully unnerving. She tucked her chin into her chest but was a fraction of a second too late. A flood of light came, followed by the sudden clear vision of a frightened young girl cowering in a crawlspace.

The woman's lips moved, but no sound emerged—at least none Janice could hear through the din clogging her ears—yet she knew the girl was calling for mercy from someone who was stalking her beyond the crawlspace. The vision lasted no more than thirty seconds before it began to fade, yet Janice attempted to hold on to it, hoping for a chance to memorize the young girl's face. It was a struggle; the more she tried to center her mind's eye on the girl, the more someone or something pushed the image from her mind.

And then the vision evaporated completely, leaving her dizzy and light-headed. The solarium room walls swam back into view and her gaze latched onto the drawing room set center stage and to reality. The buzzing in her ears ceased, and once again, Bette Midler's dulcet tones filled her ears. On stage, Ginger rematerialized in Adrian's arms and he lowered his mouth to hers. As their lips met, waves of nausea rocked Janice's stomach and it took all of what was left of her flagging energy not to black out under the phantom jolt. And then, like thieves fleeing down a darkened alley, both Adrian and Ginger vanished from sight. Her nausea and pain fled with them, leaving her even more lightheaded. A second later, one perfect red rose appeared on the floor in their place. In her ears, Janice heard a last haunting refrain: "In the spring, becomes the rose."

Chapter 10

FRIDAY—MINUTES LATER

Janice held her breath, her whole body wedded to the music. As the last tender strains of guitar strings faded away, the spotlight on the rose dimmed and the rose vanished from sight. At first, there was no movement or sound and Janice felt immense relief. It was heaven to have her pulse quieting and returning to normal.

Center stage, the birdcage began to twirl on the tabletop and though the tune was distinctly familiar, for the life of her Janice couldn't remember its title. No matter, the sweet sound was like the tinkle of crystal bells and acted as a welcome tonic to her frayed nerves. And then the soft, breathless sound of Michael Crawford sprang from the speakers. With seductive entreaty, he identified himself as the Angel of Music and called out to his ladylove, Christine.

In response to the musical plea, the drapes over the window casing began to slide back. The mood music changed from mysterious to romantic. Tremulous organ chords gave way to strings and percussion, and a single spotlight came up on the drapes highlighting the window frame. To Janice's surprise, the draperies revealed not a window as expected, but a life-size picture frame with blank canvas.

In sweet syncopation to the music, color began to seep through the pores of the canvas material and Janice gasped along with the others. Before their eyes, the blank canvas began to take shape and form, transforming itself into a life-size portrait of Adrian in all his Victorian splendor. And then the portrait came to life and Adrian stepped from it into the den.

Janice caught her lower lip between her teeth in surprise. He was good. Damn good—just as her sister had raved.

Mesmerized by his appearance, her eyes followed the seductive lift of his hands back toward the painting. A warm glow flowed through her as the painting transformed itself once again. Going blank, it rearranged colors, and to Janice's delight, reformed into a portrait of Ginger seated upon a garden swing. And then the spangles on her spectacular gown took on life, shimmering profusely, and Ginger stepped from the swing into Adrian's waiting embrace. They shared a brief kiss and the music swelled in perfect harmony.

Janice heard a low, pleasurable sigh emanating deep within her own throat and swallowed hard to keep it from being heard. She kept her gaze glued to the clinging couple, leaning forward in her chair, awed by the fusion of music and movement. Never had she seen it so skillfully blended or so ably executed. That it had been designed to create an emotional impact on the five physical senses was clear, right down to the seductive, soft fragrance of jasmine permeating the air. She realized Adrian had meant to move the viewer with the romantic beauty of the piece, and she knew that no viewer would be immune. She was moved by the illusion, sensed by their reverent silence the others were, too.

On stage, Ginger fled Adrian's embrace, drew close to the portrait and vanished once more to still life. Adrian reacted instantly, raising his hand to the portrait hanging above the fireplace. With split-second timing, the two portraits traded places. Stunned by the quick change, Janice emitted another sigh of appreciation. She studied Adrian's profile and saw his concentration was intense as he stared at the portraits. What was the secret? Where was the power? How was he able to maintain such a high level of energy, while being drained so physically and psychically?

The answer suddenly struck her. His hands! The power emanated from his hands. They were beautiful under the lights, expressive, mesmerizing. His entire act and stage presence were built around them. The way he smiled at the audience, flicked his hands. The way he paused for effect, like now, teasing them into catching their breath, making as if he were losing his concentration and the illusion would be lost. It was an incredible stage ploy designed to pull the heart out of an audience and cement them to him. It worked simply because it was the perfect symbiosis of his mind, heart, and soul with theirs.

Hearing the music swell, Janice returned her gaze to the portraits. They were shifting again, but now with an unexpected twist. Ginger's portrait vanished, replaced by a portrait of a woman with flaming red hair. Janice recognized the painting at once, as did Lloyd beside her. He stirred in his chair with a gargled croak. Turning her head, she found him tossing on his glasses so he could inspect the window frame more closely. By the look on his face, it was clear that he had recognized the painting as an exact duplicate of Princess Lisette in the gallery across the hall. Janice saw his mouth form the word "how?" She didn't know and the shake of her head told him so. He returned his glasses to his shirt pocket, stuffed them down and refocused his attention on the window frame. She did the same, though in her ear, she heard him mutter beneath his breath.

"He's too damn good."

Janice agreed completely, but before she could express the sentiment openly, the music peaked. The finale was in sight and she suspected its ending would be masterful and emotionally draining. She steeled herself for the onslaught and was surprised when a flicker of apprehension coursed through her. A quick, disturbing thought asserted itself like a neon sign in her mind. *Danger. Watch out.* Where had that thought come from? She must still be on edge from her earlier vision. She brushed at the goose bumps that pricked her skin and searched her mind. Nothing now. The thought had fluttered away as quickly as it had come.

Leaning forward in her chair, eager to be drawn into the last fusion of music and movement, Janice listened carefully as the Phantom's words beckoned, offered her to share one love, one lifetime. One love, one lifetime. The words began to echo over and over in her head and she couldn't make them stop. She shook her head for relief and felt an unwelcome sense of inadequacy sweep over her, followed by a light throbbing along her temple. Not again! She willed the pain away with another shake of her head and focused her attention on the continuing illusion. She'd not give into another aggravating vision. One a day was plenty.

The original painting reclaimed its home over the fireplace, Lisette's portrait vanishing. Janice's gaze flew to the windowpane, anticipating Ginger's arrival. The canvas went blank, seeped bright colors but showed no distinct new pattern forming.

Janice stole a peek at Adrian's face and her heart skipped a beat. He was in trouble, his concentration unraveling. She wasn't sure how she knew; his expression telegraphed no sign of distress. It was his hands, she realized. They were giving him away. They were struggling for—no against—something.

Suddenly, she saw him break off in mid-concentration, grasp his temple and double over as if in pain. Simultaneously, she felt her own mind plunge into a vortex of white light. Grabbing the arms of her chair, she fought to anchor herself to reality. Heavens, she was slipping again. Only this time she was going to sink deeper than before. Her throbbing temple was visible proof of the danger. She heard muffled groans all around her and knew this time she was not alone. Each of them was sinking like a heavy stone to the bottom of a bright white sea.

In sheer desperation, Janice forced her head to turn, her hand groping for Muriel's for support. Or was it guidance? Icy fear snaked around her heart when her fingers collided with Muriel's only to find them pried to the chair arms like steel bands. Janice forced her vision to clear through the misty white. Promptly, she was rewarded with the sight of Jasper, head in hand, fighting off his own set of pain. Muriel sat staring vacantly into space, her face deadly calm. She seemed to be in no pain, but her blank expression scared Janice more than if her body was besieged and wracked by uncontrollable shudders. Someone unknown was controlling her.

Flashing images across the white light cut off Janice's thoughts and she clutched her head in self-defense. Disjointed, garbled sounds began to assail her ears again and again. First came the knockings, rappings—distorted voices scrambling through her head. They all shouted for her to get out. Then she heard tortured cries, pleadings for mercy. Through the light, she caught sight of her earlier vision. Once again, a young girl in a cramped crawlspace reached out begging for mercy, her hands emphasizing her entreaty. Hands! Clawing hands! Adrian's hands!

Janice felt a cold touch on her arm and jumped sky-high. Her elbow jammed against cold steel and the pain was so intense it brought her out of her reverie and back into the solarium room. The gut-wrenching image dimmed, leaving Janice immobile, her heart hammering wildly against her ribcage.

"Jan-ice!" Lloyd's cry was breathless as if spoken through gritted teeth.

Janice turned her head, almost blacking out in the process. She clutched the chair arms again and braced herself. She must get a grip on reality, no matter the pain. Blinking rapidly, she forced her eyes to look at Lloyd, who was clearly struggling to control and center his own thoughts. With sheer force of will, he threw off the pain long enough to lift a finger and point center stage.

Though it was a struggle, Janice swung her head around again and guessed she was searching for Adrian. Her rapid eye movement made her head spin and she willed it to stop. She had to find Adrian. Screams began to sizzle through her ears once more, sending waves of nausea to the pit of her stomach. She willed the screams and nausea to stop. Where was Adrian? She needed Adrian. Why did she need Adrian?

Out of nowhere, the screams and pain died down, allowing her to fight past the blinding light and perceive him. He was struggling to his feet, balancing his head carefully atop his neck. Though he moved like a slug, Janice thought him lucky. He seemed to be the only one of them capable of moving inside the pain with any degree of success. She watched as he struggled to his knees, clutching the sofa for needed support. Semi-upright, he dragged his body sideways, away from the window frame. At the outer edge of the sofa, he went still and Janice wondered if he had blacked out. She couldn't tell since his prone figure was backlit by the proscenium lights, which were fast becoming cloaked in a transparent blue haze. The jasmine scent was suddenly everywhere, causing Janice to wish she could cover her nose to keep from inhaling the noxious smell. God, would this nightmare never end? Her stomach was heaving enough already without the smell. As if on cue, her mind cleared to see a thin blue mist begin to seep slowly through the pores of the canvas frame.

"Janice!" The groan was anxious and she turned to Adrian, grateful he had moved again, this time able to reach the opposite end of the sofa. "Janice!" The call was more urgent this time. Filled with her own desperation now that the blue mist was rising upward more quickly, she stammered hoarsely.

"Here."

"Get behind me," he ordered. When she didn't move, an emphatic growl followed. "Get behind me!"

Janice's blood chilled at the command. Get behind him? What for? She tried to connect her mind to his but was thwarted. All she felt was emptiness, but the power of that emptiness propelled her from her seat. Bolting up the ramp, she scurried to the haven of Adrian's side in less than fifteen seconds.

He was on his feet now, more in control of his body and moving past the pain. He pulled Janice behind his back, sheltering her from the mist that now hung in wide strips in front of the painting. Janice peered over his shoulder at the shimmering shape transforming itself into a distinctly feminine form.

"I don't sense a threat, do you?" she whispered. Her fingers plucked at his shirt back for reassurance. The feel of his body heat seeping through the material steadied her as she awaited his reply.

"She's waiting."

"For what?"

"I don't know," he barked over his shoulder.

"Well, don't take it out on me!" Janice barked back.

At their heated words, the shape before them surged upward, shimmering from blue to angry red. Janice's heart dropped to her toes and she took a hasty step back. Adrian had the good sense to do the same. Had the mist sensed their anger? It must have. Why else would it continue to alternate from red to blue repeatedly as if soaking up their emotions?

Eyes glued to the mist, they watched and waited for a sign. When none came, Adrian called out loudly to the others.

"Can you move, Lloyd?"

His reply was swift.

"Think so."

"Get over here."

Seconds later, Janice felt her right shoulder shaded by a second barrier.

"Jasper?"

"Blinding headache, I'm afraid. Vision's gone. No help to you."

"Muriel," Janice called out, casting a half-glance his way. "She's out."

At her words, he reached out and groped for Muriel's pulse point. Locating it, he wrapped his fingers around her wrist.

"Can't see her face clearly, my vision's fogged, but her pulse is strong. She's unhurt."

"You better move away from her, Jasper," Adrian cautioned as the mist began to drift down and away from the painting. "Our lady friend is about to make herself known to us, I think."

Janice heard the scrape of Jasper's chair and knew he had followed Adrian's warning. It was a good warning, Janice surmised as she peered between the men's shoulders and saw the mist had finished its transformation. Before them now floated a curvaceous, womanly shape.

"For three centuries, I have been empty."

The voice was so startling clear that for a moment Janice thought it had come from the mist itself. But when Adrian and Lloyd swung their heads to the right, Janice realized she had erred. Muriel had spoken, or at least a melodious voice similar to Muriel's had spoken. It spoke again, repeating itself.

"For three centuries, I have been empty."

The spirit paused, obviously expecting a return reply. When none came, the spirit tried again.

"I cannot harm you. I am spirit, lost and empty. I seek release, only release, nothing more. I seek to speak to the woman. Will she speak to me?"

Adrian made a protective gesture as if to deny the spirit, but Janice thwarted him by slipping between the men's shoulders. She felt Adrian's fingers tug at her sweater back and was cheered by the support.

"I will speak with you. My name is Janice."

"For three centuries I have been empty, Janice."

"I'm sorry. I don't understand the meaning of your words. Will you tell me what they mean?"

"Across time, I have come to show you their meaning."

"Show?"

"Through you and the man."

"Man?"

"The one who stands behind. The one who pretends to dislike you so."

Adrian's fingers twitched on her waist and Janice found herself liking the misty cloud. It didn't beat around the bush. The spirit seemed to sense her acceptance.

"In the spirit world, all has purpose. Believe you this?"

Janice sobered, nodding her head.

"I believe it."

"Then believe my single words. Another has interfered with my destiny. Altered its purpose. For that, I am imprisoned in emptiness."

"In a crawlspace?" Janice asked, suddenly understanding her earlier vision.

"You have said it."

"You seek the crawlspace?"

"Non, I seek not it. It is matter, nothing more. Rien plus."

"I don't know what you seek then."

"Aubert. Until I am one with Aubert, there is only emptiness. That is my destiny. Do you understand this?"

"No, I don't."

The spirit drifted closer then, causing Janice to take a hasty step back. Adrian's hand slipped around her waist to keep her from treading on his toes.

"Does the man who transforms matter understand my words?"

"I'm afraid not," Adrian replied.

"Then believe you this. Until I am one with Aubert, this house shall serve as prison, as my soul is imprisoned." The spirit waved her hand, and all around them, Janice heard the sound of sizzling fire. Outside the solarium windows, the night sky exploded with a fiery, red glow.

"What the hell? . . . "

Lloyd's curse was cut off as Adrian slammed his elbow hard against Lloyd's ribcage. The spirit waivered, and in the distant regions of the house below and above, there was the rending sound of bolts soldered into place.

The spirit moved then, floating upward, startling them all with her agility. Janice took a half-turn back, colliding again with Adrian. She clutched his shirt collar for support, wondering briefly how much more abuse his toes could take. If she got any closer to him, they'd be breathing out of the same pair of lungs. Cautiously, she watched the mist drift its way back to the window frame and begin to dissipate into the canvas pores.

"Lisette?" Janice called out uneasily.

The mist paused in its evaporation. Through Muriel, it spoke again, its tone sad and wistful.

"That which was Lisette is non plus. Her body is lost, now remains only her spirit. Soon, without release, even that will be lost."

The mist began to dissipate again, seeping through the canvas, leaving a collage of undecipherable patterns staining the canvas in its wake. From her chair, Muriel called out sadly.

"I ache. Je faire."

As the words faded away, Janice saw Muriel's head slump to her chest. Immediately, Janice's mind link with the spirit and the others severed completely. Janice's knees gave way and she would have collapsed totally if not for Adrian's tightening embrace. Moving with an agility she didn't expect, he spun her around and deposited her into the folds of the deep cushions of the sofa. Wearily, he plopped down beside her, brushing at the beads of sweat coating his forehead.

Across the room, Muriel gave a soft groan and her plump body began to slide from the chair. Jasper bolted from his seat, snatching her up as she came awake. It was obvious by her expression she was shocked to find herself being propped stiffly into the chair. Janice saw her inspect Jasper's face first and then her gaze sought each of them in succession.

"Damn, I've missed the best part, haven't I? A ghost?"

Janice saw her look to Jasper for confirmation. He patted her hand and nodded.

"A rather pretty one, Muree."

Muriel's face lit up even though it was clear she was disappointed.

"Was I her voice? I seem to remember a very pretty voice somewhere far off."

Jasper nodded again.

"My dear, you were wonderful. The star attraction."

Muriel waved him away and Janice sensed her annoyance.

"Well, I'm mad as hell. I hate missing all the fun. I was so enjoying Adrian's performance. Wouldn't you think ghosts could learn better manners?"

"Or better timing," Adrian muttered wryly.

Muriel was the only one to laugh at his sarcasm.

"Dear me, Adrian, has your ego been inconvenienced?"

Amused by her cheerful barb, Adrian laughed—the first genuine laugh Janice had heard him utter since they had met. It was undiluted, deep, warm and rich. Hearing it, she realized they had all been wrong about him. He was far kinder than he wanted anyone to know. She found the thought disturbing—what had happened to make him jaded and callous enough over the years to hide his kindness?

At the foot of the stage, Muriel pushed herself up from her chair, then gave a start when she caught sight of the red hue blazing outside the window.

"What's happening outside? Is there a fire?"

All smiles vanished at once, no one eager to be the one to explain things to Muriel just yet. Sensing their reluctance, she re-sat herself murmuring softly.

Jasper patted her hand and an uncomfortable silence descended now that the shared danger was at an end. For a moment, each stared out the window, mesmerized by the fiery red glow. And then a thunderous pounding erupted from the window seat box stage right, startling them all and sending Adrian to his feet with an anxious shout.

"Ginger!"

Lloyd sprang forward with Adrian, Janice following on their heels. Ginger's cries were muted from the box at first, unintelligible, but as Adrian flung back the seat cover, she exploded in venomous rage.

"Damn you to hell, Adrian! How dare you lock me inside this box! You made me pass out! I near suffocated." She hauled up her crinolines and climbed over the edge of the box. Tripping slightly, she knocked Adrian's hand away as he offered help. "I suppose you think that was damn funny."

"Ginger, I can explain."

"It had better be good. "

She took a stance so intimidating Janice thought even the bravest of heroes would wither under the scrutiny. That Adrian was rattled by it was clear; he struggled to find adequate words to describe the last few minutes. Janice didn't envy him. Nor could she help him. She hadn't the foggiest notion of how to tell a rational, sensible woman that she had just missed conversing with a ghostly apparition. Finally, out of sheer desperation Janice supposed, Adrian settled for the truth.

"Oh, hell, Ginger. The illusion was stopped by a ghost. She broke my concentration."

The slap was so unexpected and thrown with such incredible force that Janice almost felt its impact from where she stood. Though Adrian had been struck, it was she who took a step back, while the others remained frozen in place at the bottom of the stage ramp. The silence in the room became as chilled as a sheet of glazed ice. Ginger's eyes never left Adrian's face as she railed.

"I'm not some dumb bimbo you picked up outside your stage door, Adrian. Don't you ever treat me again as if I were."

She moved then, storming past the trio, down the ramp and toward the exit door. Halfway down the solarium, she spotted the red glow outside the window and veered sharply toward it. The group dashed after her, calling a simultaneous warning. Lloyd was the first to reach her; however, he was a fraction of a second too late as he made a grab for her hand to prevent it colliding with the glass pane. A red electrical charge snaked out and swiped at her fingertips. Ginger jumped back, too stunned to cry out. Eyes wide as saucers, she inched her way backward, slamming into Janice who steadied her. From the look on her face, Janice knew she needed rational confirmation that she wasn't hallucinating. Her gaze finally swung from the window to Janice.

"We're trapped?"

"Yes."

"By a ghost?"

"Yes."

Her gaze flew to Adrian for comfort but Janice saw his stare was centered on the red glow outside. By the stoic set of his shoulders, it was clear he wasn't going to forgive Ginger for the slap. Ginger's face fell and Janice's maternal instincts kicked in. She stifled an urge to kick Adrian in the shins for his brutal hostility. He had no right to be so ugly to Ginger, or blame her for what had transpired. It wasn't her fault. It was none of their faults.

Draping an arm around Ginger, Janice squeezed her shoulders in sympathy.

"We were all powerless to stop what occurred. Even Adrian, as brilliant a psychic as he is."

Muriel shadowed her other side, slipping an arm around Ginger's waist.

"Janice is right. It was out of our hands. Even if you had been awake, it wouldn't have done any good."

A tearful sob escaped Ginger's lips as she embraced their waists in gratitude. Together, the trio turned and faced the window. Beyond the pane, the night sky fired up, turning an even brighter, angrier shade of red.

Chapter 11

FRIDAY—10:30 PM

Wake up! The stark command sizzled through Janice's brain and she came full awake, almost tumbling off the window seat she was perched on. Heart racing, she righted herself and swung her gaze to the dimly lit room behind her. Had she heard Lloyd's voice? Squinting, she surveyed the shadows. Nothing. There had been no human voice calling, she realized, only her own inner voice chiding her to stay awake until the men came back from their foraging. She nibbled at her lower lip, wondering how long before the men would return. It had been an hour since they had disappeared into the main part of the chateau on a scouting expedition. What had they found? She shook her head, not at all sure she really wanted to know.

Nothing had changed outside the window in the last hour either. The fiery red glow stood vigil outside the solarium window, guarding them and the house. Prisoners! The word chilled her and Janice bit her lip again, this time tasting blood. Uncurling her feet from beneath her, she let them slide to full length along the window seat ledge. She felt the heated vibration on her pant leg and shifted her legs away. Oh no, you don't, she admonished the glow silently. Once was enough.

Leaning her head back against the window frame, she sighed deeply. She knew in times of crises someone always seemed to remain calm and rational while everyone else involved fell to pieces. But why did it have to be her? She let her gaze travel to the reclining figures stretched out on the sofas pulled a few yards from where she sat and knew why. She was holding herself together for Muriel and Ginger's benefit. For some inexplicable reason, she felt compelled to mask her growing anxieties from the women and project a confidence they could rely on. The question now was could she maintain the mask indefinitely?

She gave a sudden shiver, wondering if the purpose of this crazy situation was to sacrifice a human life for . . . what had Lisette's spirit said? The release of her soul? Janice pushed the terrifying thought away. No, the spirit hadn't seemed revengeful or heartless, only in great pain.

Turning her head, Janice rested her other cheek on her knees. She stared into the dark shadows of the room and felt her eyelids flutter wearily. Sleep, blessed sleep. If only she could succumb to its entreaty. Her eyelids flickered open immediately. She mustn't sleep. Not until the men came back and she knew for sure how hopelessly stuck they were.

The human shadow came so quietly across the space that at first Janice thought she had imagined it. But as it neared and took form, she reared her head up quickly. Lloyd! In a flash, she was off the window seat and by his side. Her rapid movement alerted the two women on the sofas, who also sprang up.

"Anything?" Janice asked as the trio circled his form.

His expression was one of defeat.

"Nothing. It's the same all over. The energy field is everywhere, blocking every window and exit." His defeat changed to distress and Janice touched his arm.

"What is it, Lloyd? Are you ill?"

His expression grew more distressed and Janice sensed an inner panic within him.

"I can't find Suzie, the serving girl who set the buffet. I've searched thoroughly. Nothing."

"The glow outside has probably frightened her into hiding," Muriel suggested. "She looked awfully young."

"Barely out of her teens." His scowl deepened. "What if she takes refuge in a hiding place?"

His meaning was clear and Janice found herself fumbling blindly for a chair to drop into.

"You do know where all the crawlspaces are, don't you, Lloyd?"

He didn't answer but stiffened at the question. Janice licked her lips nervously again. God, sometimes history repeated itself. Sometimes a spirit took a fiendish delight in creating déjà vu. She pushed the thought away as Ginger sank into a chair alongside her, dusting her hands nervously.

"Where are the others?" she asked.

"Still searching. They've gone to investigate the chapel on the top floor." Lloyd fell silent and Janice saw his brooding scowl. She reached out and squeezed his hand.

"You mustn't blame yourself for what's occurred, Lloyd."

"Of course I'm to blame," he barked. "There were warning signs I simply ignored. I'm gifted. I can read people as easily as they read their watches. Why didn't I see this coming?" He pounded his leg in emphasis. "I should've seen this coming."

The self-censure in his voice touched Janice and she wished she had answers to give him. Since she didn't, she felt it best to turn all their minds to something more constructive.

"What do you suppose is on the other side of that red field?" she asked. "I mean, what are the people across the water seeing when they look this way?"

"That's an odd tack on things," Lloyd declared. Janice knew her diversion had worked.

"But important."

"How so, my dear?" Muriel asked.

"Is the glow we see real?" Janice responded. "Or are our minds being cleverly manipulated to make it seem so?"

She heard Lloyd's snort as he tossed his head.

"The force field is real. Just ask Ginger there. When she made to touch it, it leapt out and sniped at her. You saw it. She felt the charge."

Ginger shivered beside her and Janice knew Adrian's assistant would rather not remember that moment.

"You think we're imagining all this?" Muriel asked. "All of us linked somehow to experience the same vision as reality, like the headaches?"

"Part of me suspects that. But the energy that it would take to sustain the vision for seconds at a time, not to mention a full hour . . . no, I don't think we could do it. One of us would give way. Crack under the mental strain."

"We're exceptional psychics, Jan," Lloyd reminded her bitterly.

Janice shook her head.

"No, there's only one exceptional psychic here, Lloyd, and that's Adrian Magus. The rest of us have only one specific talent. He has myriad skills."

Lloyd finally took a seat and hunched over, interrupting Janice.

"Adrian is a clever illusionist, nothing more."

Janice gave him a black-layered look.

"How can you be so obtuse after sitting through his performance? The man transforms matter, Lloyd. He is a telepath, has precognition . . . he knew what was coming. I swear it. I saw it. It was in his hands."

Lloyd scoffed with a wave.

"He was paralyzed by the pain like the rest of us. He succumbed to it."

"But he moved through it all. While we were rooted to our chairs and to the pain, he moved through it. He knew before any of us that Lisette was coming across and he sensed at once she was looking for me. He sensed danger long before we did. Only an exceptional psychic could do that."

"So, what's your point?"

"Lisette asked Adrian if he understood her words to me."

"And he denied knowing their meaning. I believe him, don't you?"

"I don't know." Janice shrugged. "Jasper says throughout his life, Adrian has had a recurring vision of a red-headed woman. He says it's me, but in the portrait gallery earlier, you mentioned how much I reminded you of Lisette. Suppose Adrian's image in reality is Lisette? Suppose she planted it there?" She broke off, seeing the determined shake of Lloyd's head. "Well, why not?"

"Because the image was you, Janice. I've seen it."

"You've seen it? Where? When?"

He didn't answer right away and Janice knew the question made him uncomfortable. She watched a range of emotions ebb and flow across his face before he finally gave a shrug and answered.

"Interrogating Adrian in Iraq was hell. He was on overload, absorbing the volatile emotions of the soldiers dying around him. As a parapsychologist, I did what I could to help under the circumstances, saw to it he was shipped home, but not before I garnered a brief glance of the image. It was you, but I never put two and two together. Not even after you and I met at the university. In fact, I never realized you were that woman until tonight when I saw the look on Adrian's face as you walked in to dinner. Everything clicked in place, like the glass shattering."

Janice's heart skipped a beat.

"It was a forewarning none of us picked up on," Lloyd continued. "Adrian wasn't holding that glass tight. We all saw that. Still it shattered. Why?" He leaned in closer, his gaze steady. "Do you remember feeling anything unusual at the time, Janice?"

"Unusual?" Janice hoped the question sounded thoughtful, because inside her chest, her heart was beginning a strange tattoo along her ribcage and her lungs were beginning to constrict rapidly, like they always did when she prepared to tell a lie. Should she tell Lloyd about her mind link with Adrian? And the brief image of limbs entwined in sexual combat? She studied the inquisitive face leaning into her, waiting patiently for her answer. No, she couldn't tell Lloyd. The image was too disturbing. At first, she had surmised the entwined limbs were hers and Adrian's. But, now that Lisette had revealed her need to be reunited with Aubert, it was possible she and Adrian had tapped into Lisette and Aubert sharing an extremely pleasurable interlude. But she had to be sure before confiding.

"Janice?"

"Sorry. I was trying to relive the incident to see if there was anything useful for us to know about it. I can't think of a thing. It happened so rapidly. Perhaps, Adrian could offer more. You might ask him."

"That question will have to wait." Muriel stated. "Our first priority has to be figuring out Lisette's time line before she died. Tell us about her, Lloyd. How did she die?"

"Most people would want to know how she lived," Lloyd countered.

"Well, then, how did she live? Who was she?"

"She was the Earl of Montagne's first cousin. Spent her early life tucked away in a cold-as-ice convent. Her parents betrothed her to Baron Dumas when she was nine, he twenty. He owned a fleet of cargo ships. Sailed the waters to and from America for years and came to love the savagery of the new land. He decided to make his fortune and future here so he bought land and built Witchwood. When Lisette was eighteen, he sent for her, arranged a mammoth wedding."

"Sounds like an idyllic love story," Ginger interjected. "Boy meets girl, boy gets girl. What went wrong?"

"The records are sketchy but I've managed to piece together some of what must have occurred. They were to be married in the chapel upstairs. The day of the wedding, the staff rose early, eager to get a head start on the wedding preparations. You can imagine the scullery maid's terror when she found the baron's severed head sitting atop the banister stairwell. Her blood-curdling screams echoed up three levels of stairs. They found the baron's upper torso in the West wing's library. His lower torso rested in the East wing master bedroom."

Janice gave an uncontrollable shiver.

"Mutilation?"

"Hmm. Gruesome, isn't it?"

"Too much so. And Lisette?"

He gave an impatient shrug.

"Disappeared without a trace."

"Locked in a crawlspace, you mean," Janice replied. "Terrified and hiding. But from whom, do you think?"

Lloyd shook his head and Janice knew he had no answer. Leaning back, she realized their survival depended on learning the answer to who had killed the baron. It was somewhere through a heavy mist. Could they break through it?

An unexpected touch on her shoulder startled her to the present. Clutching her chest, she looked up to find Adrian staring down at her. He patted her shoulder lightly.

"Sorry, didn't mean to scare the hell out of you." He drew up a chair to hers and straddled it. "I assume you're trying to piece together Lisette's life?"

Before she could nod her assent, Jasper pulled a chair alongside Muriel and straddled it. His expression was grim as he cautioned.

"We better come up with something soon. Our investigation of the chateau has been fruitless." His gaze found Janice's. "We are truly trapped. Our only option is to reason this whole nightmare out amongst ourselves."

Janice couldn't agree more. The sooner they discovered Lisette's murderer—and Janice was sure that being sealed in a tiny crawlspace whatever the reason did constitute murder—the better off they'd be. She leaned in, studying the men's faces.

"Do either of you feel we are living in an illusion created by our own minds?"

"Impossible," Jasper stated immediately. "We couldn't maintain that type of illusion for any length of time."

"Maybe one of us could," Lloyd interjected and Janice knew he was recalling their earlier discussion. Beside her, she felt Adrian stiffen. She turned to find his gaze boring into her own.

"I assume Janice has been trying to convince you I've created this illusion somehow? A continuation of my Vegas performance, perhaps?"

Janice didn't miss the smoldering anger beneath his sarcasm. Lloyd came to her defense without hesitation.

"She thinks nothing of the kind. If truth be told, Adrian, she finds you exceptionally gifted. Admires you tremendously for how you held us all together during the mind link."

Janice felt her cheeks flame under Adrian's sudden scrutiny of her face. He was speechless in his surprise and so was she. Damn Lloyd's runaway tongue! She had voiced no such opinion of Adrian. Out loud, that is. Damn and double damn! She hoped the semi-darkness of the room hid the flush in her cheeks adequately or there would be hell to pay. Obviously sensing her discomfort, Adrian turned his gaze from her and then studied each face in turn.

"I'm going to say this once, and only once. I don't know what's going on. I'm as much in the dark as any of you."

"I believe you, Adrian." Muriel's voice was filled with a defiance that dared anyone to say differently, and Janice found her protective instincts endearing. "We all have to work through this together," Muriel continued, "if we want to get out of here alive, that is."

"We're all getting out of here alive," Adrian countered. "Nothing else is acceptable. So, what's our first move? Besides admitting the obvious bullshit that we're trapped by a ghost who wants her soul freed."

"No." Janice corrected. "She wants to be reunited with Aubert. To be one with Aubert, that's what she said."

"Do we know anything about this Aubert?" Adrian asked Lloyd.

"Death by mutilation."

"Horrible death," Jasper muttered. "Is it possible his soul is trapped and needs release?"

Janice's eyes lit up at his words.

"That makes sense. Lisette implied her destiny had been interfered with. Altered in some way. Is it possible that her soul is tied to Aubert's and if we release his soul, we also release hers?"

"How do normal people release a dead spirit's soul?" Ginger asked with a shiver.

"Good question, Ginger," Adrian complimented. "Only one way I can think of is to backtrack and find Aubert's murderer."

Lloyd gave a busted laugh.

"Are you crazy? Do you know how long that would take? He

died centuries ago. We don't know a damn thing about his life or his enemies. There's no way to backtrack, not fully enough."

"Oh yes, there is," Janice piped up. "The old wing, Lloyd. You said it's still intact. Rooms, treasures, everything intact."

She saw his thoughtful frown.

"Yes, but . . . "

Muriel leaned forward, catching Janice's excitement.

"Is there a library in the old wing, Lloyd?" At his nod, Muriel clapped her hands once. "There'll be records, hordes of them. They wrote everything down back in those days. Diaries . . . "

Adrian slapped his thigh, smiling with satisfaction.

"We start there. We go through every book and if that doesn't work, we split up in teams and search the chateau thoroughly, every room! Agreed?"

Every head nodded in assent and Muriel added as a last thought.

"With our second sight, we should be able to time slip, tap in and put ourselves back there. Experience the moment. Alone, we'd never do it, but together, we might get away with it."

"Can you really do that tap in thing?" Ginger asked with another nervous half-giggle. Lloyd reached over and patted her hand affectionately.

"Only in mind, not in body."

Ginger's face relaxed and Janice saw her give her first genuine smile since the dinner table.

"Thank God. I suddenly had visions of you all exploding into fragments like the glass did. Or worse, beaming up like they do in a *Star Trek* transporter."

"Speaking of that glass, Adrian," Lloyd said, turning back to the group. "I was telling Janice earlier that the shattering was a warning we failed to pick up on. Do you remember anything unusual at the time it happened? Janice says she recalls nothing."

Janice could hear her teeth grinding into her jawbone at the pronouncement. Damn Lloyd's free-spirited tongue. Why was he revealing their conversation to Adrian? Didn't they have enough trouble without adding more fuel to an already out-of-control fire? She stole a peek at Adrian's countenance. Would he reveal their mind link to the group? He disliked her enough to. His gaze locked with hers and Janice felt the air in her lungs suddenly drain. To her surprise, a silent message passed between them. Adrian was the first to pull his gaze away.

"I only know one thing," he replied, flashing a grin at the group. "Things would be so much easier if ghosts came with a set of instructions."

The group laughed at his remark and Janice felt her muscles relax. It was a good ploy on Adrian's part to make them laugh. After all, if they were busy laughing, there would be no time for screaming. She glanced at Lloyd, who gave her the "thumbs up" sign and then stood. He signaled for them all to follow. Uncurling her legs, Janice rose, only to find Adrian blocking her way.

"Did you really say you admired me tremendously, Janice?"

"Of course not," she replied. "If I focused everyone's attention on your tremendous talent and skills, I'd no longer be the center of attention, and God knows, it's all about me and the limelight."

He had the sense to look embarrassed at her obvious reference to his earlier shredding of her character and for a moment, Janice almost felt sorry for him. Then she shook herself mentally. No, it was his fault they were enemies, not hers. She held his gaze, not about to be the first to look away this time. A niggling question surfaced as their glances remained locked in a silent battle of wills. Was Jasper right? Was he pretending to dislike her to cover up some irrational fear he had of her? No, that was ludicrous. She couldn't see him wasting time with pretenses. Especially when he could use barbed insults so effectively.

Seeing his glance falter, Janice steeled herself for the upcoming insult and dropped her gaze. When it didn't come, her glance shot up to find him grinning at her.

"Go ahead and say it, Miss Kelly."

"Say what?" she hedged.

"That you find my humor provocative and extremely sexy."

Janice's eyes widened at his audacious wit. He was teasing her again, damn him. Well, she was through battling with his jaded wit. Squaring her shoulders, she met his gaze.

"Do something for me, Adrian?"

"What? "

"Go to hell!"

He bowed immediately.

"Yes, ma'am. I'm on my way."

With a springy bounce, he was gone, striding across the room to join the others. Once there, he took hold of Ginger's shoulders and pushed her out into the corridor ahead of him. Laughter spilled back through the door and as it faded away, Janice knew she'd wasted her insult.

With a reluctant sigh, she took the same path to the door. Must Adrian's every movement remind her of his sexual attractiveness? She rounded the doorframe and caught sight of Lloyd waving from the hallway landing. Behind him, the others were already disappearing up the staircase. As she reached the stairwell, she offered her hand to Lloyd, who squeezed it affectionately. Hand in hand, they ascended the staircase and soon caught up with the waiting group. Two flights later, the group had worked their way into the unused section of the manor. By the time they reached the mammoth library and spotted the massive bookshelves surrounding them, their expressions clouded over with worry. Ginger was the first to speak.

"How will we ever wade through all these books in such a short time?"

Seeing the same perplexed expressions all around, Janice took up the reins of command and stepped forward.

"Nothing ventured, nothing gained," she quoted brightly.

Crossing to a bookshelf, she took down two large volumes from the top shelf and placed them on the floor, then repeated the pattern. Beside her, Adrian did the same, starting his own stack alongside hers.

"Spread out. Take a wall," he urged.

Out of the corner of her eye, Janice saw the others split in three directions. Soon, the floor was carpeted with stacks of books. Janice tried not to let the enormity of their task daunt her. Somewhere in these stacks was a bridge back through the strings of time. They'd find it and cross it. They'd relive that last horrendous day and somehow make sense of it.

Pulling a gray wingback directly beneath the overhead chandelier, Janice dropped onto its plush cushions. Around her, the others did the same. Grabbing the top book of her stack, she ran her fingertips efficiently across the ragged book edge. Concentrating, she tried to tap in to its pages. Nothing. She closed the book, took another. Again, she ran her fingers across and along the bindings. Nothing. She took another, then a fourth. Soon, her first stack began to dwindle and soon, the only audible sound in the room was the careful, slow turning of book pages.

Chapter 12

FRIDAY—MIDNIGHT

For the fifth time in as many minutes, Adrian found his gaze straying from the printed text to the white brocade sofa where the women sat. His gaze centered on brilliant colored hair then dropped to view high cheekbones tinged with a musk-rose flush. If only he could explain this tendency he had to stare at Janice. Even now, he couldn't stop thinking how arresting her face was in the glow of the off-white lighting. How the blue of her angora sweater heightened the translucence of her neck and face. It was insane to go on this way, a slave to an unknown prickling along his scalp.

Still, he couldn't seem to budge his mind from thoughts of Janice. His gaze raked her face again, tracing the ridge of her Grecian nose, to the full lips rounded over even white teeth. Her eyes were hidden from him at the moment as she sat poring over the stack of books in her lap. Still, it didn't matter. He didn't need to see to recall their color. He had memorized those eyes the moment their glance had locked across the rim of the shattered glass in his hand. He would always remember their color, even when this hell they were currently experiencing was over. He would always remember her eyes, not because of her per se, but because they brought back the same stirring he felt as a child when he gazed at the sea-green water of Rocky Reef Cove.

Adrian let his gaze drop to her fingers as they skimmed each book edge with the expertise of a Braille reader. She was scanning three books to his one and it was apparent by the growing stack at her feet that she possessed an extraordinary talent in her hands. With just the delicate touch of flesh to paper, she was tuning into some long ago memory of the book owner. He wondered if she knew how transparent her face was in relaying the emotions she sensed beneath her fingers.

Adrian drew his gaze back to the book clasped in his own grip. Inwardly, he gave a sigh and willed his mind back to its task. His mind obeyed for a few moments, then it wandered off, choosing instead to drift into a vague, shadowy fugue of its own.

In his mind's eye, a picture formed. He stood on one side of a large chasm, Janice on the other. The chasm was steadily breaking apart, taking her from his sight and from his life. The vision made his stomach curl as if an army of snakes were slithering in its pit. He scowled, wondering how he came to be acting like a love-struck fool. He—a man recently crowned the darling of Las Vegas—brought so low as to moon over the beauty of a woman. He clenched his jaw tighter. Next, he'd be down on all fours, baying like a lonely hound dog.

Taking himself to task again, more harshly this time, Adrian forced his mind into accepting reality. He had no woman to complicate his life. That was that. So what if for a few moments he had fantasized that Janice was his? A good fantasy never hurt a male ego. And what did it matter if he had allowed himself to hope that Janice's abrupt arrival into his life meant an end to his empty, meaningless existence wowing crowds and indulging in wild parties? That didn't mean a thing either. Hadn't his life been empty and meaningless twice before? And hadn't he come through both holocausts with the minutest of scars?

Pensively, he looked out across the room. Was his life empty? Yes, at the moment it appeared to be. Was it meaningless? No. Somewhere there was a woman for him, and she would be his life preserver on his stormy sea. With a will of its own, his glance again found Janice's shapely form. Was Janice that woman? He didn't know and not knowing rattled him. His gut instinct told him she mustn't be and that worried him. Why, he wasn't sure. He only sensed that when she returned to her life in Colorado, he would feel an extraordinary void worse than his present one.

Out of nowhere, Adrian felt a muscle spasm in the small of his back and grimaced. Damn the useless, wooded chair! He shifted on the padded cushion to release the kink. If only he could drown his aches and doubts in a good, stiff drink.

Snapping the book in his hand closed, he slid it along the tabletop and reached for another from the stack to his right. Flipping it open, he wondered if the others were experiencing small fugues of their own. Did they feel as drained as he did? He gave a cursory glance at each of their faces. Yes, they appeared tired, and worse, on edge. Who would be the first to crack under the strain of their captivity?

He slid his gaze right and studied the woman seated cross-legged on the floor, rubbing her back against the edge of the sofa. She was flipping through a stack of pages, and as she did so, her face collapsed into a complex set of wrinkles, her mouth puckered into a tiny rosette. Instantly, he realized Ginger was the one who would crack under the pressure. And soon. As he watched her begin to nibble at her lower lip, he once again felt that reptilian army marching in the pit of his stomach. Damn Lloyd for inviting him here and damn his own arrogant cowardice for coming. He hadn't wanted to face the weekend reunion alone and in his self-absorption he hadn't even given the briefest thought to what Ginger wanted.

Adrian shifted in his seat again, trying to stem the shooting pain that had now traveled to the middle of his back. How many more hours could he endure reading these damnable pages? He'd like nothing better than to hurl the stack of books to the floor and indulge in a drink, a smoke, and a woman.

As if conjured from his thoughts, a book sailed through his line of vision, hit the floor, skidded a few yards and then rammed the leg of the table where he sat. Adrian blinked in surprise, sure he was crossing over into some mind dementia where inanimate objects came mysteriously to life.

"I can't do this anymore!" The whine was brimming with distaste. Around him, heads shot up, as startled as he by Ginger's emotional outburst. She scrambled to her feet and stared at each one of them in turn, seeming to dare them to object to her words. "I want out!"

Her words were said in a rush and Adrian realized she meant to storm from the room in a huff. Knowing it wasn't safe for any of them to travel alone at the moment, he bolted from his chair, intercepting her as she came round his table.

"You're tired, Ginger. We all are. Use the couch over there. Get some rest."

Her eyes iced over immediately.

"I want out of this house now, Adrian," she declared, pursing her lips.

"It's not possible at the moment," Adrian reminded. "You know that." She made a move to shove past him but he threw out his arm. Her face paled in anger.

"Let me by, Adrian."

Adrian stood his ground, not about to let her pass. The snakes in his stomach inched up and around his ribcage.

"It's not wise for any of us to split up, Ginger. Now, stay put."

Her eyes took on an even more ferocious glitter.

"Get out of my way, Adrian, or I'll hit you again, I swear it!"

A chill, black silence descended as her words sank in. Rapidly, the group came out of their seats, intent on warding off another ugly confrontation. Adrian should've been pleased by their concern but felt angered instead. Their hovering made him lash out at Ginger, the last thing he intended to do.

"Dammit, Ginger, you are *not* going out that door. I'll tie you down if I have to!"

The threat pushed her over the edge and she flew at him like a shrew. Using both hands, she shoved him hard. Adrian stumbled back, knocking his hip against the table edge and emitting a muffled "oof." It was all the time Ginger needed. Rocket-like, she was past him and dashing out of the library.

Stumbling up, Adrian swung about, ready to charge after her. Something snatched his elbow back roughly, halting his flight.

Sharp fingernails dug into his sweater sleeve as Janice called sharply to Lloyd.

"Go after her, Lloyd. She'll never find her way back to the main chateau alone."

Adrian felt rather than saw Lloyd's nod as he bolted past the table. He disappeared through the doorframe, calling sharply for Ginger to hold up. The rich timbre of his voice faded away along with receding footsteps and Adrian felt his stomach heave. Those snakes were having a picnic in his stomach now, hissing and coiling, preparing to strike. Janice's voice cut through their din.

"Calm down, Adrian. Lloyd will see to Ginger. Her outburst is understandable. She's scared."

"Well, who the hell in the room isn't!" he snapped.

"It's different for her and you know it. She didn't grow up in our kind of world."

"Babying her won't help the situation!" Adrian countered.

Janice's accusing retort stabbed the air.

"A little understanding from your heart instead of your mouth would be a welcome relief to us all, Adrian. My God, why can't you have some compassion for Ginger and look at this nightmare from her side? She must feel like an animal in a cage, who, even if the door was open, wouldn't dare come out. We talk of ghosts and spirits the way she talks of music and composers. To her, we must resemble creatures from another world."

"Or hell," Adrian commented wryly.

Janice shot him a cold look, rancor sharpening her tone.

"Give your mouth a rest, Adrian. It'll thank you for it."

With a sweep of his hands, Adrian returned her sarcasm.

"Ginger's got to stay tough and brazen her fears out with the rest of us. I don't know what Lisette has in mind next for us, do you?"

"Of course not!"

"Well, my gut instinct tells me things are going to get tougher, not easier. If you weren't so busy coddling Ginger just to spite me, you'd sense that!"

"Spite you!" Janice's eyes flashed green ice. "I resent that remark from you, Adrian, I really do. I genuinely like Ginger. And if I'm coddling her as you say, it's because I do feel sorry for her. Not because we're trapped here like mice in a maze, but because I remember what it's like to hang around an insensitive bastard twenty-four hours a day!"

Her words were meant to sting him to the core, Adrian realized, but it had the opposite effect. She was obviously comparing him to her ex-husband. The snakes in his stomach quieted, infusing him with an unexpected streak of honesty.

"I've been ugly to you, Janice. I don't deny it. If I had a heart of stone, it wouldn't be so bad being here with you, looking at you, wanting to make love to you . . ."

He cut off his sentence in mid-stream as startled as she by the confession. Her confusion quickly turned to subdued anger. One look at the fiery glint in her eyes and Adrian knew she had misinterpreted his words. She thought them another of his ploys to be especially nasty to her. She stepped back and he guessed she was about to deliver the second stinging slap to his cheek in one night.

Inwardly, Adrian groaned, a part of him hoping she would hit him. If she struck him, there would be an end to the mounting dislike between them. If she hit him, both of them would be released—free to concentrate on getting rid of Lisette's hold over them.

Adrian waited for the blow, his eyes locked in a silent battle of wills with Janice. Like cunning dogs defending their turf, they both assessed the other's anger, neither giving way. When the silence between them deepened, Janice put out her hand, palm up to him. Adrian glanced at it, confused.

"My compass," she said quietly.

Adrian nodded. She was leaving the room like Ginger before her. But she was going away in quiet dignity. Knowing he couldn't allow her to go off on her own either, Adrian dipped his fingers into his shirt lining pretending to search for her compass. He came up empty and shrugged in dismay at her.

"Sorry. Must've dropped it in the solarium in all the excitement."

Her face fell in disappointment and she withdrew her hand. Adrian heard a small sigh escape her lips as she took a step around him and headed for the doorway. Lightning-quick, he grabbed her elbow and spun her back around.

"We've got to stay together. You know that." Her withering glare set the snakes in his stomach hissing again and he let loose her arm. Clenching his teeth, he swatted the air impatiently. "All right, go ahead. Get lost out there." She remained motionless and he repeated his gesture. "Go on. Take your tight little ass out of my sight!"

She was gone with a graceful spin before he even finished the sentence and her retreat had him groaning aloud this time. Smooth, real smooth, he congratulated himself.

Staring at the empty doorway, Adrian parked himself along the edge of the table and wondered what to do now. His damnable luck when it came to women was still holding and then some. He reached into his shirt lining and withdrew Janice's compass, curling his fingers around the cylinder. He sensed her life force immediately. Abruptly, his subconscious tossed up a single word. Anna. He tightened his hold on the compass, seeking Anna's identity. Nothing came, only the word Anna singed in his mind. Anna. Anna was everything to Janice. Quickly, he shut the memory out, stared again at the empty doorway.

"Way to blow it, Adrian, old buddy," he chided, mimicking Todd's usual catch-phrase. "You never thought she'd walk out, did you?"

A discreet cough sounded behind him and Adrian sprang from the table, casting a furtive glance over his shoulder. Dammit all to hell! He had forgotten the Grisombs were even in the room. He groaned aloud. Sweet Jesus! They had heard every word between him and Janice.

Rapidly, his mouth went dry and he sought some witty comeback to cover his discomfort. Finding none, he re-parked himself along the edge of the table and began tossing the compass into the air and down again.

Mercifully, the pair kept silent, sparing him further embarrassment. Their silence allowed him a moment to regain his composure and, forcing a remote dignity to his tone, he finally dipped his head.

"I think I handled that rather well, don't you?" Muriel's laugh gave him a small, satisfying victory and he shrugged his shoulders. Seconds later, his gaze floundered under Jasper's keenly observant stare. "I know what you're thinking," he stated. "I should go after her."

Jasper heaved himself from the sofa at once, coming to rest alongside the table.

"No. Actually, I was thinking how well suited you and Janice seem to be."

"Well suited! She can't abide the sight of me!"

The older man grasped Adrian's shoulder and shook him firmly.

"Nonsense. If you rub two sticks together long enough, you're bound to ignite a fire."

Muriel echoed his sentiment.

"Jasper's right. Conflict is a natural state of affairs and the wonderful thing about conflict is that it stimulates one to new insights about themselves."

Adrian gave a busted laugh.

"Insights! You saw her leave. She'd rather take her chances with a ghost than to stay in the same room with me."

Muriel gave his forearm a pat.

"Yes, well, as a Don Juan, you have about as much finesse as a sloth on Librium."

Adrian threw his head back, a genuine laugh spilling over. Muriel was a priceless pearl. She had coined a phrase out of his own barbed wit. Touched by her warm support, Adrian reached out and gave her an exuberant hug.

"You're so like my foster father. I could never fool him for a minute either."

She was obviously pleased by his words and squeezed his arm affectionately.

"There must've been a wonderful little boy inside you once, Adrian. What happened to him?"

"He got lost somewhere . . . like a bead from a broken string." The admission was dredged from somewhere beyond logic and reason, and Adrian was astonished at the sense of fulfillment he felt in admitting it. A gentle caress raked his forearm and when he turned, Muriel's eyes were filled with compassion. Before she could speak, he pocketed the compass and hopped from the table. "Too drained to explain further," he supplied as he made for the door. "Let's find Janice. I'm feeling uneasy all of a sudden."

In two steps, they were at his side, ready to help in his search. Adrian signaled Muriel out first and she went quickly. About to follow, Adrian was halted by a clamp on his wrist. Instantly, his mind collided with Jasper's and he heard the question as clearly as if it had been spoken between them.

"What really happened between you and Janice when the glass shattered at dinner?"

For a second, he thought of evading the question, then realized the futility of it. If Jasper really wanted to, he could find the answer by simply diving deeper into Adrian's mind. But it wasn't his style, Adrian realized. He didn't intrude where he wasn't invited. Their eyes met as the two exchanged a pact.

"A mind meld. A memory. An image of rough, raw lovemaking . . . " he said aloud, then paused, aware that Muriel had returned and was staring at him curiously. "I don't know what it was," he finished lamely.

Jasper released his wrist, nodding with a hesitant shrug.

"Are you afraid the vision you saw is about to happen with Janice?"

"Worse. I'm afraid it's *not* going to happen."

His candid reply shocked both of them, but he didn't wait around to see the look on their faces. Instead, he whipped past and strode down the corridor. A short moment later, he heard their footsteps tapping on the oak floor behind him.

Reaching an intersection, Adrian signaled the Grisombs.

"The main staircase is just beyond there. I'm going to circle back through the wing and pick up Janice."

"You're sure she's back there?" Jasper asked with a tilt of his lips.

"Yes, because she's blind as a bat without her compass." Seeing Muriel's mouth open, Adrian lifted his hand. "You're right. It was a despicable thing to do, letting her leave without it. I'll apologize as soon as I see her."

He gave the pair no chance to cast any further slurs on his character and strode back the way they had come. Now, if only Janice would be as kind to him when he finally found her.

Chapter 13

SATURDAY—1:35 AM

Staring down the expanse of a dimly lit assembly hall, Janice held back a childish desire to stamp her foot. Curse her rotten luck! She was right back where she had started from and more lost than ever. The swords and crossbows hanging like vultures on the crossbeams above her head were the same ones she had passed only minutes ago. Sighing, she finally admitted she had no idea where she was or how far she had come from the library. One thing was for certain though, she was traveling in circles and each minute that passed had her more unsure as to which corridor she should take. Damn her stupid pride! And damn Adrian Magus for not giving her the compass!

Janice swiped at an angry tear forming. He had her compass, the lying swine! She'd stake six months' royalty checks on it. Why hadn't she challenged him in the library to return it to her instead of fleeing like a stupid thief in the night? And why was he refusing to give the compass to her in the first place? He knew she couldn't find her way alone without it. Why was he being such a donkey's ass?

Janice did stamp her foot then, wishing the worst tortures of hell on him. And also on herself. She had let his barbed tongue goad her into leaving the library and it was a childish, foolish thing to do. What had she gained by it? Nothing. He was safe. She was lost.

"He wanted to keep you from wandering the chateau alone. He senses the danger coming."

Janice stiffened, hearing the voice in her head as clearly as if someone had spoken it aloud. Damn it all to hell, go away, she commanded the voice. It drifted away at once, leaving her to notice a tangy aroma permeating the air.

"Raspberries," she muttered beneath her breath. The word sent a sudden suspicious chill up her spine and tossing her head, she ventured a tentative question to the air. "Lisette?"

No response came and Janice stifled a chuckle. If her sense of humor hadn't suddenly skipped town, her penchant for talking to ghosts that weren't there would be hysterically funny. After all, hadn't she promised Captain Bowers only this afternoon she wouldn't spook any ghosts while here? So much for keeping that promise.

She cast a hasty glance left and right, swallowing the thick knot that was suddenly forming in her throat. She had to get out of here any way she could. Any door she could. Her gaze scoured the massive white pillars nearby and she shivered. Should she go back that way? Yes, she had to find Lloyd, Adrian, anybody real. If she didn't, she'd run into an insane panic.

Squaring her shoulders, she stepped forward, treading the wood floor as if walking on eggshells. With each step, she forced herself to take deep, calming breaths. Breathe in, breathe out.

Reaching the pillars, a new chill seized Janice, a frozen, frightened thing in her heart and, unnerved, she whirled. In the distance, she heard footsteps drumming on wood. Her hand fluttered to her heart as it began to thump wildly against her ribcage. Dear God, could ghosts produce human footsteps? No way, she cautioned, ghosts were spirit, nothing more. It was Adrian or the Grisombs coming to fetch her.

A single tear formed in the corner of her right eye as she peered through the shadows of the room toward its farthest end. Please be someone I know, she prayed fervently. She closed her eyes and listened, catching her breath as the footsteps paused, then suddenly resumed, moving away from her. They were leaving her!

Panicking, Janice tore down the hall toward the receding footsteps and a blot of minuscule light emanating beyond the doorway. Halfway there, she skidded to a halt as a shadow loomed up in the doorway. Adrian. It was Adrian. Bless him. He really didn't hate her as much as he implied.

Janice picked up her pace again, clamping her lips to imprison a sob of relief. She didn't care how much he insulted her from here on out. She had never been so glad to see anyone in her life.

He stepped into the room, spying her speeding figure and Janice slowed her steps, realizing how stupid she must look to him. *No need to rush*, she berated herself, *you're safe at last*. Her heart slowed its wild thumping, calmed by her confident words. She could see Adrian's face clearly as he neared and it cheered her. In a few steps, she would be touching him, touching his ruffled shirt to prove he was real, not just a hysterical delusion her panicked mind manufactured.

Halting inches from him, Janice lifted her gaze to his face. She thought she saw a

pensive shimmer in the shadow of his eyes and had an unexpected, disturbing desire all at once to flee back the way she had come. In the next instant, he greeted her, his voice thick and unsteady.

"Hallo, Izzy, ma petite fleur." Janice froze, stunned by the greeting. Izzy? Who was Izzy! A hand came out to stroke her hair and she drew back from the touch. "Non, cherie, do not shrink from the touch of my hand on your hair. Vous êtes toujours avec moi quoi que nous avons toujours partie." The dark eyes clung to hers and Janice's breath caught in her throat. Was that tenderness in Adrian's expression and voice? And why the devil was he calling her Izzy and speaking French? And then it hit her. Izzy—Lisette! This wasn't Adrian at all. In a suffocated whisper, she quizzed.

"Aubert?"

"Oui, mon amie."

He spoke again, his voice almost a caress. He reached out and this time Janice let his hand brush a stray tendril of hair from her neck. "Do you know what a prized beauty you are? Your hair a tribute to rubies? For three centuries, I have hungered to see you, to feel the melting softness of your body." His hand smoothed her hair, moved on to her cheekbone.

Janice held her breath, hypnotized by the invisible warmth of his touch. His knuckles caressed the line of her cheekbone and he was looking at her face as if he were photographing it for all time. Janice's heart suddenly swelled with a feeling she thought long dead. Not since Jimmy had she felt so consumed by naked desire.

Before her stood, not Adrian, but Baron Aubert Dumas. And he believed her to be Lisette, was seeking Lisette.

"Never touched, always touching." His husky murmur cut into Janice's thoughts, accelerating her pulse. His hand slipped to the nape of her neck and pulled her toward him. "For three centuries I have hungered to feel your lips on mine." He was going to kiss her, Janice sensed, unlock his heart and soul to her. The idea sent her spirits soaring, her knees trembling, and the blood pounding in her ears. "Embrassez moi. Come kiss me, Izzy." His voice was sensually seductive as he lowered his head and his uneven breathing teased her cheek. She felt tears smarting behind her eyes and he saw them. His own gleamed more fiercely. "You have nothing to fear from me, cherie. I am your salvation." His head dipped lower, his lips hovering inches from hers. Janice's pulse skittered in alarm as his head blocked out all light.

"Adrian!" she called, scarcely aware she had called his name.

As if struck by a spasm, the lips halted their journey. Janice watched the eyes darken in pain, reflect glimmers of light, adjust, then regard her with a speculative stare.

"Was I about to kiss you?"

The question was crisp and clear, with a hint of sarcasm, and Janice knew the baron had vanished, letting Adrian's consciousness take over again. Suddenly tongue-tied, Janice managed a suffocated whisper.

"No, *you* weren't. Baron Dumas was."

Adrian's eyes narrowed suspiciously and he lifted his head away from her. Taking a step back, he stared at her in waiting silence. Janice could see her answer had rattled him and for a long moment, they merely looked at one another curiously. And then his eyes grew openly amused.

"I get it. You're doing this to get back at me—for what I said to you in the library."

Floored by such a ludicrous suggestion, Janice laughed.

"No, I'm not. The baron was here. You were him. He was you. Using you to talk to me . . . " she corrected herself instantly, "to talk to Lisette."

Adrian threw up a hand, cutting off her words. With his free hand, he fished into his shirt lining and came up with her compass. He held it out to her, offering an apology.

"All right, I admit I'm an insensitive jerk. I should've given it to you. I don't know why I didn't. Take it."

Janice hesitated, seeing suddenly for the first time how much like a recalcitrant child he was. As if he had been caught with his hand in a cookie jar and now he needed to make excuses for being caught.

"You didn't give it to me, Adrian, because you didn't want me wandering the chateau alone," Janice stated. "There's danger ahead." His shocked expression told her she had hit the mark. She pressed her point. "I'm not lying to you, Adrian. The baron was here. The baron was you. He's seeking Lisette."

Janice made him the victim of her stare and she could see her words took him beyond merely rattled to completely unnerved. Recovering quickly, he pushed the compass toward her and chided lightly.

"Take the god-dammed compass and let's get the hell back to the others."

Janice nodded, taking her prize. Immediately, she felt a thrumming in the middle of her palm and a wave of grayness washed over her. In her head, she heard a blood-curdling scream that rose severely in pitch and soon clamored in her throat to get out. Her body suddenly jerked as if struck by lightning.

"Janice!"

The call came from a distance but she couldn't center on it. The voice was worried, asking if she was all right. No, she wasn't all right. She was drowning. Someone was pushing her mind aside, pushing her consciousness down into a black vortex.

Disoriented, Janice threw her hands out, fumbling blindly to latch on to Adrian's shirt front. She heard a dull clink and wondered what it was. Down, down. She was being swept away. Down to darkness. Down to emptiness. Down to nothingness.

Finally, she hit bottom and floated aimlessly.

Chapter 14

SATURDAY—1:40 AM

For a second, no more, Adrian froze. He heard a dull clink as Janice's compass hit the floor. Thinking fast, he reached out and caught her light frame as it slammed into his chest. For a second he thought they were both going down, but miraculously, his knees locked and held, allowing him to secure her weight. Quickly and carefully, he sank to one knee, using his raised thigh as a cushion for her back. He tapped her cheekbone.

"Janice!"

Her eyelids remained closed and Adrian felt a wrenching, jagged lurch in the pit of his stomach. She was out like a light. Now what? In his ears, he heard a thunderous pounding like horses' hooves and realized the sound was his racing heart. Blood was sliding through his veins like cold needles and he was scared by Janice's blank expression and seemingly non-existent breathing.

Pushing aside his fear, Adrian's fingers darted to Janice's nose to assure himself she was breathing. He felt a fan of air trail along his fingers but wasn't encouraged. Somehow, Janice was literally being swept away from him and he didn't know how to call her back. *Think, Magus, think.* She was probably only mesmerized by a marvelous ballet taking place in her head—her thoughts like gliding clouds, floating in and out of the heavens. When she woke . . . *if* she woke . . . the thought froze Adrian's brain. His fingers shot to Janice's neck artery, seeking a pulse point.

"Don't you leave me, Janice Kelly," he commanded. "We still have unfinished business, you and I."

Adrian detected a distant movement beneath his fingers. Yes, there it was. He pressed the knobby ridge harder. Steady, strong and vibrant. He exhaled, euphoria replacing his panic. Janice wasn't lost to him yet. She was alive physically. It was her mind that was in question. Where was it? What was happening to it? Remembering her earlier taunt about the baron, he had a sudden thought.

"Lisette?"

"Je suis ici."

The words were an alluring whisper and for a second Adrian could only stare at Janice's lips. Had they actually moved? A second later, his scalp prickled and he glanced over his shoulder. Above his head, the air stirred and he caught wind of a sickly, sweet fragrance. Jasmine. Lisette's scent.

Adrian searched the crossbeams for any sign of her presence. Nothing. Instinctively, he gathered Janice closer. She'd have to go through him to get to Janice. He'd see to that. Almost at once, he was rewarded with another ripple along his scalp and knew she was nearby.

Willing his pulse to slow, Adrian peeked at Janice's face, startled when he found her ice green eyes sweeping over his face with approval. She didn't speak, but it didn't matter. The pull of those eyes probed his soul and sucked him down. And then she reached up her hand and caressed his cheekbone.

"Je suis ici," she repeated lyrically.

The soft touch on his cheek bespoke tenderness and Adrian's skin tingled at the contact. Again, he caught a whiff of sweet jasmine. Lisette was purposely making him dizzy and light-headed. He had to stop her assault. She was shattering the hard shell he had built to keep Janice out. Janice! Sweet Jesus! He had to make Lisette send Janice back from wherever she had sent her. But how did he communicate when he found it almost impossible to breathe? He knew no French, yet he fought to translate Lisette's words. Systematically, he tried to think them through. *Je suis . . . je suis . . .* I am. I am what? *Ici . . .* no, that was lost to him.

"I am here."

She startled Adrian with her casual reading of his thoughts, then he sensed she wasn't reading his thoughts at all. Rather, she was responding to the lure of an earlier lover's call. Her caress skimmed his cheekbone, moved through his hair to the back of his head.

"I welcome thy kiss, *mon ami. Je faim.*" With a firm tug, she pulled Adrian's head toward her own. Over and over, he heard her urge him sweetly. *Je faim. I hunger for your kiss. Je faim.*

Her lips hovered dangerously close before Adrian stayed his head. If he kissed Lisette, he'd violate Janice. He'd gain a kiss but would lose the thing he craved most from her—her respect. Adrian gripped the arm tugging at his head and pulled it away.

"No," he murmured firmly.

At his denial, a keening wail tore from Janice's lips and rose up into the shadows above his head. Its loud frequency plucked at the nerves in Adrian's scalp. On and on the wail keened, until finally it dissipated into the very crossbeams around him.

Janice's body gave a violent jerk in his arms and she came back to reality with a quick intake of breath, followed by a ragged, choking sound and a desperate gulp for air.

Adrian clutched her neck, hoping to anchor her to reality. The touch worked. She turned her head, hunched over and gripped his arm, squeezing the muscle to assure herself it was real flesh and blood.

Adrian exhaled. Thank God. She was back from whatever hell Lisette had sent her to. And it had to have been hell because she was shaking like a leaf and her fingernails were cutting a deep groove into his skin, right through the fabric of his shirt sleeve.

For a moment, no more, Janice clung to him, and then Adrian felt her body stiffen. She dropped her hands into her lap and Adrian knew she was ordering herself to get a grip on reality. He gripped her hands, stilling the fluttering fingers.

"You're all right. You're safe."

She looked up at him then and Adrian heard a tearing sob leave her throat as she fully recognized him. She flopped onto his chest with a second busted sob and Adrian breathed a sigh of relief. Tears were a good sign. When you opened the floodgates, the torment had a chance to find its way out.

"So dark out there . . . so awful . . . so empty."

Her sputtered words seemed to come from the depths of her soul and Adrian knew memories were crowding in like hidden currents. Once more, he patted her cheekbone and spoke softly, hoping to lull her into a relaxed mood.

"You're back, safe and sound."

She gave a small hiccup and Adrian heard wonder in her voice.

"Lisette?"

"Yes."

"She sent me down to a gray nothingness. She wanted me to feel her emptiness. My mind just floated, went nowhere. I felt a great ache. Her ache." She broke off and Adrian realized she didn't want to remember the ache. He touched her cheek, this time with a wistful gesture.

"I don't think she really meant to harm you. She was responding to the baron on some primitive, physical level."

Both sat quietly digesting that thought and Adrian let her sit conquering her fears for a moment longer, then seeing her shudders subside, he pushed her head from his chest. Holding her close was proving dangerous to his frame of mind. Lisette's sickly scent had departed with her wail, and now, in its wake, Janice's fruity blend of perfume was making him heady in a different way. The smell of her hair tantalized him and he longed to lean down and nuzzle its texture. What would she do if he did?

As if sensing the question, she scooted along the floor away from him.

"Why didn't you kiss Lisette?" she asked, swiping at her drenched cheeks.

Adrian grinned, brushing a stray tear forgotten by her fingers.

"How do you know I didn't?"

"I would have remembered your kiss."

Adrian turned his grin up a notch.

"You were out like a light, Janice. A herd of elephants could have stampeded in this room and you wouldn't have heard them."

"I would have remembered your kiss," she repeated in a more composed voice. "I think women remember your kisses."

"Careful, Miss Kelly. That sounds suspiciously like a compliment, perhaps even an invitation."

Her hackles rose instantly, as Adrian hoped they would. They were treading on dangerous ground with their talk of kissing. He had to swing their thoughts to a safer subject. Her tears and anger he could handle. But her prying into his motives for not kissing Lisette? No, he wasn't willing to discuss that with her yet.

She pushed a section of her hair back across her shoulders with an impatient flick and gave him a cool stare.

"Very clever, Adrian. You knew calling me Miss Kelly in that condescending way would divert my mind from Lisette. You don't want to talk about what just happened, do you?" Adrian hedged, looking off into the shadows. "*Do you?*" She pushed him now, defiance written in her tone as well as a subtle challenge. Adrian wished he could pretend not to understand her look. Her mouth curved in faint amusement suddenly.

"My God, she rattled you. Big, strong Adrian rattled by a ghost. It's priceless."

Adrian's lips puckered in annoyance at her obvious glee.

"Don't gloat, it's unbecoming." He swung his hand out, groping for her shoulder. "How about helping me to my feet? My leg has one hell of a cramp in it."

She scrambled up instantly, grabbing Adrian's arm and hauling him up behind her. Adrian staggered once, caught his balance and then hobbled in a small circle to work out the kink.

"Thank you, Adrian."

He looked up from his shuffle.

"For what? Not kissing you?"

"That and for not abandoning my mind to Lisette."

Adrian flexed his knee.

"Don't thank me yet. You may, before long, wish I had kissed you. We aren't out of danger."

"No. And now we're facing a second spirit's will as well. Any suggestions as to how we end this nightmare before it reaches the point of no return?"

Adrian eyed her suspiciously.

"We both have a pretty good idea where this entrapment is leading and where it will end. We both know, though we pretend to each other we don't. Lisette's intentions are getting clearer by the minute."

"What we're thinking is preposterous. A person can't be forced to commit an act against their will. I've seen it proven time and time again with patients under hypnosis. You can't make them do anything that is abhorrent to their basic, moral structure, no matter how hard you press."

Her confident tone impressed Adrian.

"I hope that proves true in this case because I don't remember a damn thing during those minutes you claim I was the baron. And as for you, I could have made love to you ten times over and you wouldn't have known it. Your body was in my arms but your mind was gone." Adrian saw her shudder at the remembrance.

"We have to talk to Lloyd immediately. He works with psychic minds all the time. He may know how to combat this. There has to be a way to keep our consciousness from being manipulated so easily."

Adrian didn't feel compelled to agree out loud, instead, he took Janice's elbow and nudged her forward.

"Let's go find the others. I don't relish the thought of reliving the last five minutes, do you?"

Her grim expression was answer enough for him. Gripping her elbow more firmly, he pulled her along behind him. Six steps later, she yanked away from him and swung about.

"Wait, my compass."

She back-tracked their steps and dropped to the floor in search of the fallen cylinder. Adrian gritted his teeth. She was actually delaying their departure over a dropped compass.

"Forget the compass, Janice," he called sharply. Her hands swept in a wider arc, ignoring him.

"No. It means too much to me. It was a gift."

From Anna. Adrian's head finished the sentence, then danced on. Anna meant everything to Janice, and Anna was dead. It wasn't the compass Janice feared losing. It was the memories the compass kept alive. Still, he couldn't let her jeopardize their lives this way. Bending down, Adrian stopped Janice's arm in mid-motion.

"Dammit, Janice, forget the compass. We'll come back for it later with the others."

"I'm not going without it."

She jerked free of his grasp and skimmed the wood at a much more frantic pace. Watching her frenetic fingers, Adrian felt a glimmer of anger surface. Of all the stupid . . . no compass could be more important than her life. Hadn't she just learned that lesson?

Losing patience, Adrian bent down and hauled Janice to her feet. "I said, forget the god-dammed compass!"

She gave him an odd stare, and Adrian had the strangest feeling he had impressed her in some way. He had no time to quiz her on it before a vicious shove propelled him sideways and away from her.

"What the hell do you think you're doing, Adrian?"

Adrian stumbled back, stunned by Lloyd's assault. What in the hell did he *think* Adrian was doing? He was protecting Janice, that's what. He had no further time to speculate as the rest of the group spilled into the room and rushed their way. Ginger reached him first, slipping her arm into his and laying her cheek against his sleeve.

"Thank God we found you, Adrian. Jasper's been acting like a crazed man for the last five minutes. He's tapped into something—I don't remember what he called it—but it's made him, well, not at all Christian."

She shivered and Adrian realized she had good reason to be scared. Jasper's sudden touch on his sleeve derailed his thoughts.

"Time slip. Someone's coming over."

Adrian tensed at once.

"Lisette?"

Jasper gave a quick shake of his head.

"No. Someone else."

Adrian pushed Ginger toward Muriel's plump form.

"Go stand with Muriel. I don't have time to explain." Ginger left his arms into Muriel's protective embrace and Adrian swung his gaze to Jasper. "I think you're about to be introduced to the Baron Dumas," he stated.

The air stirred briefly and each member of the group glanced overhead. Adrian's glance dropped to Janice, who was staring at him with a look of pure horror on her face. He shook his head.

"Relax. It's the baron."

But if anything, she looked more alarmed by his words. Adrian turned to Jasper. He didn't know how much time he had before the baron's appearance. But he was sure that once he lost consciousness, he'd be of no help to anyone. He surveyed Jasper's face as intently as Jasper was surveying the crossbeams around them.

"Anything?" he prodded.

Jasper's gaze never wavered from the crossbeams.

"Thirty seconds. Maybe forty."

Adrian's stomach lurched.

"Whatever happens, keep me away from Janice. It's in her best interest."

Jasper held up a warning finger.

"It isn't the baron," he remarked.

"What!"

Adrian's hand sliced through his hair with blurring speed. A raised finger silenced him again.

"Three, two, one . . . "

His voice drifted off precisely the moment a series of purple sparkles drifted from the wood beam. The sparkles swirled erratically at first, no vague shape or discernible form, and then a hideous putrid stench assailed the room. The last of the sparkles shot from the beam with a burst and the cloud reshaped itself into one big scribble of pulsing lights.

A hand gripped Adrian's shirtsleeve and he jumped, startled by the unexpected touch.

"Sorry," Janice stated with a shiver. "I had to touch something real."

Adrian knew what she meant. The room and stench now resembled something out of a late-night sci-fi movie.

A fiendish laugh suddenly swept from the cloud like rumbling phlegm. It shot over their heads and bounced off the walls, growing in pitch and intensity.

"God damn, what is that?"

The question came from Adrian's left, but he didn't have time to offer a guess. The cloud intensified its crackling, festering like the hiss of a broom on wet cement. The laugh turned darker, as if feeding off the group's agitation and its pulsing lights turned a darker, richer purple. The laugh then went sour, becoming a malicious, hideous sound.

"God damn, what *is* that?" Lloyd asked again and Adrian heard the panic in the question. Again, Adrian didn't answer. He didn't think Lloyd would like the answer he supplied.

The cloud ripped apart suddenly, relieving itself of objects like the muted crack of icicles. Before they knew it, the floor in front of them was littered with a myriad of books and trinkets. The laugh hooted wildly again, shooting by them and evaporating back into the cloud with a sizzling whistle. The dazzling blur crackled once, twice more, and then vanished back into the crossbeams as if sucked through a vortex.

The group stood in their stunned huddle, no one having the courage to break the unease that had been left behind. Then Adrian seized the moment. With a quick intake of breath, he dropped to his knees and riffled through the objects. His action galvanized the group out of their stupors.

"What is it, Adrian?" Ginger queried, peering over his shoulder curiously.

Adrian picked up a round cylinder, offering it to Janice.

"Your compass, I believe."

She took it from him, turning it over in her palm.

"But how?"

Her words trailed off as Adrian picked up a second round object and offered it to Muriel.

"Your wedding ring, Muriel."

She took it from him, just as confused by its appearance.

"You were going to use it for the rehearsal," she reminded.

Adrian met her curious stare.

"Actually I had it in my shirt lining only five minutes ago."

Muriel didn't comment, merely slipped it on to her finger once more and stepped closer to Jasper's side.

"But, what does this all mean, Adrian?" Ginger insisted. "What is Lisette trying to tell us?"

Instead of answering, Adrian picked up a book and handed it to Jasper, who dropped to his haunches inspecting the treasure. He began to thumb through the book casually.

"Looks like a ship's log. Old as hell, but maybe readable."

"From the baron," Janice supplied, leaning down to inspect the book. "He's aiding us in our search."

"And this is Lisette's diary," Lloyd stated, picking up a second journal. A glazed, faraway look entered his eyes. "I've always sensed she kept a diary. Never could find it among the books, though."

"Is this your ring, Adrian?" Ginger asked, holding a large ring out to him. Adrian scanned its markings and then shook his head.

"Could it be the baron's?" Muriel asked, curiously.

"It could be . . . " He broke off. Could the ring belong to a third spirit? A spirit with a laugh that spoke of dreaded things? "Perhaps it belongs to Lisette's murderer," he commented as if the answer was obvious.

"Three spirits," Jasper said, spacing the words evenly.

"We can't fight three spirits at the same time, can we?"

Ginger's question had them all staring at the ring Adrian held between his fingers as if it were a crystal ball. When it remained silent, offering no verbal communication, Adrian chuckled.

"If wishes were horses . . . " he stated, wryly.

The group laughed and the sound ignited a strange ballet in Adrian's head. One that housed a bizarre twist of fate. Were they about to relive that fateful day three hundred years ago? If he were Aubert and Janice was Lisette, that meant one member of the remaining group was to be the murderer. He felt Ginger's fingers on his shoulder and he shook his head, stalling her question.

"No, I don't know what lies ahead, but my guess is we'll soon find out." He scanned each face in turn. "From here on out, none of us stays alone. Agreed?" Each head dipped in agreement. Exhaling, he slipped the ring back into his shirt lining. "Good. Now let's get the hell out of here and find a more suitable place to study our treasures."

They each scooped up one of the scattered items and headed for the door, Lloyd first, Ginger next. Reaching the door, Adrian paused, letting Muriel and Jasper go through ahead of him and then noticing Janice's lagging gait, he waited for her. His eyebrow raised in surprise when she stopped by his side instead of exiting.

"Problem?"

"I had a horrible thought a moment ago."

Adrian let his lips twitch slightly.

"Let's hear it."

"What if we're about to relive the murder?"

Her intuition was so disturbingly like his own, it unnerved Adrian. It was time to divert their minds again with his special brand of sarcasm.

"Correct me if I'm wrong, Miss Kelly, but I sense that if you were given the choice between making love to me and seeing me murdered and mutilated, you'd choose the latter."

"God, what a horrid thing to say! I don't want you dead."

"How encouraging. And to think that only a few hours ago I dismissed you as a cold and sexless kewpie doll."

Her lips twitched and then she laughed outright. Satisfaction pursed his mouth as she taunted.

"Would it be considered absolutely diabolical if I saved the ghosts the trouble and killed you myself?"

Adrian answered with a mock bow before he signaled her out. She slipped past him in a flash and he grinned appreciatively. He had been right not to kiss her. Now, there was a tangible bond between them that would be hard to break. Awareness, invitation, acceptance, all in a few seconds. The knowledge sent a surge of blood scurrying along his pulse and a rush of adrenalin to his legs. Quickly, they hurried to catch up with the disappearing group.

Chapter 15

Janice knew by her shaking hands that she was coming unglued at last. Why now when she was safely ensconced with the others? Because now she was grounded to reality again and could feel the overwhelming fears burning in the pit of her stomach. She raised her head to study the speckled green wallpaper surrounding the dressing table. It should be reassuring to recognize a chair as a chair and a table as a table. To distinguish colors. Why wasn't it? She knew the answer to that, too. Her mind had been stripped from her too easily. Sent to some empty hole to exist alone in an alternate dimension and she hadn't been able to stop it from happening.

Janice studied her reflection in the mirror. She had been lucky. She could've been left in that void if Adrian hadn't grounded her. Shivering, she dismissed the thought. Better not to think of Adrian, either. Leaning forward, she studied the green eyes reflected in the glass before her. Was she looking at the face of a woman who had undergone some kind of mad rebirth? Yes. In just a short twinkling of time, a transformation had occurred deep within her. She had traded places with another's soul, experienced that soul's life essence in a momentary flash, and had been thrust back into her own life, lucky enough to come away unscathed. Or at least partly unscathed.

Somewhere in the exchange with Lisette, Janice gained a new power. She had become empathic. There was no other word to describe it. Nothing else explained her heightened sense of awareness of space and time and things. Colors were brighter, voices were louder, matter seemed more real. Even now, through the open double doors, she could easily identify the murmurs of her companions. She could feel their movement, even their lack of it. What did it all mean?

Janice ran a finger along the rim of her lower eyelid. Surely she had aged decades in the last sixty minutes. Where were the lines? And where was her courage? It had suddenly gone underground. With a moan of distress, she pressed her hands over her flushed cheeks.

"Here, drink this," came a husky voice, "it's only soda but it tastes heavenly."

The words drifted to Janice's consciousness, followed by a cool wetness on the back of her right hand. She clutched the sweating glass, forcing herself to settle down. She took a deep breath, punctuated with several even gasps.

"You're a peach, Ginger," she applauded between gasps, "I'm tired, but most of all, I'm hungry and thirsty."

"I've got just the thing," Muriel remarked from the doorway. "I've fixed us some sandwiches."

She bustled over the threshold, silver tray in hand, and Janice spun around on her stool. Food. She was starved. Not waiting for the tray to be set down, she scooped several of the sliced sandwiches as Muriel passed.

"I could eat a bear," she declared, popping the first morsel into her mouth. She chewed it with relish.

"Bear is not on the menu, I'm afraid," Muriel teased, dropping into the print wingback and setting the tray on the footstool between them. Like Janice, she popped the morsel of a sandwich into her mouth and savored its taste. "One thing about ghost hunting," she remarked, "it creates an astounding appetite."

"Don't tell me the men are munching on finger sandwiches," Janice exclaimed. She slipped a second wedge, this time egg salad, into her mouth.

"Those overgrown clods! They're devouring giant double-decker sandwiches and it is NOT a pretty sight!"

Janice took a second sip of Coke and gave Muriel a bemused smile. "You're sounding chipper, Muriel."

"I'm positively glowing," she replied, "such mystery and intrigue!"

"You can't mean you're enjoying all this?" Ginger interrupted, shocked, her hand hovering over a tuna salad slice. "No one could possibly enjoy this insane captivity."

"It's not a matter of enjoying it, Ginger. It's a matter of accepting the situation and adjusting to it. Once you do that, victory is possible."

Janice wagged her head in agreement.

"You're right. We've got to accept the problem and confront it."

"Confront Lisette?" Ginger choked. "We shouldn't get her mad, should we?"

Janice could see the genuine fright in Ginger's eyes as she spirited away a tiny slip of tuna salad from her lower lip.

"She's a kind spirit," Janice reminded. "She's not dangerous, just determined. She wouldn't hurt a fly."

"Is that why the men have let us have some breathing space?" Ginger asked. "I thought we were supposed to stay together." She gave a familiar shiver.

Muriel bent over and patted her fingers.

"You can relax, my dear. Jasper's on watch. His precognition has returned and he's assured me that he'll know in plenty of time if we're about to encounter one of our ghosts."

"Then why is Adrian afraid for Janice?" Ginger asked.

Afraid! The word chilled Janice and she took a long, cool sip of Coke, thinking on it. Why was Adrian afraid for her? Unsure, she inclined her head toward Ginger.

"Is he?"

"While we were fixing sandwiches a moment ago, he was comparing notes with Lloyd," Muriel cut in. "Adrian's concerned about his apparent blackout as the baron . . . my dear, was he really the baron?" Muriel broke off, not quite used to the story yet.

"He was."

Muriel clucked sympathetically, picking up the tale again.

"It worries him. He has no recollection of the takeover, while you, according to Adrian, had an extreme physical jolt and displacement as Lisette."

Janice jiggled the ice against the side of her glass and watched the carbonation fizz.

"It's not as odd as it seems. Adrian uses his telepathic abilities daily. He has great practice moving in and out of the two worlds he lives in. I, on the other hand, have to wait for the other side to contact me with the message or picture."

"So Lisette had no trouble breaking through your mental barriers," Ginger surmised astutely. "Then why did she displace your mind?"

Janice dipped her head.

"I believe she felt if I experienced her pain and loneliness, I might be more agreeable to helping her. And from that, I might encourage all of you to help her."

"And has she convinced you?" Muriel asked. "To help her, I mean?"

Janice felt as if a hand had closed around her throat. Was she convinced? Not if it meant surrendering her body to Adrian's masterful seduction. If only she could openly express her growing fear to the women. More and more, the solution to their freedom seemed to hinge on her and Adrian. Aware that Muriel was still waiting, she arched her eyebrow and gave a hesitant shrug. Muriel leaned forward.

"Let's be frank between us women. Something happened between you and Adrian when the glass shattered this evening at dinner. Adrian will only admit to seeing an image. I would like to know what that image was. In fact, I believe we all have a right to know. Though I pretend to be composed, I'm not. I don't relish being murdered in a crawlspace."

Janice saw Ginger's apprehensive jerk at the image, and contained one of her own.

"Neither do I," she agreed.

Muriel's frown deepened. "If you're hesitating to spare Ginger's feelings, we can't afford the luxury of being considerate at the moment. I sense what you saw was . . . embarrassing in some way?"

Janice lowered her voice.

"More unnerving than embarrassing. The image was an erotic one and extremely graphic."

"The baron and Lisette," Ginger exclaimed with a smile.

"That's what I thought at first, too," Janice agreed, pleased to hear someone else jump to the most obvious conclusion.

"But something has changed your mind," Muriel coaxed. "You don't believe anymore that's what you saw."

Janice marveled at Muriel's accurately reading her thoughts. She leaned forward, eager to relieve her mind and conscience.

"Remember the portrait of Lisette down in the gallery? According to Lloyd, she came to America straight from the convent life. Yet, when I saw the portrait for the first time, I was filled with a sense of wildness. That portrait is *not* an innocent young maiden."

Ginger shifted in her chair and Janice saw her face light with eagerness. She was getting into the mystery.

"She had a lover," she concluded seconds later. "That's the only answer."

"But she was only eighteen and convent-raised," Janice countered.

"Girls matured early in those days, were sold off to older husbands," Ginger reinforced quickly. "She was young and beautiful. Perhaps an admirer seduced her."

"No." Janice shook her head decisively.

"Why do you say that so emphatically?" Muriel asked. "Ginger's right, not all girls back then came to their wedding beds as virgins."

"She was. I'd swear to it."

"But why?"

"Because of the baron."

A thoughtful silence fell among the women and Janice took that time to relive the moment in the assembly room when the baron had sought her kiss. He had been gentle in his asking, a considerate lover, one approaching an innocent virgin.

"What did the baron want, Janice?"

She didn't pretend ignorance.

"To kiss Lisette."

"How utterly romantic!" Muriel responded. Janice felt a warm flush steal over her cheeks at Muriel's glib phrase. "And did you oblige the baron?" Muriel prodded.

"No, of course not!" Janice scoffed. "It wasn't really the baron."

"You just said you spoke to the baron."

"I did. But he was speaking through Adrian."

"Yet Adrian admits he has no recollection of the takeover, so technically you wouldn't have been kissing Adrian, would you?"

Janice felt a streak of anger begin to saw at her stomach muscles. Why was Muriel being so obstinate in her probing?

"This is not about kissing Adrian and you know it!"

"Isn't it?"

The two simple words sent Janice's head reeling and the question took seed within her. Of course it was. It was about kissing Adrian. Seeing her unease, Muriel continued digging.

"You might as well tell us about the image. I'm quite relentless when I set my mind to knowing a thing."

Fine, she'd stop beating around the bush.

"Who do I suspect was the couple in the image? I'm not sure."

"Let me rephrase that then. Who does Adrian suspect is the couple?"

As if wired, Janice's fingers suddenly curled into fists. Her glance locked once more with Muriel's.

"He suspects it's the two of us."

A smile of satisfaction broke out on Muriel's face. Leaning forward, she patted Janice's clenched fingers.

"Well there, it's finally out. That wasn't so bad, was it?"

Janice uncurled her fingers, grimacing at Muriel's subtle ploy to get the truth from her.

"Yes, it was," she admitted. "The idea is utterly preposterous."

"Do you think so? For myself, I'm relieved. I would so much rather be manipulated by romantic ghosts than murderous ones, wouldn't you?"

Janice gave an unexpected shudder and alongside her Ginger did the same.

"I don't see how you can joke about something so serious, Muriel," Ginger chided.

"If I don't, I shall start screaming hysterically. It's not an appealing option." She scooted to the front of her chair. "I will admit you and Adrian seem to be the main focus of Lisette at the moment, but we mustn't forget that we were all brought here to serve a purpose. I act as the bridge for communication with Lisette. Actually, I think our spirit friends are being overly accommodating. When they find us slow to act, they prod us quite quickly." Muriel paused and Janice saw her features grow taut. "We must speak with Lisette again. And if she won't come, we'll summon the baron."

"And if he won't come?"

"We'll summon our third friend."

Friend. That fiendish laugh echoed in Janice's ears. She'd rather not talk with that spirit if they didn't have to. She'd bet it didn't know what the word friend meant.

"We won't take no for an answer," Muriel muttered crossly. "We've got to end this growing tension. Now, how to convince Jasper of my doing it."

She fell silent and Janice knew her mind was sorting and discarding all her options. Options! What options? Quickly, Janice wrenched her mind from the terrifying absurdity that they'd never get out alive. They had to get out of the house. That was the only option.

Chapter 16

The aroma of pipe smoke permeated Adrian's nose, and he broke off reading, glad of the distraction. Over the last several minutes, the printed words had begun blurring and his back had stiffened with a pressing pain.

Straightening, he raised his elbows, finding his arm muscles stiff as well. He heard a distinct crack as he flexed his shoulders. And then, arching his back, he brought his spine to an even deeper curve. Again, he heard a crack, this one louder than the first. He was tired. The resounding crack proved it. He was warm again, though, thanks to Lloyd's quick scrounging in a nearby closet. His newly donned shirt and trousers fit loosely, but their warmth more than made up for their bagginess.

He closed the book in front of him with a decisive snap. He was journaled out. It was time for his mind to digest what it had learned, just as his stomach was currently digesting that sub sandwich. He stole a peek at his companions and realized they too were digesting—both in mind and body.

Leaning back, Adrian propped his legs on the coffee table and let his gaze focus on the smoke rings drifting in upward spirals around Lloyd's head. He supposed he should break the silence, but for the moment, he couldn't summon the energy.

Out of the corner of his eye, he detected a movement. Jasper, too, was coming out of his stupor, stretching his arms above his head to restore circulation.

"I could use sleep in a real bed," he commented. "Dare we try to sleep for a couple of hours?"

"You've got my vote," Lloyd seconded, coming to life. He

withdrew his pipe, stifling a yawn.

Adrian roused himself as well.

"I suppose we should give a shot at interpreting these journals first," he advised. He swallowed down his own yawn and dropped his feet to the carpeted floor. Idly, he pushed the sheaths of paper back and forth with his fingers. "We've each read the journals, so what do we know?"

Neither man across from him ventured a guess and Adrian realized everyone was waiting for someone else to speculate first. Finally, with a resigned sigh, Lloyd rose from his chair and crossed to the fireplace. There he tapped the pipe stem against the palm of his hand, then deposited the ash into the glowing embers. Pocketing the stem, he sat again, his glance meeting Adrian's.

"They set sail from France in the spring," he began, "expecting to arrive in the Americas in late summer. Captain Enoch Waters was in charge, Lieutenant James Arthur, his first mate . . ." Lloyd broke off suddenly, his glance moving past Adrian's shoulder.

Hearing movement behind him, Adrian swung about and spied the women. Muriel came first, dropping onto the couch alongside Jasper, who laced his fingers within hers in welcome. Adrian greeted Ginger with a brief shift along the couch and a swift pat of the cushions alongside him. Bringing up the rear, Janice propped herself on the arm of Lloyd's wingback and Adrian saw her give their host's arm an affectionate squeeze.

The women took one look at the closed journals on the coffee table, waiting for an update. When no one took up the tale, Janice piped up curiously.

"What have you found?"

"More than we bargained for," Adrian drawled. "Go ahead, Lloyd."

Lloyd leaned forward, flipping the closed journal open once more. He tapped a page.

"The passenger list consisted of Lisette; her abigail, the Lady LaCoer; and a cousin the captain refers to as Simone Villashay, most likely Lisette's best friend. The baron's younger brother, Chase, was also a passenger. His destination was New York City, though why he was going there isn't stipulated anywhere."

Lloyd fell silent and Jasper took up the tale.

"We know the voyage was good at the start. Captain Waters writes so. However, a month into the voyage the weather turned nasty. The ship spent three additional weeks skirting the storm." Jasper leaned forward and flipped through the journal, never losing his train of thought. "It's obvious Waters and young Chase became enemies early in the voyage. At least eighty percent of the captain's log entries refer to the boy as 'that deviant bastard,'" Jasper paused in his riffling to give the group a speculative glance. "I suppose if the boy was a mental case, he might be our third spirit with the hideous laugh."

Adrian nodded and leaned over the journal, following Jasper's current train of thought.

"Waters also makes reference to 'the rutting rake,' though we can't be sure if that's the first mate Arthur or for young Dumas," Adrian added. "A trip of that length must've been hard on the balls . . . " He broke off, realizing the women were present. "Sorry. It's hard to imagine any of the men aboard remaining celibate for the entire voyage. They had to have craved sex with Lisette."

"Or the abigail," Jasper countered. "The captain describes her as . . . " he paused and leaned over an ear-marked page. "'a well-put together widow, with ample breasts.'" Jasper looked once more at Adrian and then the women. "Our captain seems a trifle deviant himself. Perhaps he lusted after the fair Lisette, too."

"Not exactly a lunch bucket type of crowd," Adrian agreed. He continued the tale this time. "They arrived in late September, minus young Chase. The baron was in Philadelphia when the ship anchored, so Waters deposited the girls in a coach-and-four sent from Witchwood. The captain ends his log entries with a final cryptic entry." Adrian flipped to the end of the journal and read aloud. "'Tis well rid of the scurvy lot, I am. God take the whoremonger and his whore. May their souls burn in the everlasting pits of Hades.'" Adrian looked up from the pages. "Anyone care to hazard a guess about that wretched curse?"

Jasper shook his head, clearly stumped. Muriel offered the only comment.

"It could've been any pairing. The boy, the cousin, the abigail, the first mate . . ." She leaned back with a frustrated groan and Adrian knew the feeling. They were going to waste precious hours piecing together what had occurred once the passengers had departed the ship. Lisette's diary had shed no light on the matter. Once the ship docked, the entries in her diary were relatively scarce.

Leaning back, Adrian gave a half-smile.

"More and more, it looks as though the murder was a crime of passion."

"Any mention of ages?" Janice asked, curiously.

Adrian reached out and tossed Lisette's diary to her. She caught it deftly and her fingers thumbed through it casually as he answered her question.

"We know Lisette was eighteen. It appears the other women were in their early twenties. We suspect the first mate was also in his twenties. The brother was possibly fourteen or fifteen."

"Sixteen," Janice interjected swiftly. "He was cloddish, suffered with a hare-lip." At her pronouncement, every head swirled about, impaling her with direct stares. Her eyes lifted in surprise. "I don't know how I knew that," she stuttered. She followed the confession with a small, uncomfortable laugh. "Just an intuitive flash, nothing more." She tossed the diary back to the coffee table obviously, confused by the momentary insight. Lloyd must've sensed her discomfort too, because he captured her fingers and squeezed them with a small shake. Adrian saw her flash him a brief smile and then she turned her attention to the group once more.

"If the baron's brother was only sixteen," Jasper continued aloud, "why wasn't he accompanied by a man servant and why was his destination New York instead of Witchwood?"

"Perhaps he stowed away," Ginger guessed. "A boy that age might long for a sea adventure, especially if he suffered from low self-esteem."

"Very intuitive, Ginger," Jasper applauded. "But there's no mention of the word stowaway, just 'deviant bastard.'"

"You're sure the phrase was meant for him?" Muriel asked, swinging about. "Deviant bastard brings to mind a rather older rake. One who's had some years to build a naughty reputation." She hesitated. "I suppose boys became notorious rakes early in those days. He might've been a hellion."

Adrian gave the papers in front of him an impatient shove.

"Guessing, that's all we doing. We're no further along than we were an hour ago. And at the rate we're going . . . " he left the sentence unfinished.

"Let me solve the problem," Muriel offered. "Let me channel one of the passengers. We know what questions to ask now, so let's ask them."

Jasper clamped Muriel's arm, a frown surfacing on his brow.

"No. Until we learn which of them owns that hideous laugh we heard an hour ago, I don't want you channeling. If our friend is the baron's brother, he intends harm. And you will be especially vulnerable as the channeler. I won't risk your life in such a slip-shod fashion and I won't let anyone else do it either!" His look to the rest of the group spoke volumes and an uncomfortable silence descended among them.

"We'll sleep on it," Adrian finally stated. He saw Jasper's dark glare and ignored it.

"Is it safe to sleep?" Ginger asked, slipping her arm through Adrian's while trying to suppress a shiver. Adrian sighed loudly.

"Safe or not, we're going to. We all look like hell. Sleep is the cure. We'll sleep in pairs though. Jasper, you and Muriel take the west bedroom." He dipped his head left then right. "Lloyd, you and Janice, the east bedroom. Ginger and I will make do on the couches here." The group rose at the command and started toward their designated areas. "Move the beds as close to the doorways as you can," Adrian called to their backs. "That way, we'll be within earshot of each other. Remember, if you feel dizzy or strange or sense anything out of the ordinary, shout out!"

The group disappeared from view. Seconds later, Adrian heard a vitriolic curse, followed by Janice's bubbling laughter. Looking over, he saw the outline of a huge canopy close in on the doorway. Looking left, another silhouette appeared in the west bedroom doorway. Satisfied the group was taking his advice, he swung his own couch to a ninety degree angle alongside Ginger's to ensure he could see both doorways. Lloyd re-entered the room, blankets in hand.

"The room should stay warm for a couple of hours at least but here's covers just in case." He tossed a pink blanket to Ginger, who snuggled under it gratefully. Pivoting, Lloyd tossed the remaining blanket his way. Adrian caught it and settled quickly into the cushions. He didn't know if sleep were possible but at least he'd give his body a rest. What his mind chose to do was its own business.

Rolling the blanket in a ball, he tucked it beneath his head. Nearby, he heard a shifting motion and the room went dark around him. A tired sigh told Adrian that Ginger was falling off to sleep in rapid fashion.

Stretching out full along the couch, he listened to the settling quiet and closed his eyes. Blessed sleep. He needed it badly. Soon, the only sound he heard was the occasional snap of wood chips in the fireplace. Muscles relaxing, he let his mind drift into a thin veil of half-sleep.

Chapter 17

SATURDAY—3:15 AM

Through a distant grayness, Janice heard a frightened shout. At first she ignored it, continuing to float along in her dreamless state. Then it hit her—someone was in trouble. She came awake with a start, her eyelids flying open with alarm. Someone was calling, needed her help. Rolling over, she oriented herself to the room and squinted into the surrounding darkness. She searched the shadows for an identifiable shape. Who had called for her help? Lloyd?

Propping herself on her elbow, Janice located his shadowy form. A light, continuous snore assailed her ears, and she realized he was dead to the world. Had he called out in his sleep? Not likely.

Rolling back around, Janice slid to the edge of the bed and hung out over it. Was it Muriel? Blinking rapidly again, she adjusted her eyes to the gloominess of the interior living room. Across the way, she could just make out two dim silhouettes and a bed. The Grisombs appeared to be soundly asleep, too. Adrian?

She swung her head, locating the angled couch. He was sprawled out, and like the others, appeared to be in no difficulty. Still, she couldn't shake the nagging notion something was wrong. Something odd was beginning and it was nearby. It was up to her to check it out. None of the others seemed to sense it.

Swinging up, she slid from the bed and tiptoed into the darkened living room. The room's iciness hit her full blast. Damn! Of all the times for the fire to go out. She cast a glance toward the fireplace and froze. The wood chips were burning as bright as ever. The hairs on her arm prickled suddenly and she knew instinctively she was not standing alone in the darkness. *Light, Janice.* Turn on the light, she urged herself. She whirled on point then skidded to a stop. *Wake someone. You need a witness.* She was at the angled couches in three seconds flat, bending down and calling Adrian's name.

He came full awake, even as her whisper left her lips. His face loomed close to hers and Janice was taken back at his alertness.

"What is it?" he whispered.

His breath fanned her cheeks and there was a gentle softness in his tone.

"The room's cold."

"The fire's gone out," he commented, as if the answer was obvious.

"No, it hasn't."

He came up rapidly, not bothering to check over his shoulder, and Janice could've kissed him for believing her without question. Did he know how endearing that made him to her at the moment? She pushed the thought away as she found her fingers clenched tightly. In the next instance, she was trailing behind him in the dark, heading for the light switch on the far wall. Once there, Adrian snapped the light on. Around them, the room filled with light and its sudden, shocking glare brought the sleeping couple in the west bedroom off the bed in a hurry and on to their feet.

"What is it?" Jasper asked, circling the bed and stepping into the living room. His gaze darted about, seeking answers.

Janice and Adrian did the same, swiveling their heads in search of their unknown intruder. And there was an intruder. Janice was sure of it now. The hairs on her neck had joined the ones on her arm in a stand-up salute.

"Fuck!"

Adrian's muffled oath sent Janice's stomach into a dizzy flip-flop and above her ribs, her heart began a clumsy foot race with her lungs. The hand holding hers trembled then jerked, and Janice followed Adrian's gaze upward.

Oh, shit.

From the ceiling directly above Ginger's sleeping form, a white mist was showering down droplets. Reacting, Janice made a movement to warn Ginger and found herself hauled back roughly.

"Don't be an idiot!" Adrian barked. "It's our fiendish friend."

Janice wondered how he could identify anything from only a white mist. She got her answer immediately. A familiar stench rolled over them, and above them, the mist turned into a haze of shimmering purple lights. It laced itself down and stretched lengthwise over Ginger's prone form.

"Do something, Adrian," Janice whispered.

As the words left her lips, Ginger stirred on the couch, sensing the light and voices. Her eyes popped open. She didn't see the cloud of lights at first, her gaze searching for Adrian on the companion couch. Not finding him there, her glance swiveled right and left, the first sign of apprehension appearing on her face. And then she glanced up. Absolute terror erased all other emotions, and Janice didn't know what kept Ginger from screaming. The sparkling mist was descending now, stalking her form, as if aware she was about to bolt.

"Ad..ri . . . an!"

Her voice squeaked the last syllable. Ginger was working to be brave on the outside, but her stutter was a dead giveaway that she was frightened beyond belief. The cloud sagged suddenly and Ginger slid from the couch, seeking refuge against the side wall.

It was a good try at escape, and any other day, it might have worked. But the cloud had anticipated her flight and followed immediately, stalking her cowering figure and galvanizing Janice into action. Tearing at Adrian's fingers, Janice attempted to pry her wrist loose.

"Let go, Adrian."

"God damn it, Janice, be still! She'll be all right."

As if to mock Adrian, the mist ballooned out, encircling Ginger and cocooning her with its sparkling form. The swift attack galvanized the men forward in one fell swoop. Anticipating their approach and suddenly angered by it, the cloud billowed upward, transforming part of itself into a new shape. When it was finished, it resembled a misty octopus with shimmering ionized tentacles that hung high over the couch. The tube-like pincers sprayed outward toward the approaching men as if to rend them apart. The air sizzled around their heads like the crack of whip meeting flesh, and Janice quaked uncontrollably. In front of her, Adrian and Jasper ducked under the spray of electricity, just barely managing to dodge its stinger.

The spirit was furious with their show of bravado, had every intention of punishing them for their audacity. Falling back, the men crowded into the women, forming a protective shield against the tentacle of light. Seeing the maneuver, the cloud doubled its show of force. Two more tentacles snaked upward, releasing a menacing hiss from somewhere in its central core. The sound chilled Janice's soul as she clutched Adrian's shirt back, ready to solder herself to it. The hiss continued like a steam boiler about to burst which unnerved the men as well, Janice realized when she heard Lloyd's shaky curse.

"God damn bastard! He's not going to let us near her."

At his words, the tentacles halted in midflight and held their station. As if now having proved their superiority, they no longer needed to intimidate. This spirit was indeed arrogant, Janice thought. With an ugly, vindictive nature.

Above their heads, the sparkling lights danced and curled for a brief second longer, then vanished completely. With the dissipation, the main cloud of light returned to cocooning Ginger. Again, the room was filled with the sound of crackling static and suddenly the cloud thinned, exposing Ginger's rigid form to the group's stare. Through the opaqueness, Janice could see her fright and a stain of tears. The sight of them brought a tight knot to Janice's throat. It wasn't fair for anyone to be so incredibly terrified.

"Somebody *do* something, or I will," she stated defiantly.

Lloyd stepped in close to her body and lowered his voice so Ginger couldn't hear. Or maybe so the spirit wouldn't hear, Janice thought bleakly.

"I don't think we have any choice now but to let Muriel channel the spirit," he stated.

"I forbid it!" Jasper growled, overhearing. "That spirit is deranged. It would just as well kill us as look at us. Muriel could end up being its pawn."

"We've got to do something," Lloyd argued.

"We can't leave Ginger stranded this way," Janice stressed. "Please don't abandon her."

"We won't have to," Jasper intervened, signaling toward the sparkling lights. "Our friend is tired of baiting us. Look."

The group swung around in unison. Across the way, there was a new change. The lights surrounding Ginger's form were increasing in intensity and obliterating her from their sight once more.

"Is she all right? Can anyone tell?"

Janice felt her heart plummet along with a sinking feeling they were all doomed. One by one, they'd be picked off by this malevolent spirit. The men beside her closed their eyes. Jasper was the first to respond.

"She's about to blackout."

True to his pronouncement, Ginger toppled from the cloud of light. She slid to the carpet, ending in a crumpled heap at the foot of the couch. No one moved to help her. Rushing to her aid was out of the question, Janice knew. The cloud was still her hovering guardian, although Janice suspected that circumstance could change any second. No sooner had she finished the thought when the spirit shifted shapes again, this time morphing into a snake-like appendage streaming across the flat ceiling. If the situation weren't so horrifying, Janice could admire the spirit's ability to transform itself at will. It ballooned, it mushroomed, it re-energized itself with little effort. How wonderful to control such freedom of time and space.

Janice quelled her preposterous mind rambling, reminding herself that the spirit was not *admirable*. It was dangerous and they had no idea what trick it would play next. It might intend a second victim. And she might be that victim. Janice's heart rate quickened at the thought, and as fast as her heart began to pound was as fast as the cloud began to crawl across the ceiling toward the side wall and down. It snaked its way, sure of its destination.

As it approached the wall mirror to their left, Janice's fingers dug into Adrian's shirt back and came away wet. He was sweating, sweating profusely in an ice-caked room. Well, she couldn't blame him. Her own pullover felt damp against her ribcage.

"Dare we try to get to Ginger now?" Muriel asked, plucking at Janice's sweater sleeve.

"In a moment," Adrian cautioned. His gaze remained glued to the cloud's misty form, which was now disappearing behind the wall mirror and seeping into the paint pores. When the last of its white tail vanished behind the mirror, Adrian moved fast. Janice moved with him, not about to stay put any longer. The others must have had the same idea because they all reached Ginger's crumpled form within seconds of each other.

Adrian lifted Ginger to the couch swiftly, as Jasper grasped her wrist in search of her pulse point. His eyes closed, delving deep into the recesses of Ginger's mind, and Janice chewed on her lower lip. He was back again quickly and she saw the worry increase on his brow.

"She's not? . . . " Janice left the sentence unfinished. She couldn't say the word they all dreaded.

"No!" Adrian's snarl was emphatic. He hovered closer to Ginger. "Don't anybody say it!"

Janice's glance locked with Jasper for reassurance. He nodded briefly.

"She's out like a light but her pulse is strong. Her mind is intact, no damage to her brain. She's simply . . . " he paused, struggling to find the right word.

"Free floating?"

He nodded quickly.

"Yes, that's good, Janice. Was that what you felt when Lisette displaced you?"

"Yes. And a great darkness that was terrifying."

"How long can she maintain this free floating episode, Lloyd?" Muriel asked. She reached out and brushed a stray blond curl back from Ginger's face. "You must've seen some kind of mind control in your work with the students. Can her physical body maintain this type of stress for any lengthy period of time?"

No answer came and Janice turned along with the others, surprised to find Lloyd missing from their huddle. A quick look backward and they found him still frozen in place, his gaze centered on the mirror to their left. What was he looking at?

"Lloyd?" He ignored her call. "Lloyd!"

He swung about as if stung by the sharpness of her tone.

"What!" His tone was belligerent, almost hostile and Janice flinched. She had the inescapable feeling he resented her intrusion on his thoughts.

"Have you seen this kind of mind controlling before, Lloyd, in any of your experiments with the students?"

He didn't answer. Instead, his gaze gravitated back to the mirror.

"Filthy bastard! Sneaking around! Why doesn't he just show himself and tell us what he wants? No, instead, he swats at us like a cat teasing a grass yard lizard. Damn his mocking presence! Damn his fucking impertinence!"

The curse was heated, sliced with raw anger and Janice was shocked to hear the tirade. True, the episode was scary for them all, but Lloyd's tone was distinctly edgy. If she didn't know better, she'd swear he was coming unglued at the seams. Though his posture showed no stress, his behavior reminded her of the dinner table scene in *Alien*. One minute the crew had been dining, chatting happily; the next a terrifying alien popped from their crewmate's ribcage.

"Jesus, Mary and Joseph! Look!"

Lloyd's voice broke off and Janice swept her gaze to the mirror. Her pulse skyrocketed at once. Reflected in the glass was a human feminine face—a quiet oval face, dark and rather delicate. Billowing hair blew about the face and the beginning of a smile tipped the corners of a rosette mouth. And then the image changed. Now a bulbous nose dominated meaty features—a glum-faced man whose mouth was pulled into a sour grin. And then the derisive grin changed to an open, friendly smile and it was feminine again. This time ebony curls swung about proud shoulders. No, now the hair was fiery red. Now, a cobweb of silvery gold.

Janice couldn't keep up with the shifting features. Like a slide cassette gone berserk, images danced and alternated in lightning speed across the glass. What were they seeing? Faces from the ship's log? The images began to repeat and Janice found herself moving toward the mirror. She stood before it, mesmerized by the ballet of color-laden images. Her suspicions had to be correct. They were seeing images of Lisette, the ships' passengers, and crew.

Janice felt a light touch on her elbow but she didn't turn.

"My dear, didn't I say our ghosts were most accommodating?" Muriel whispered. "When we're slow, they prod us."

"But I don't believe Lisette is producing these images in the mirror," Janice replied, turning back to the reflections. "I think our third spirit is."

"But why?"

"To draw Lisette out," Lloyd snarled, his voice still thick and unsteady.

Fortunately, no one noticed the tremor in her own voice as she asked matter-of-factly. "Why draw her out, Lloyd?"

She was instantly sorry she had asked the question. Lloyd's eyes narrowed and his back became ramrod straight. Janice felt that same nervous tic in the pit of her stomach. The look on Lloyd's face said she was a fool not to know the answer.

"It wants to kill her."

Janice was surprised by the declaration.

"But, Lloyd, it has already killed her. Three hundred years ago."

A touch of madness came into Lloyd's eyes at her words and Janice flinched under his withering stare.

"You fool! It killed her body, not her soul! It wants her soul. It will kill all of us to get it. I've got to stop it."

Before Janice knew it, Lloyd seized an ashtray from a nearby tabletop, and hurled it at the mirror, shattering the glass and spewing shards in all directions. Flabbergasted, Janice jumped away. Could this nightmare get any worse? She stepped back to study the jagged fragments still intact in the mirror and became conscious of a low, tortured sob.

Instinctively, Janice knew a terrible regret was assailing Lloyd for what he had done. Cracking under the strain, his face was bleak with sorrow and his teeth were starting to chatter.

Janice closed her eyes, her heart aching for him. Is this what they all had to look forward to? To succumb to a torment eating at them from the inside out? She kept her eyes tightly closed, unable to bear the sight of Lloyd without breaking down herself. It was wretched to feel so helpless. And then the sobs moved away and Janice opened her eyes.

Jasper was leading Lloyd away with Muriel trailing several paces behind. Janice felt a sick yearning to have this nightmare over—even if it meant sacrificing her body to a hot tide of passion with Adrian. Making love would be a humiliation but one she could quickly forget. If making love to Adrian . . . she broke off her thoughts and sank into the nearest chair. My God, she was actually entertaining the thought of making love to Adrian without the proper safe-sex precautions. Was she out of her mind? Yes, that was it. She was losing her grip on reality, like Lloyd. She clasped her fingers together in her lap and stared down at them. She hoped when it came, her breakdown would be swift and that she'd have no recollection of it. It was all right to be insane if you couldn't remember the details.. A tear dropped onto her thumb and she felt movement in front of her. Strong fingers appeared and covered her white-knuckled ones.

"That won't happen to you," Adrian stated.

Janice met Adrian's dark eyes. She released her fingers from his grasp and scrubbed at the wetness on her cheeks. Though her mouth felt like paper, dry and dusty, she managed a shaky reply.

"I wouldn't have thought it would happen to him either. Lloyd's the strongest man I know."

"Let's not judge him until we have all the facts."

"You mean his behavior may have been manipulated on purpose?"

"Yes. To cause dissension among us. To split us apart."

Denial flew from Janice's lips immediately.

"But you're wrong. It isn't to split us apart. It's to bring you and me closer together."

Surprise siphoned the blood from Adrian's face and he stared at her as if she had suddenly grown a new head. Then his face twisted into a lopsided grin and he patted her fists lightly.

"Can't be done. If ever two people were worlds apart, it's you and me. I hate you. You hate me."

"I don't hate you, Adrian."

"Of course you do. I'm an arrogant bastard, you said so yourself."

"Well, you are. But I don't hate you for it."

Adrian cocked his head and Janice had the feeling he was staring into her very soul.

"Do you want to make love to me, Janice Kelly?"

Weary of the question, her answer was half-hearted.

"I don't know."

"You *are* cracking up." His retort dripped with sarcasm and he withdrew his hands from hers. Acknowledging his sarcasm, she pressed her hands over her eyes.

"I must be. There's no other explanation for such stupidity."

Adrian stood then, bringing her up with him. He swept her into the circle of his arms and his lips descended on hers. It was an empty kiss, lacking real heart and emotion, but still the pit of Janice's stomach did a wild somersault. When he raised his head again and they were staring curiously at each other, Adrian sent her a wry grin.

"There now, we've got the damn kiss behind us. We both felt nothing. Now, maybe we can concentrate on getting the hell out of this place."

He swung about and strode to the bedroom, leaving Janice to stare after him in alarm. Did he think that empty kiss settled matters between them? If so, he was a fool. The kiss had made things worse, if not for him, at least for her.

Janice sat down hard again in her chair, pressing her hands once again over her eyes. He probably thought a cold kiss would prove to their captors the futility of pushing them together. The kiss had started a funny kind of singing in her veins and on her lips. Her whole being was filled with unanswered longing. Janice gave an impatient groan. Damn Adrian! He had doomed them. She hadn't been fooled by that ice-caked kiss, and if she wasn't fooled by it, the ghosts certainly weren't either.

Chapter 18

The west bedroom was swathed in half shadow, half light, and from where she stood in the doorway, it was hard for Janice to imagine a more serene picture. Yet she knew the chain of events that had occurred in the last hour didn't even remotely resemble serene. Nothing seemed real in the last ten minutes. Not Ginger's cocooning, not Lloyd's breakdown, not Adrian's empty kiss. It was if time had simply surrendered itself into Rod Serling's *Twilight Zone*.

Adjusting her eyes to the dim light, Janice studied the four-poster bed silhouetted before her. It stood like a giant wasp, an alien creature with tasseled wings. In its stomach, Lloyd slept peacefully, oblivious to the world, barely seeming to breathe. Muriel was alongside the bed, her arm draped on the coverlet. Janice watched her fingers pluck continuously at the tufted quilting as she kept a vigilant eye on Lloyd's rhythmic breathing. Stepping into the room, Janice headed for the bed.

"How is he?"

A silent wave signaled her to a chair and she sank into the deep green cushions, glad to be able to give her own body some restful downtime. She rubbed her eyelids and then settled her gaze on Muriel, who was thoughtfully contemplating Lloyd's sleeping form.

"How is he?" Janice asked again. Muriel's whispered response was low and filled with compassion.

"He's asleep at last. Poor man, he's exhausted. It must be hell to be so defenseless. To have to listen to garbled voices in your head and not be able to cast them out!"

Janice stole a peek at Lloyd's sleeping form. If there were voices chattering in his head, it wasn't apparent on the surface.

He seemed lifeless, almost comatose. Janice wondered if he was somehow slipping away from them on purpose, out of self-preservation. What was he hearing in his head? It was awful not to know. Perhaps if they did, they could help him ease the pain.

Janice returned her gaze to Muriel, averting her thoughts from Lloyd's breakdown. "You don't look so refreshed yourself, Muriel," she commented softly. She hoped the worry in her tone was adequately disguised. They all had enough troubles without saying the obvious.

"Too much excitement," Muriel replied. "And not enough time to process it. It's as if time has been suddenly suspended and what we do in the next few moments will seal our destinies."

"Perhaps it will," Janice remarked. The women exchanged knowing glances and Janice found herself leaning forward, stilling Muriel's restless fingers. "Do you trust me, Muriel?"

Muriel's eyes widened in surprise at her question.

"My dear, how can you even ask that? Surely you know I've grown exceedingly fond of you. It is my dearest wish that when this nightmare is over, you'll let Jasper and me come and visit you in Colorado. I want to meet that precious daughter of yours."

Janice felt a rising knot in her throat and swallowed it down. Muriel had to be the dearest, the sweetest woman she had ever met. If only things weren't so muddled. She squeezed the fingers in her palm affectionately.

"I've grown very fond of you too, Muriel. That's why you must listen to what I am going to say with an open mind."

"I'm a trance channeler. If there's one thing I've got, it's an open mind."

Janice stifled an urge to laugh. Muriel was incorrigible, her sense of humor indestructible. Even now, when things were at their worst, she was still able to poke fun at their plight. Janice felt a sudden inner pang; she envied Muriel's ability to remain buoyant no matter the adversity. Perhaps if she herself had a better outlook on what was occurring, she would be able to handle the gnawing ache in the pit of her stomach. As it was, continuing to hold back the pain set her teeth on edge more and more, she realized. She had to make Muriel see things as she did. Leaning in, Janice took the initiative.

"I can't stand what's happening to us, Muriel. If I have to stand by and watch another one of you shut down like Ginger, I'll go out of my mind."

"My dear, who's to say that you won't be next? We don't know what our spirit friends intend."

"I know," Janice replied. "I've known ever since I met the baron. What's happening here is between Lisette and the baron. It's that simple."

"What are you suggesting, Janice?"

"Help me convince Adrian that we must separate from the rest of you."

Muriel pinched Janice's fingers.

"My dear, that's nonsense. None of us stands a chance alone. We must stick together."

"But we won't be alone. Adrian and I will be together." Muriel's frown deepened and Janice added quickly, "Don't think I haven't thought of the danger. But if this nightmare is to have an end, it will be because of me, of what I do. There's no use lying to ourselves anymore. Lisette intends to free her soul and only I have the power to free all of you. Though we all skirt the issue, I am the key. Lisette needs me, needs my physical body."

Muriel's fingers pinched Janice's again, her horror apparent.

"Surely you're not intending to give yourself over to Lisette? That's crazy talk. Though she seems a benevolent spirit, we could be misinterpreting her pain. She could be lying, preying on our goodness."

"I wouldn't really be giving myself over to her. When she comes, I don't have any recollection of it. Whatever she makes me do, I won't remember it."

"And Adrian?"

"He won't remember either."

"I don't like it!" Muriel scoffed. "For you and Adrian to sacrifice your bodies . . . I don't like it!"

"If there's another way, I'm willing to listen to it," Janice commented. She saw Muriel's frown pucker deeper.

"I don't know any other way."

"Then you'll help me convince Adrian?"

"It's useless, my dear. Adrian will never agree to it, and I say, thank God!"

"He'll agree. He's attracted to me physically."

"And that's just why he won't agree to it." Muriel argued. She gave Janice's hand a sympathetic pat, meeting her baffled gaze straight on. "Can you imagine Adrian agreeing to make love to you knowing full well he won't remember it when it's over? He won't do it. Mark my words."

"He has to. Because he knows the same as I that if he doesn't, he will put the rest of you in jeopardy. For all his jaded wit, I don't think he'll let that happen. He'll agree—if you and Jasper convince him of it."

A look of alarm crossed Muriel's face at once and she lowered her voice so only Janice could hear her words.

"I can't burden Jasper with this. He's a man of the cloth. It's his job to counsel unmarried couples to abstain from sex, not indulge in it."

Janice felt a warm flush stain her cheeks. Heavens, she had never thought how perverse her suggestion might sound to a minister. Lord, had she lost all shreds of decency? Her hands sought the shelter of her lap once more and she stiffened her resolve. No, she'd not change her mind. No matter how sinful a minister thought it was. She was going to end this nightmare.

Across the way, Muriel shifted in her chair, remaining silent to allow Janice a chance to regain her composure. Pulling her thoughts back in line, Janice let her gaze drift back to Muriel, who took charge again.

"No, I won't discuss this with Jasper. But I will talk to Adrian."

Janice felt immense relief well up.

"Bless you, Muriel."

A warning finger flashed before her eyes.

"I'll talk with Adrian. But I won't press him."

Janice had a moment of indecision, but she stamped it down where it belonged. They were getting out of here alive. All of them. Anything else was unthinkable.

"I trust Lisette, Muriel. I know it's foolish to believe a ghost, but I don't think she will let any harm come to me. And I don't think the baron will harm Adrian."

"If we were just dealing with the baron and Lisette I should feel safer. But that fiend of a spirit intends harm to you. To Lisette."

Janice brought her hands to Muriel's and cupped them for a change.

"You let me worry about that horrid, spiteful ghost. Besides, what could you do to keep it from harming me this very minute if it wanted to? You saw it before. We were powerless to stop it."

Muriel slipped her hands from beneath Janice's.

"I hate it when you're right." She plucked at the collar of her dress. "That hateful ghost has made me quite cross. And I intend to tell it that if it dares to show itself again."

Janice did smile then, knowing full well Muriel wouldn't do any such thing. For all their bravado, each of them was sufficiently kowtowed by the spiteful cloud.

Muriel gave a busted sigh, bringing Janice's attention back to the matter at hand.

"Well, sitting here won't get the thing done," she remarked, rising. She padded across the carpet and was gone before Janice could offer a heartfelt thank you.

Leaning back, all bravery gone now that her task had been accomplished, Janice sighed. It would soon be over. They'd be going home. A tear welled up suddenly, saturating her lower eyelid. No tears, she chastised herself, swiping at the bead. The time for crying is long past. Another tear followed the first and soon Janice found herself continuously dabbing at her wet cheeks. *Janice Marie Mignon Kelly, you are the stupidest of fools. Just because you have to sacrifice every shred of decency in you and make love to the handsomest, most infuriating man you've ever met . . .* her thoughts derailed instantly. Heavens, that wasn't why she was crying at all. She wasn't crying because of what she had to do. She was crying because she wouldn't recall one wonderful minute of doing it.

*

"Driving yourself this way is foolish, Adrian."

Warm fingers descended on Adrian's collar and probed the cords along his neck. Adrian dropped his head forward, enjoying Muriel's fingers as they massaged a knotted ridge along his upper back.

"I feel so useless," he stated. He stole a peek at the comatose woman alongside the ottoman where he sat. "I know she can't see or hear me, but I at least have to prove to myself I didn't abandon her."

The fingers dug deeper into his flesh, massaging a stubborn kink.

"Ginger knows, Adrian. She trusts you completely."

Adrian raised his head at the comment, his lips curling to a sneer.

"She'll never speak to me again when this is over. And she'd be a fool if she did. I had no right to bring her with me. I just couldn't face this reunion alone. Damn my egotistical pride!"

The fingers on his neck paused and soon, Adrian saw a flash of pink. When he looked up, Muriel was settling in a chair in front of him.

"You brought Ginger along to entertain Lloyd's guests. It was exceedingly smart on your part to do it. So if you want me to feel sorry for you because things haven't turned out as you expected, let me tell you right now, I won't do it. None of us had any choice in this arrangement. We were all called to this moment, for good or ill."

"One of God's never-ending jokes on mankind," Adrian quipped, then fell silent as a disapproving frown appeared on Muriel's brow. He inspected her clouded expression closely. He hoped his own was guarded because he didn't want her to see how worried he was by her appearance and words. She looked drained. The wrinkles along her cheekbone seemed more pronounced than he remembered. Take a look in the mirror, he chided himself at once. *You might be surprised by your own face.* Living through hell on earth tends to age one quickly, he informed his alter-ego. Still, he hoped his face wasn't as easy to read as Muriel's. Something was on her mind. She was staring at him with the same intensity as he was at her.

"Has something happened?" he asked, when Muriel continued to keep her own counsel.

"Janice wants me to convince you it is necessary for you and her to separate from the rest of us."

Adrian felt a tremor explode deep in the pit of his stomach.

"Has the woman gone completely insane? We can't split up. It's out of the question."

"Is it because you are afraid to be alone with her, Adrian?"

"What!" Adrian barely kept his seat but managed to put a leash on his temper. What was Janice concocting against him now? He had apologized to her for being a surly bastard. What more did she want from him? He shot Muriel a heated glare. "Has Janice been black mouthing me to you, Muriel?"

"Of course not. You know she never would. I merely asked that question because Janice sincerely thinks that if you two separate from the rest of us, Lisette will follow and the rest of us will be safe."

"She's right of course. That will happen. But that also leaves both of us in a potentially dangerous position."

"Yes," Muriel agreed. "Janice believes the ghosts will quickly take over your physical bodies. She believes Lisette intends to consummate her love for the baron, thereby releasing both their souls."

"And do you believe that?" Adrian asked, surprised to find himself banking on her answer. No, he chastised himself, he was really seeking her approval.

"The idea has merit, although I wouldn't admit as much to Janice. She's quite the bravest woman I've met in years. It's not every woman who would sacrifice herself to a man to save people who were unknown to her only several hours ago."

Adrian's mood blackened and a deep scowl etched his eyebrows.

"Don't you mean it's not every woman who would sacrifice herself to *me* to save lives?"

"No, I didn't mean that at all," Muriel intervened. "I think you are quite the bravest man I've met next to Jasper."

Adrian felt his lips twitch unexpectedly.

"Well, at least I'm in good company."

"Be serious, Adrian. I need to know what you think. I've told Janice you won't do it."

"And I won't."

"Yes," Muriel nodded at him. "You strike me as a man who relishes the feel of a woman. I don't think your manly pride could stand making love to an unconscious woman."

Adrian's lips twitched to a broad grin.

"Guilty on all counts." He found himself sobering suddenly. "And I don't relish making love to a woman when I don't know I'm doing it."

"Exactly," Muriel concurred, "then we're both agreed. You and Janice will stay with the rest of us." Adrian found himself nodding, although he wished he hadn't when Muriel's next words washed over him. "You'll have to tell Janice. I haven't the heart. I don't think she will take it well. She seems sure that this is the only way to end this predicament. I'm not sure I don't agree with her."

"I'm not making love to Janice," Adrian stated flatly.

"Yes, I can see you've quite made up your mind." Muriel eased herself from the chair and Adrian came to his feet, gently taking her elbow. As he did so, she slanted a peek at him. "You know, of course, when you tell her, it will end any chance you have of winning her?"

"Winning her?" He looked down at the eyes boring into his.

"She'll never forgive you. And when the rest of us become victims like Ginger, she'll do everything in her power to see that you pay for it."

"Is she as bloodthirsty as all that?"

"This is not a laughing matter, Adrian. Think carefully before you turn down Janice's suggestion. If, as she says, we are taken down like Ginger one by one, the result will be the same. You and she will be left alone to face Lisette and the baron."

Adrian gripped Muriel's elbow tighter.

"I'll talk to her. I'll judge for myself whether she's got a point or not."

"And if she does?"

"We'll separate from the rest of you." A long sigh emanated and Adrian sucked in his own breath. "No promises, Muriel. I think my answer will be the same. I'll not make love to Janice."

"Not even to save my life or Jasper's?"

An ice-cold chill trickled up Adrian's spine. Put so baldly, his words proved him to be a horse's ass, uncaring and unfeeling. Did Muriel think him that way?

"I don't intend you or Jasper to come to harm, Muriel. You have my word on it."

Muriel gave a grave nod.

"Janice knows you far better than you realize. She said you'd do the right thing." Adrian chuckled, and hearing his amusement, Muriel urged, "Now, don't make me cross, Adrian. My part in this discussion is ended. You and Janice must make the decisions from here."

"You're washing your hands of us, eh?" He stepped forward and Muriel did the same.

"I should say so. Old folks should leave young folks to work out problems by themselves."

"Yes, Grandma," Adrian mocked. "Well, let's go and see if we can convince Janice to give up this hysterical crap she's suggesting."

"I hope you're going to be more subtle than that with her."

"Of course."

He saw her skeptical glance and pinched her arm good-naturedly.

"Trust me, Muriel. I'll be discretion itself. C'mon."

Chapter 19

SATURDAY—4:30 AM

What was keeping Muriel? Surely a simple yes didn't take a full five minutes. He was refusing to agree to her plan. That was all there was to it. Janice choked back a despairing sob, willing herself not to cry again. What would she do if Adrian refused? Lord, she hadn't figured on that. She'd strike out on her own, that's what. Then Adrian would have to follow her. Her runaway thoughts stopped in midstream as Janice felt nauseous at the thought of traveling the house alone. No, she wasn't going anywhere in the house alone. No one could make her. As if to prove it, she snuggled deeper into the folds of her chair. Absently, she began to pluck at the textured arm. There had to be a way to convince Adrian she was right.

"How long have you been playing nursemaid?"

The crabby question startled Janice. Her head shot up and whipped around. Probing eyes met hers and she immediately sprang from her chair in relief. Across the way, Jasper shot to his feet, charging around the bedpost directly opposite her. In a flash, he was bending over Lloyd.

"How are you feeling?"

"As if the top of my head has been sawed off," Lloyd exclaimed. "How long have I been out?"

Janice's hand glided through the air to his shoulder.

"About thirty minutes."

He gave another muttered groan and let his head sink deeper into the pillows. Janice knew he was experiencing the same feeling of disorientation and time lag as the rest of them.

"Feels like a century," he remarked. He swiveled his head to keep Janice in view. A bleak look came into his eyes and he raked his fingers through his hair as if trying to push something aside. Seeing the movement, Janice tensed, steeling herself for the possibility of a recurring attack of madness. Madness was tricky, she knew. It could come and go at will, like the cushioning silence of fog. "Did I hurt anyone?" The question was sane and sensible and Janice felt an instant spark of relief. Lloyd couldn't be going mad if he was worried about harming them.

"No," Janice assured him quickly. "No one is hurt."

"Thank God!" His relief was immense and so was Janice's. For a brief moment, she felt invincible. Lloyd had beaten the evil mist at its own game, and if Lloyd could come back from the brink, there was hope for each of them when their turn came.

"Do you remember anything at all?" Jasper asked, dropping onto the edge of the bed and studying Lloyd's face.

"I heard a snap in my head, followed by a tremendous flood of hate and an insatiable desire to kill someone…anyone…everything goes blank from there," he finished.

"Are the voices still bothering your head, Lloyd?" Janice asked, trying to keep the conversation light and away from murders and mutilations.

"No, they've gone." He rolled over and propped himself on his elbow and Janice saw him survey the shadows again. "I've got to see Ginger," he muttered, suddenly. Again, Janice pushed him down into the pillows.

"Ginger's fine, Lloyd. She's in no pain."

"It's all my fault," he stressed, grasping her fingers and pushing them away from his chest. "Don't coddle me as if I need babysitting. I'm back among the living again. I won't hurt you." He struggled to a sitting position and Janice took a step back, stung by his sharpness.

"I never thought you would, Lloyd."

He didn't believe her. Janice could see it in the set of his chin and the scrutiny of his gaze on her face. His next words confirmed it.

"I'm no fool. You all think I planned this damn insanity— brought you here for it."

"Lloyd, I assure you none of us believes that for a moment," Janice stated.

"Janice is right," Jasper added. "None of us believes this is your fault."

"Lloyd, how wonderful to see you awake." Janice turned, suppressing a sigh as Muriel breezed through the doorway and charged the bed, pleasure written all over her face at the sight of Lloyd sitting up and chatting. Rounding the bedpost, she flicked her fingers at Janice, who slid gracefully from the bed. "You're looking much better, Lloyd," she said. "We were so frightened for you. How are you feeling?"

He was ready with a curt reply.

"Spaced out."

"Yes, well, you have a right to be. Your mind has certainly taken you for a ride."

Janice saw Lloyd nod again and his shoulders slouched as he commented brusquely.

"I'm tired."

"Of course you are," Muriel soothed, "that's why you're going to take another short nap." She reached for the coverlet and he started to object but her clucking defiance cut him off. Capitulating, he dragged his body back to the center of the bed, gave them all a brief smile, turned his head and closed his eyes.

"I'll sit with him," Janice offered.

"No, you go and sit with Adrian. He needs cheering up."

Janice cast a glance over her shoulder to the doorway where Adrian lounged. He certainly didn't seem as if he needed cheering up. He was watching the proceedings with his usual disinterested expression.

Reluctantly, Janice crossed the carpet. As she passed Adrian, she had the uncanny feeling she was going to be the one to need cheering up. By the look on his face, the next few minutes would not be pleasant. At least not for her. Behind her, she heard movement and knew he had hoisted himself from the doorframe. She quickened her steps.

Heading for the ottoman by the sofa, Janice reminded herself she could be very persistent when she chose and she had no intention of letting Adrian browbeat her into submission. She sank to the ottoman only to find her wrist snatched roughly and her body propelled back up and pushed toward the outside hallway.

"We can talk out in the hall," Adrian stated.

They were out the door in seconds with Janice barely remembering how they got there. He was being polite, she noted, extremely polite. Intuitively, she sensed Adrian was at his deadliest when being extremely polite. What was she in for?

Stepping onto the corridor landing, Janice heard the door slam closed behind them. Deep inside, she heard a similar slam, as if the door to her heart had suddenly shut, too. She began shoring up her reasoning for the battle to com. What argument could she offer Adrian to make him see the sense in separating from the others?

Studiously, Janice looked out over the banister to the floor three stories below. The distance between hers and Adrian's hearts was as far from where she stood to the ground floor below. How could she ever hope to win Adrian over when he so plainly refused to like her?

Beside her, Janice heard a cough and knew Adrian's patience was wearing thin. Out of the corner of her eye, she saw him begin to pace the corridor. He strode away, past pewter candlesticks and back again. He repeated the pattern a second time, his rapid pacing that of a caged animal, anxious for release. Yes, he resembled an animal ready to pounce while she was a coiled spring ready to snap. She withdrew her gaze from Adrian and searched the ceiling overhead again.

"Where do you suppose the mist will strike from next?" she asked, finally breaking the silence. Adrian halted his stride and gave her a dismissive shrug.

"It won't for a while. We aren't stressed enough yet. It'll give us plenty of time to imagine the worst. It wants us to anticipate our downfall."

"I understand the cloud's behavior," Janice stated. "As you say, the longer it stays away, the more effective its power over us. But what holds Lisette at bay? She knows I'm willing to help her."

Adrian stopped pacing and perched his bottom on the banister rail. He hooked one leg around a brass pole to hold his balance. His countenance turned thoughtful before he announced brusquely:

"Fear."

"Of her soul being snatched from her?" Janice saw Adrian's nod. "No, I can't buy that. It's against all the principles I know to be true about the other side. Something else keeps her away."

"Release of her soul is a pretty powerful hunger. Don't underestimate it or her. In her own way, she's as dangerous as the sparkling lights. It would be a good idea for you to remember that."

Janice swung about, reflecting on Adrian's remark. Lisette did have a powerful motive, she wasn't denying that. So why lay back? What was Lisette really waiting for? Approval! The word flashed into Janice's mind and her heart leapt in surprise. Yes, that was it. She was waiting for approval. Not hers but Adrian's approval. She wondered why she hadn't thought of it before. Swinging back to Adrian, Janice couldn't keep the eagerness from her tone.

"She's waiting for you, Adrian. She knows you're reluctant to help me. Until you agree, she'll stay away."

"She'll have a long wait," Adrian stated. "I have no intention of making love to you to get us out of here."

Two hours ago, Adrian's pronouncement would have thrilled her, but at the moment she found it disconcerting. Quite suddenly, she wondered what she had done to make Adrian change his mind. Muriel had been so sure that Adrian was attracted to her, she had let herself believe it too. Had Muriel been mistaken?

Janice quieted her racing thoughts. Who cared what Adrian thought? *You do*, her pride nagged stubbornly. Her marriage to Jimmy taught her that men never refused an offer of free sex, so why was Adrian turning her down?

When no satisfying answer came, Janice let the small of her back rest gently against the banister. She began to chew on her lower lip. She stole a peek at him out of the corner of her eye. Like her moments earlier, he was studying the ground floor below showing the same thoughtful intensity. She looked away. Why didn't Adrian want to make love to her anymore?

"Janice?" He snapped his fingers to catch her eye. She picked up the threads of conversation instantly.

"I don't know why I'm surprised. Muriel did warn me you would refuse."

"How could you think I'd agree?" Adrian asked. He shifted his torso as if to relieve a knotted kink.

"I guess I thought you of all people would see the sense of it," Janice replied.

"Sense! Where's the sense of putting our minds purposely in danger?" As if shot from a cannon, Adrian hopped from the banister, sliding past Janice to an alcove surmounted with a huge Georgian shell. He fingered the shell absently. "If you were so eager for me to put my life in danger, why couldn't you ask me first instead of going to Muriel? You've worried her unnecessarily."

"I knew you wouldn't agree if I asked you myself," Janice argued. Foolishly, she found herself staring at the edges of the brass rail instead of Adrian. She began to finger it. "You've been as nasty as you can be to me. And all because of an image in your head. Though I didn't put it there, you blame me for it. I went to Muriel because I thought she could accomplish what I never would. You seem so genuinely fond of her."

"I am. And because I am, I don't upset her needlessly."

Janice flushed, hearing the censure in Adrian's remark. Blast it! Why did he have to be right? She had been extremely inconsiderate of Muriel but it was just as rude of him to point it out. What did they do now? She stopped fingering the banister, coloring even more fiercely. She lifted her gaze and caught Adrian's eye.

"I was wrong. I see it now. I'm sorry, Adrian. Fool that I am, I believed that you wanted this nightmare to end, too."

"I do want it to end. Apparently more than you do."

"How can you say that? I have a child waiting for me at home and the thought of never seeing her again hurts so much that I am willing to risk my sanity to get home to her." Janice pushed her point. "If we separate from the others, you know the ghosts will follow, Adrian."

"You're damn right they will and so will our murderous friend. What's to keep it from possessing one of us?"

"Lisette will."

Intense astonishment stained Adrian's face and Janice knew her words had floored him. Not to her surprise, he stopped fingering the shell and riffled his hair in exasperation.

"How can you stand there and tell me you're putting your faith in a ghost who not more than a few hours ago displaced your mind and abused your body?"

"I don't know but I am."

Adrian's fingers trailed down his temple.

"You're nuts, you know that? As crazy as Marks in there."

"Why? Because I'm willing to end this madness right now and you aren't?"

"No. Because you're willing to end it by giving yourself over to Lisette and the baron without a fight. And you expect me to do the same."

"I don't expect you to go willingly, Adrian."

"That's a relief. You're not a total airhead!"

Janice shot up from the banister with an annoyed hiss. Why had Adrian's jaded wit chosen this moment to resurface?

"You can't fight off the baron, Adrian," she snapped.

"I won't know until I try. And neither will you." He advanced a few steps toward her and Janice saw his hands arc through the air in emphasis. "We have the ship's log and Lisette's diary. They contain all we need to get out of here."

Janice's disdain turned quickly to exasperation. Was she the only one with any brains left between the two of them? Couldn't he see they wouldn't have time to decipher the logs? She took a deep breath, hoping to disguise her irritation long enough to reason sensibly with him.

"I don't believe we'll be allowed the time to decipher the logs.

If we piece together the events in their correct sequence, we will have identified Lisette's murderer. Knowing that, we will have the power to release her soul. The cloud isn't going to let us get that far. No . . . " Janice added, with a slight smile of defiance. "We've reached a dead-end here. What's it going to take to make you see that? When Muriel's mind is spun around like Lloyd's? Or Jasper's? And Ginger . . . " Janice broke off, stepping forward. "Change your mind, Adrian, please! How can either of us be so selfish as to leave Ginger like that? Let's separate from the others and save them. Let's face the ghosts one on one. If we don't, the others will be shut down and in the end, we will still face the ghosts one on one."

She paused to catch her breath and Adrian seized the moment to comment brusquely.

"Suppose we both blackout and only one of us wakes up? Have you ever thought of that?"

Janice disguised her unease. She had thought of that. In fact, she thought the possibility was quite likely. But if she admitted as much to Adrian, he would never agree to help her. Mulishly, she remained silent, withstanding Adrian's penetrating gaze without dropping her own.

"Has it ever occurred to you that we could both blackout and *neither* of us wakes up?" Adrian persisted.

Janice swung about, glancing back across the space to the red glow silhouetted in the stained glass panel. Death! At the word, a memory ruffled through her mind like wind on water and Janice deliberately let her mind run backward. A name lingered around the edges of her mind.

"For days after my sister Anna died, I had recurring visions of her standing at the edge of a lake. She was healthy and whole, no sign of the muscular dystrophy that had ravaged her body since birth. She stood waving at me . . . " Janice felt the familiar prickle of tears. She swung around to find Adrian's face a misty blur. "I wonder if you can imagine it. Anna standing. Anna who had never experienced a day without Mama forcing her little legs to try harder. Anna who only saw the world through a bedroom window. She was standing, Adrian. And each night in the vision she waved to me. And each night she was farther away from the edge of the lake and harder for me to see. I may have been only six years old but I suddenly knew what complete happiness was. I understood that in death Anna was free from pain and joyously happy. And she wanted me to know it."

Janice felt her throat constrict and her gaze miraculously cleared, locking with Adrian's. "A moment ago you wondered how I could conceive of putting my faith in a ghost. Anna's the reason why. Anna's soul was freed from physical torment and it was blissfully free to move on. Lisette seeks that same bliss, nothing more. And I don't have the courage to deny her that. If our positions were reversed, she'd sacrifice herself willingly for me. I have to do the same. If I don't, it would be as if I were betraying Anna somehow. Can you understand that?" Janice felt a hot tear slip down her cheek and swiped at it hastily. "Damn! I wish I wouldn't cry when talking about Anna. It's such a childish thing to do!" She whirled around, offering Adrian her back. It was bad enough when she cried in front of Bibi, but to cry in front of a man she hardly knew was just plain ridiculous. Quite suddenly, she felt a presence at her back and Adrian's voice was oddly gentle as he echoed her own longings.

"If I agree to separate from the others, you must promise me that if there is another way out of this nightmare beyond the physical, you'll take it."

Janice whirled about, a smile breaking across her mouth.

"I'll take it," she promised. "Besides, I can't imagine you want to make love with me anymore that I want to with you."

"You underestimate your beauty, Janice. You really do."

"Beauty?" Janice stuttered in surprise.

"Don't fish for compliments! I know you own a mirror." He pushed her toward the closed door. "And right now, your coyness is as scary as changing a flat tire on a congested freeway."

"And obviously as popular as a tax increase."

The tip of her shoulder was pushed roughly again.

"You're giving me a King Kong headache, Miss Kelly. Open the door!"

Janice did as she was ordered, grasping the doorknob and pressing the door with her fingertips. When it refused to open, she jiggled the handle harder.

"It's stuck." She smacked the panel.

Strong hands thrust her roughly aside.

"Get out of the way." Gripping the door handle, Adrian heaved his shoulder against the wood. A seam cracked, but the door remained tightly wedged. "Son of a bitch!"

Above her head, Janice felt the air stir and the hairs on the back of her neck felt the light prickle. Instant panic seized her and she muttered in Adrian's ear.

"The door, Adrian! We've got to get inside. Hurry!"

Adrian slammed his shoulder against the door more forcefully but even though the seam cracked, adding a second stitch, the door held its placement. Tucking herself into the doorframe, Janice began to pound on the wood.

"Muriel! Jasper! Open the door!"

"Save your breath," Adrian cautioned, stepping back in a hurry. He captured Janice's hand and she realized he was experiencing a new stirring. Looking up, they both studied the cathedral ceiling overhead.

"Which one is it?" Janice asked. "Can you tell?" His guess never materialized as above their heads a purple flash ignited. "Oh, shit!"

"Right," Adrian drawled quickly.

Jerking Janice forward, he bolted for the stairs, ignoring her pained yelp as he accidentally twisted her wrist. Before she knew it, they were barreling down the staircase like frenzied rabbits fleeing a pack of hungry foxes. Tripping onto the second level stairwell landing, Janice had no idea where they were heading. And at the moment, where didn't matter. They had to find shelter. Lisette's murderer was coming for them. She could tell by the smell and the ruptured hiss trailing down the staircase behind them.

Chapter 20

SATURDAY—4:40 AM

Footsteps clattering down first one flight, then a second, Adrian could only hope that Janice was hot on his heels. He didn't dare take time to look for her over his shoulder. They had to get away as far and as fast as they could from the roaring din swirling about their heads. Myriad garbled sounds, voices, murmurs, and poppings were thrumming like pigeon's feet on a roof and each second that passed, the din grew louder and closer to them.

As if in a foot race, Adrian increased his pace down the stairs, taking the last two steps to the main floor in one jump. When sure of his footing, he twisted around in search of Janice only to find himself slammed back hard as she barreled into his chest, arms flailing. Thinking fast, he managed to lock his knees and capture her waist, miraculously keeping them both from crashing to the floor.

"Which way?" she gasped, clutching his shirt front with knotted fingers.

Adrian spun her around and shoved her toward the arched columns a few yards ahead of them.

"The back staircase," he muttered between a labored gasp.

She whirled back around, eyes wide as saucers. From the look of alarm permeating her face, Adrian knew she hated the thought of thundering down another set of staircases. Her legs probably felt as bad as his, the leg muscles cramping from the sudden, fevered use. Still, he hardened his heart. They had only one option—to keep moving until they could find a safe hiding place.

Snatching her hand, he bolted down the corridor and shot through the columns only to skid to a halt as disjointed sounds and strangled groans began to mewl and wail in the distance ahead. Out of the sounds, Adrian saw the showering sparkle of purple lights.

"Wily bastard," he snarled. He gave a quick glance left and right, searching for any feasible bypass they could use to outfox the lights. Finding none, he whirled, hauling Janice back through the columns and into the front hall of the house again.

Reaching the southern staircase, the pair began a rapid climb back the way they had come. Hitting the second level, Adrian veered off sharply, racing down a side corridor and into the back part of the chateau. The yammering mewls were muffled from their hearing and Adrian wished he had the breath to waste on a hearty thank you. But he couldn't. They had to take advantage of their good fortune by continuing to distance themselves from the lower levels.

Once again, Adrian veered off sharply, ducking into yet another side corridor and new staircase. Reaching it, he started up, taking the steps two at a time. For two levels, he felt Janice shadowing him closely and then her foot must have miscalculated a step because he heard her stumble. Stopping dead in his tracks, he whirled, hoping to right her before she crashed into the banister. Miraculously, she regained her footing without his help and flashed past him, on up the staircase to the next level. Adrian overtook her at the top and began to rush them down a corridor back to the front of the house. In tune again, they tore through the second floor corridor, past the solarium into the connecting hallway. Adrian could only hope their erratic dash had confused their tracker. Jesus, forget their tracker. He was confused. He had no earthly idea where they were or where they were headed.

Rounding into the south third floor wing, Adrian felt a stabbing pain in his chest and knew his lungs were caving in. They were stressed to the max and screaming to shut down. Drawing up, he bent over and gave into a spasm of hacking coughs. The coughs elicited a sharp twinge between his shoulder blades and he shot upright again, clutching his chest. Jesus, now the muscles on the right side of his ribcage were screaming for relief. He rubbed the sore spot vigorously, feeling his heartbeat thumping erratically in his chest. Suddenly remembering Janice, he glanced over his shoulder to see how she was faring.

She was sitting on a marble bench off to the left, her hands tugging at the neckline of her sweater. Even disheveled and out of breath, she was a knock-out. Her cheeks were scarlet from the climb and her hair was a tangled web etched around her head. Thanks to their frantic dash, her colorful hair clips had literally gone with the wind. She licked her lips and swallowed hard, and Adrian fought down an urge to cross the space and sweep her into his arms. He thrust the thought away, cursing himself. Why was he thinking of kissing Janice when he should be thinking of escape?

Escape! The word triggered his adrenalin and he came alive. Though they were both exhausted, he knew they couldn't spare another moment to rest. Not now. They had only two flights left to hide in and he didn't like the absolute silence that now surrounded them. Their stalker was up to a new trick. He could feel it along the edges of his mind.

Holding out his hand, Adrian summoned Janice with a wiggle of his fingers. She took one look at his hand and shook her head.

"Leave me. I can't climb another step."

Right, he was going to leave her. What kind of horse's ass did she think he was? He saw her cradle her head with one trembling hand and wave him away with the other. Adrian strode to the bench.

"Get up, Janice. Get up or you're going to die!" His words washed over her as if never spoken. She remained impassive, choosing to ignore the warning. Didn't she care that they got away from the stalking cloud of lights? Labeling the thought absurd, Adrian bent over, stretched his arm across her shoulder and barked a more serious warning. "Get on your feet, Janice, or that precious daughter of yours will be an orphan by morning!" She bolted from the bench immediately, all signs of exhaustion submerged. She looked to him for directions and he managed a tight smile for her. "Don't count us out yet. We have time on our side. We don't have to transform matter to get where we're going. It does."

Grabbing her elbow, he steered her forward and they were on their way again, mind and bodies finally moving through the space together. Reaching the fifth floor columned arches, Adrian caught a whiff of a sharp, carbolic odor and drew up. The smell reminded him of sweat and piss, and he drew Janice into the protection of his arm. Ahead, through the arches, a barricade of sparkling lights stretched itself from wall to wall.

"Clever bastard!" He felt Janice's shiver of unease and encouraged softly. "Relax. We'll outsmart it."

"I don't see how," she stuttered. Her fingers inched up his shirt and Adrian stilled them.

"I thought you wanted to face the ghosts one on one," he stated. "Well, here we are."

"I never thought we'd actually have to do it."

"Now, you tell me," Adrian quipped. He pushed Janice from his arms. "Let's see how badly it wants to stop us. When I say go, pretend to head back to the stairs. The cloud should follow. That will open up the corridor ahead of us. The chapel's beyond. Make for it."

Spinning on her toes, Janice swung out of his arms. Immediately, the barricade of light dissipated as Adrian hoped it would. It wanted Janice, wanted her badly. Following his instructions, Janice whirled on her toes and shot past him. The corridor had been left open but Adrian didn't discount the cloud's intelligence. It would see their ruse and be back with a vengeance. Swiveling around, he dashed after Janice. In seconds, he was tailing her closely and protecting her back.

The last fifty yards to the chapel door were the longest thirty seconds of his life. At every step, Adrian expected to be showered with sparkling lights and knocked unconscious. Or worse, killed outright. When he reached the chapel doors unharmed, he thrust out his arms, slammed the door open and barreled inside. Janice sailed in on his heels, and as one, they spun and slammed the doors closed with a heavy swipe. The resounding clang echoed unbelievably loud in the silence of the sanctuary, causing Adrian to grind his bottom teeth into his lower lip. Next to him, Janice gave an involuntary shudder and collapsed against the door.

Following suit, Adrian leaned his forehead on the wooden

frame, grateful for their good luck. Behind him, he could hear Janice's sudden wracking coughs. They were winded but they were alive. At least for the moment. Hoisting himself around, he found Janice staring at him between coughs.

"Why the chapel?" she stammered.

Adrian flushed, wondering if he dared tell her the truth. Why not? He couldn't appear any more foolish to her than he already did.

"Let's just say, I foolishly believe that the devil won't set foot in God's house."

To his amazement, she seemed impressed with that answer and nodded at him with complete understanding. She followed the nod with a flashing smile,

"If there's a joke in all this, I sure would like to hear it," he said.

He hands arced up and swept toward the pew, altar and crucifix.

"God's house . . . marriage . . . vows . . . Lisette . . . the baron . . . you . . . me." She began to laugh then and her laughter held a sharp edge. Adrian caught the irony immediately. They had exchanged one danger for another just as likely to take their lives. He didn't find the irony amusing in any way. Her laughter changed abruptly into an unexpected sob and Adrian darted across the space and gathered her close to him. He shook her shoulders in a firm warning.

"Don't fall apart on me now, Janice. I need you. It's going to take both our minds to outwit the ghosts."

She sobered at his warning and pushed herself from his arms. Her fingernails tapped his chest.

"I'm not going to crack. At least I think I'm not. I hope I'm not." She wiped her eyes with the back of her hands and there was a trace of laughter in her voice once more as she teased. "I hope you're taking notes on the spirit's performance. The illusion is simply spectacular. You could probably use parts of it in your act."

"Bite your tongue."

"No, I mean it. That barricade of light was simply smashing. Think of it under stage lights. The effect would be mesmerizing."

"Thanks for the advice but my act already has a finale with laser lights."

"Erotic and sexy, I'll bet," Janice added lightly.

"And all of it done with the use of satin sheets," Adrian remarked. He let his glance become lazily seductive as it traveled up and down her long-legged, slender form. His scorching gaze brought a fresh flush of color to her cheeks and he saw her shiver at the husky tone of his voice. Had that been a trembling thrill he noticed? Was she hungry for his touch and unaware of it? He stilled an impulse to reach out and gather her in his arms again, this time to do more than calm her fraying nerves.

Turning his gaze to the avant-garde crucifix over the altar, he wondered if he found Janice so desirable because she was so unattainable. No. His need for her ran deeper than that.

It was more compelling than sexual fulfillment. It crossed more barriers than just the flesh. And because it did, it stabbed his heart to know that when this hell was over she would leave him. Carefully, he blocked his mind from the cutting edge of loneliness that thought brought and tried to concentrate on the Stations of the Cross along the chapel wall.

Janice's laugh was like a whinny when it came, her smile singularly sweet.

"Muriel is right. Your jaded wit can be highly entertaining." She left him then, sliding into the back pew closest to the door. Quickly, her fingers shot to her hair, attempting to restore the curls to some semblance of sanity. Working out the kinks, she shot Adrian a serious glance.

"What do we do now?"

He moved to the pew opposite her, dropping down with a groan. He offered her a wry smile and a shrug.

"We wait."

Chapter 21

SATURDAY—4:50 AM

Stroking his chin, Jasper carefully regarded the gold doorknob. Why he thought that the door would budge under his forceful prodding this time when it had refused to budge the last five times was a mystery to him. The door was firmly sealed from the outside and they were very cleverly trapped on the inside. No use lamenting, no use pushing or prodding it. The ghosts had tired of waiting on them. They now had every intention of ending the cat and mouse game currently underway. Janice's prediction showed every sign of coming true. They would be shut down one by one in the next few minutes.

But why? Jasper couldn't imagine—well, he could—but since only crazy dogs sat uselessly baying at the moon, he decided he wasn't wasting his energy worrying when he might need that energy for something more important, like his and Muriel's survival. Something was coming, something bad. Every nerve ending in his body told him so. What had happened to Adrian and Janice?

A tattoo along his right temple had him suddenly wincing. Drat, he had been concentrating so had on piercing through the wood to find the couple that he had given himself a headache. And his precognition was blocked again, as if a shutter lens had suddenly closed to block out rays of glaring understanding. He didn't know where Adrian or Janice were—couldn't sense their life forces. But he did know one thing. His mind was being manipulated to keep the couple's whereabouts a secret from him.

Raising his gaze to the ceiling, Jasper listened to the silence surrounding them. Was the invisible tension in the air part of his mind blockage? It had to be. Otherwise, he'd be able to sense

Muriel probing his mind for answers. Quickly, he dropped his gaze and found her. Immediately, he saw the two deep lines of worry between her brows. Seated beside Ginger's sleeping form, her head was slightly bowed as she remained in an attitude of frozen stillness. She looked tired and he wondered why he hadn't noticed it before. He was usually so in tune with her life force that it was hard to tell where she ended and he began.

She sat staring at Ginger but Jasper knew she wasn't really seeing the girl at all. She was working out their new predicament in her head. Her unseeing stare signified it. Whether mildly disturbed or severely rattled, Jasper knew she had the power to shut down, go inside herself and seek God's solace and answer. He envied her that trait. For all his ministerial prowess, he was unable to connect with God's solace by the same method. By the look on her face, he guessed she was worrying about Janice and Adrian's disappearance. He had to admit she had reason. He was more than worried himself.

Unsettled by her intense concentration, Jasper had a sudden inexplicable feeling of emptiness. For a brief moment, his senses warned him he was going away from Muriel. Was his death imminent? Was that why his mind was blocked? To shut off the knowledge from him? He murmured a prayer of hope that his senses were wrong. He didn't want to leave Muree. Not quite yet.

Taking a deep, steadying breath, he shelved his worry and crossed the small distance to the ottoman where Muriel sat. He wedged himself into the seat next to her. His touch on her elbow was light, yet protective.

"They'll be all right," he said, quietly.

Not to his surprise, she came out of her reverie, understanding his words without interpretation. She scanned his face, feature by feature.

"Can you sense them, Jasper?"

"No. I'm being blocked out. I can't read any life force, not even yours."

She must have sensed the hidden worry in his word because Jasper found his hand clutched tightly. Her voice was patient and encouraging.

"It's not so surprising really. You pose the biggest danger to the spirit. With your ability to tell when it's crossing over, it can't use the element of surprise on us." She leaned her forward, her voice turning overly serious. "You've changed a lot of people's lives by pretending you can't read their future, Jasper. And I love you for it. But this is not the time to be silent. You must force your mind past the blockage. I'm worried for Janice. If forced to, she will sacrifice herself to the spirits to save us. She may have already."

Jasper dismissed the thought with an airy wave of his hand though his expression grew thoughtful.

"She's with Adrian, and he will see to it she doesn't do anything foolish."

"I'm not so sure. Janice was going to convince him they must separate from the rest of us."

"Yes, I heard."

She directed a stare at him that spoke volumes about eavesdroppers.

"Then you already know Adrian said he wouldn't agree, but what if he had no choice?" They'd both heard Janice's frantic screaming through the wooden door earlier. Even now in his own head, he could hear the panicked shout followed by a desperate pounding on the doorframe. "You heard her voice, Jasper," Muriel continued, "she was scared. Something was happening to them out there. If only we knew what it was." She lifted her eyes, seeking his comfort and Jasper immediately caught her hand in his. He squeezed her fingers with more encouragement that he actually felt.

"Adrian's not about to let anything happen to Janice. You've seen the way he looks at her. His eyes smolder with passion one minute, brim with tenderness the next. Unless I read him wrong, and I haven't," he stressed quietly. "Adrian will sacrifice his life for Janice if it comes to that."

Muriel nodded dubiously.

"Janice can be quite persuasive. And quite stubborn." Without warning, she lifted her fingers and caressed his cheekbone. "I love you, Jasper. Have I told you that today?"

Jasper's pulse skittered in response and he drank in the comfort of her nearness.

"In every glance you gave me, Muree." Unexpectedly, he found himself stilling her fingers, flipping her hand over and pressing a kiss in the center of her palm. "This isn't exactly how I envisioned this trip would turn out," he commented. "I was hoping we'd have some romantic moments together."

Her gentle laugh rippled in the air.

"Why, Jasper, we're literally surrounded by romance. Ghosts have traveled across time to rekindle a love that was lost and two young people we just met have fallen madly in love and don't know it yet. And we've been locked in a room together with two bedrooms. Now, if that isn't romantic, I don't know what is."

Jasper threw back his head and snorted good-naturedly. God, he did so love Muree's Pollyanna sense of humor. In a flash, a busted laugh joined his and he cradled her into the circle of his arms. Spirits soaring, he kissed the tip of her nose, then her eyes, and finally, his lips descended and captured her mouth.

At first her lips were warm and pliant beneath his and then like a sudden blast of icy wind, her lips turned cold and she pulled away. She raised a hand to shelter her eyes from him and Jasper had the uncanny sensation of emptiness again. *Something's coming, something bad.* The warning had him almost jumping out of his skin. He leaned forward, knotting his fingers with Muriel.

"What's going on, Muree? Tell me." Her gaze never left his face but Jasper sensed a slight withdrawal from her. "Are you ill?" he prodded again, this time more urgently.

She shook her head.

"Not ill, experiencing pain."

Something's coming, something bad. The words seemed to reverberate like an echo down a well. He let go her hands, his palms suddenly beginning to sweat.

"How long?" he quizzed. "What kind of pain?"

"I'm having difficulty concentrating," she murmured as she raised her hand to her temple to massage the flesh. "I'm short of breath and I feel an odd draining of energy, as if someone's trying to pull open a locked door."

Offering his unspoken support, Jasper touched her elbow lightly. A sharp gasp burst from her throat at the touch. Her body twitched once, twice, and then stiffened with a taut jerk. In the next instance, she threw her hands up in front of her face as if to barricade herself from some unseen presence.

"Crossover."

The word startled Jasper as she toppled forward, sinking into a sudden, total blackout.

Lightning-quick, Jasper made a dive for her slumping body. He absorbed the weight of her fall, and neatly hoisted her up and about, settling her into the deep green cushions of his vacated chair. Wrapping his fingers around her pulse point, he sought entrance to her thoughts.

He met fire. Angry fire. Waves of it. Reeling under the invisible heat, he pulled his mind back and frantically shouted toward the doorframe to his left.

"Lloyd!"

Waiting for no response, his gaze returned to Muriel, attempting to connect the mind link again. He had to know if she was all right. He shut his eyes, driving his mind deep into hers. A second later, his mind collided with two life forces instead of the one he expected.

Feeling the power of the presence, he tried to force the alien entity out of Muriel's mind. Instead, he found himself taking the brunt of a savage fire bolt along his forehead. His physical body jerked backwards, as if stung. The entity wanted him out, would drive him out if he resisted.

Well, he wasn't going. He wouldn't leave Muriel to the mercy of such blind rage.

Steeling himself, Jasper pushed his energy into overdrive, fighting to keep his mind linked to Muriel's. Shock. Anger. Fury. Hostility. Sensation after sensation of pure hate hit him, yet Jasper refused to drop his mental barriers. He intended to block the alien link with just as much force as it was blocking his.

Little by little, through the stabbing pressure, Jasper began to perceive random thoughts. The entity was furious, had been thwarted in some way. Jasper tried to fathom the impulses. Perhaps if he delved past the unintelligible thought patterns. He tried and it worked. A vivid image of a cross flashed across his mind's eye, almost severing his mind link. He threw up another mental barrier against the pain, and immediately tried to bring the image into focus. It came this time, a pure, strong shimmering shape of God's cross.

Suddenly, Jasper understood. A cross could only mean one thing. Janice and Adrian were safe, had taken refuge in the chapel one floor above. Somehow, miraculously, they had escaped the spirit's wrath and had bought precious time by hiding themselves away.

Now having been shut out by the pair, the spirit was intending to exact revenge on the remaining trio. Another searing bolt of pain rocked his forehead and he knew the spirit had deciphered and understood his own thoughts.

Gritting his teeth, Jasper shifted his mind and energy to locate Muriel. Their minds collided, held for a moment, then severed completely. Bounced from the mind link, Jasper attempted to bring one firm thought pattern with him. The one that came tore at his heart.

Muriel was wilting under the spirit's ongoing pressure and in her weakened physical state, he knew her ability to hold on was doubtful. The spirit's hammering impulses would be too much for her. Somehow he had to short-circuit the spirit's power. But what could he try?

He had no time to find out as he felt his shoulders jerked back roughly. The mind link severed completely, bringing Jasper back to the physical room around him. Something was shaking him so ferociously, he lost his grip on Muriel's wrist. In his ear, he heard Lloyd's crazed snarl.

"For God's sake, man, what's going on?"

Jasper ignored the question. He had no time to explain. He had to re-establish the mind link with Muriel. Recapturing her wrist, he clamped down, seeking entrance. He found none and he groaned as a fearful image began to build in his head. Muriel's breath cut off. Muriel's mind fluttering away. Muriel lost and broken. He pressed down on the pulse point, praying for a sign of entrance.

Her eyes flew open at his touch and, stunned, Jasper withdrew his mind. He took a small step back and felt a cold knot forming in the pit of his stomach. *Something's coming, something bad.* Hatred blazed in the blue eyes probing his and a voice that seemed to come from a long distance emerged loud and clear from Muriel's throat.

"You cannot stop me," the voice warned with cool authority.

The words washed over him, stinging his senses, and Jasper realized what Muriel's last, mysterious word "crossover" had meant. Before him now sat, not Muriel, but Lisette's murderer. The throaty voice spoke again without inflection.

"You cannot stop me. Do not try."

Disconcerted, Jasper took another step back. Beside him, Lloyd did the same. Neither spoke but they both knew the entity was beyond intimidation. It had no intention of letting them fall from its spell. Muriel's lips parted in a curved stiff smile and Jasper heard a deep breath punctuated with several even gasps. Then the voice ordered belligerently.

"I want the woman you are protecting from me."

Jasper answered quickly, hoping to stem the spirit's increasing hostility.

"We don't know what happened to her."

The spirit twisted Muriel's face into an expression of loathing and Jasper's heart chilled at the disfigurement. Again, the voice spoke, this time its tones filled with cold contempt.

"You lie. My thoughts have been yours. You know the woman is above. With the man who guards her from me. You can summon the man through your mind. I saw you do it one time."

Jasper offered no comment. Beside him, Lloyd offered a brusque warning.

"Don't tell it a damn thing. It's bluffing."

Jasper thought so, too, but at the moment they had to be cautious. Muriel's hand arced to her chest, her fingers clawing at the region as if intending to rip the chest cavity open.

"You will summon the man and woman from above or I will harm the woman's body further. She is weak, but I can prolong her pain as I choose." To prove the threat, Muriel's body pitched forward and slammed back with a vicious jerk. Immediately, her fingers fluttered to her head and sharp gasps burst from her throat.

Sickened by the defilement, Jasper didn't know how he managed to keep from launching himself across the space to Muriel's side. Probably because he knew without doubt that the spirit would terminate her life before Jasper could reach her. Still, he knew he mustn't back down from the spirit, so he shoved his hands into his pants pocket and hunched his shoulders forward. Eyes darkening with pain, he spoke in a suffocated whisper.

"Release my wife and I will summon the woman you seek."

Jasper felt an iron grip on his arm.

"It's bluffing, do you hear? If it weren't, it would have already killed Muriel. Don't let it feed off your concern for her. Make no promises. Let's see the bluff out."

Jasper removed Lloyd's iron grip from his arm.

"Stay out of this. I know what I'm doing." Jasper faced the spirit again. "You will release the woman you hold or we will not help you," he stated calmly.

At his decree, a resounding mewl spewed from Muriel's lips, and to Jasper's horror, Muriel's body was yanked to its feet. From the very air above, a circle of lights began to cascade down. An icy blast of wind followed, hitting the pair full force. They fell back at the assault, and then thinking better of it, both men planted their feet firmly on the carpet and stood their ground.

Behind them, as if propelled by an explosive force, the hallway door tore from its hinges and slammed to the floor with a walloping thud. The sound animated the whirling cyclone of lights. In a flash, it had propelled Muriel by them and through the door, leaving the air above the men's heads filled with deafening cracks of thunder.

The pair leaped through the door, in full pursuit of the cyclone. Through the corridor, down the staircase, the cyclone kept the lead. Jasper and Lloyd stayed close on its heels and before Jasper knew it, they had descended two floors and were entering the second level portrait gallery. The circle of lights sped to the south end of the room, subsiding its mewling as it stopped before the portrait of Lisette.

The men followed at a more leisurely gait, cautious of drawing too close to the spirit in its present whirlwind. And then the swirling lights turned opaque and offered Muriel's plump form to their view again. Simultaneously, the cloud shifted to the left side of the portrait and boasted arrogantly.

"I would hear from your lips the name of the woman in the portrait. If you can tell me, I will release the woman I hold."

"It's a portrait of Lisette," Lloyd whispered swiftly.

The cloud spoke again, this time its tone held a rasp of excitement.

"Be careful of the name you call out. It is possible to see what is not there. Your eyes may deceive your mind."

"It's full of shit," Lloyd said strongly.

Jasper studied the portrait before them. No, not this time. The spirit was in deadly earnest. He strode forward and examined the portrait more closely. The woman etched in oil was a vivid beauty with crackling red hair. For a moment, he could see how Janice could be mistaken for her. Their hair colors were exact. But there he thought the similarity ended. The woman in the portrait had a wild quality about her whereas he knew firsthand Janice's nature was compellingly serene. Was the portrait of Lisette? He didn't know. If only he could pierce the canvas. Sense the model.

"Arretez! Stop! I forbid it!" The command was like a thunderous cannon echoing on the battlefield, and at first, Jasper thought the spirit hurled it at him. And then he saw it. The portrait before them began changing, the colors seeping and bleeding into each other. "Stop!" The cry came again and this time, Jasper was physically thrown aside, out of the cloud's path. It swirled before the canvas, ordering loudly. "You will stop! I demand it!"

Righting himself with Lloyd's help, Jasper kept his eyes glued to the portrait. The colors were dissipating through the pores of the canvas faster, replaced by a new set of colors saturating the fabric from the reverse side.

"Non, you will not have him!" The voice raised an octave and then faded to a hushed stillness. Soon, a keening wail emerged from the center of the cloud. The wail was so tormented Jasper could almost feel the spirit's pain within his own mind. The colors were finally settling in the portrait. Through the pores, a new portrait was forming. All at once, Jasper felt his mind open up. Across the darkness, images and thoughts one after the other began to bombard him.

At first, the thoughts were disconnected, a curious form of double think, and then he was given one cold, lucid thought that replayed sickeningly in his head. Tuning into it, he suddenly knew what was coming. There, just around the corner of his mind, he caught a glimpse of the swimming future. As he picked up the strings of time, memories from the past opened before him like a curtain drawn back on a string.

And just like that, Jasper knew the identity of Lisette's murderer. Saw the undeniable truth. He cast a curious look at the circle of lights pulsing nearby. How wonderful to hold the key to the terrible secret at last.

Chapter 22

SATURDAY—5:00 AM

Seated on the lower slab of altar steps, Adrian wished he wasn't so damn bad at waiting. Since his declaration that they would wait the spirit out, the silence in the chapel had grown oppressive, making his insides feel like a taut cable wire. Though he hadn't been to church in years, he still believed in an all-powerful God, and right now he didn't think God would approve of them using his house of worship as a battleground. But what else could they do? They were safe nowhere else in the house. No crawlspace or corner would keep them immune from the cloud of sparkling light.

Frustrated, he rubbed his forehead. He had to think of a plan—any plan. However, he was currently devoid of ideas. And concentrating with such fervor to find one only forced his head to ache. He let his gaze do a long, slow slide to the chapel doors at the rear of the aisle way. What was the cloud's next trick? Would it be a fiendish revenge for their success in outwitting it so far?

He heard movement nearby and remembered he wasn't alone in his apprehension. Janice was exhibiting her fair share of nerves. In fact, her restless pacing back and forth in front of him was getting under his skin. With each turn of the room, her edginess raised a few more notches. Well, it was understandable. Fear of the unknown was knotting his own stomach. Should he reassure Janice? No, he didn't think it would calm either of their strained nerves. Anyway, he wasn't sure he wanted Janice to be calm. Fear kept the senses heightened and if Janice were scared, she wouldn't relax her mind. For the last few minutes, he couldn't chase away the unsettling thought that if either of them dropped the barriers of their minds to a relaxed state, their attacker would seize the opportunity to overwhelm them.

Adrian watched a flash of blue streak by his line of vision again. Sweet Jesus, the silence around them was enough to give anyone the screaming meemies. A blue pant leg flashed by again, striding away and then back again. Adrian stretched one leg out, barring Janice's path.

"Stop. You're making me dizzy."

She stood there, facing him, but managing not to look directly at him.

"Sorry. I keep thinking that if I don't keep moving, my mind will be snatched away."

They were on same wavelength, Adrian thought. Both sensed the same danger. Both knew the consequences. Adrian cocked his arm and patted the cold marble slab beside him.

"Come sit down. Let me entertain you." She hesitated, a momentary look of unease crossing her face. Adrian grinned, patting the slab beside him again. "C'mon. I don't mean what you think. I'm not going to touch you. I thought we might wile away the time with a little magic." Sighing, she plopped down beside him, wrapping her arms around her knees and casting him an attentive glance. Adrian reached out his hand. "Your compass, please." She forked it over quickly. As his fingers collided with the plastic, a mewling wail screeched beyond the chapel doorway, rattling the nails on its hinges, and sending both of their glances to the back of the chapel in alarm. Behind their heads, the stained glass windows began to vibrate under the bellowing wail.

"Sweet Jesus!" Janice muttered, grasping Adrian's arm and huddling closer to him.

Adrian's head whipped around, stunned to hear his favorite vulgarity leave her lips. She had been around him too long—not only was she thinking like him, she was starting to swear like him. He switched the compass to his left hand and the mewl hissed away, cascading over their heads like the hum of live power wires. Adrian squashed an urge to duck under the invisible heat. It wouldn't do to let the spirit sense their agitation. He listened to the silence that fell instead. When no other sound taunted them, he wrapped his fingers around the compass and turned to Janice, clearing his throat.

"As I was saying before I was so rudely interrupted." He raised his hand, flashing the compass at Janice, who nodded. Sure of her attention, he rhythmically moved his fingers, making the compass vanish from his right hand to his left and back again. He heard her swift intake of breath and explained, "The one thing that makes an act better than average is showmanship. Showmanship makes the ordinary extraordinary. This is called the French Drop."

Adrian began a series of now-you-see-it, now-you-don't swaps. As his fingers flexed through the motions, he felt an unexpected surge of enjoyment. It was good to see a face register obvious pleasure in his illusion. It made him feel young again, when as a boy, the joy of magic had been the center of his universe. He had done magic for the love of it then. It helped take away the edge of his loneliness. With one last flow of his fingers, he raised both hands to Janice, displaying empty palms. She inhaled sharply.

"How did you do that?"

Adrian lowered his hands.

"Tricks of the trade."

"No, really, Adrian, where is the compass?"

Adrian's lips tilted in a boyish smile, liking the way her eyes sparkled at him with a combination of disbelief and eagerness. He leaned forward, his right hand searching her left ear. Pulling back his hand, he revealed the compass once more to her. She tore it from his grasp. Wonder filled her voice as she turned it over in her palm.

"How did you do that? I was watching carefully."

Adrian's mouth snaked to a wry grin.

"Obviously not close enough."

She seemed to accept that answer, though she didn't look up at him again. Instead, she continued staring at the compass and twirling it. Adrian wondered what she found so intriguing to think about.

"What happened to you, Adrian? What happened to you to make you so jaded and cynical about life?"

She asked the question with such sincerity and caring that Adrian responded unexpectedly with the truth.

"Death. That's what happened to me."

Her head shot up then, her glance searching his.

"You lost someone you loved very much?"

Adrian tore his gaze from her searing one, to a point beyond her right shoulder.

"Not just someone. Everyone. My life is one long trail of people dying and me moving on. I never knew my parents. They were killed in a sailing accident. I was washed up with the boat wreckage and eventually found by a retired sea captain. Life was good back then. He loved me a lot. No one's ever loved me that way since, not even my ex-wife." His gaze sought Janice's face and he noticed her expression was pained, as though she had been wounded. His laugh sounded broken even to his ears.

"He recognized my gift of second sight long before I did and encouraged it. He saw how good I was with my hands. Taught me what little magic he knew. The rest came from books. He said it would help to ease the loneliness of living with a crusty old bachelor." Adrian smiled, suddenly amused. "He was right, the old salt. Magic became the center of my universe."

"You saw his death coming, didn't you?"

Adrian dropped his gaze, scanning the slim fingers caressing the compass.

"Yes. I suppose being the foolish boy I was back then, I thought my gift could overpower death. It was a devastating moment for me when I realized I couldn't save him."

Reaching over, Adrian plucked the compass from Janice's fingers and began to flip it in and out of his palm. She watched the nervous gesture a moment before commenting softly.

"I once saw a film where a character said how we face death is as important as how we face life. That thought stuck with me for a long time. In a small way, it wormed its way into my paintings, which in turn have given meaning to a lot of people who can't cope with their lives as they are."

Adrian spun the compass between his fingers. He ventured a subtle question.

"What would you tell a patient haunted by visions of a red-headed woman?"

Her reply was husky.

"Was it as bad as all that, Adrian?"

Adrian lifted his gaze from the compass.

"No, actually your image was comforting. I could always rely on it, no matter how many foster homes I was moved to. It would go away for months, but, like the proverbial bad penny, it always came back."

Slim fingers plucked the compass from his grasp and Adrian twisted his head to find Janice staring at him pensively.

"I don't suppose this will mean much to you coming from me, Adrian, but my sister Bibi saw your act in Vegas last year. She talked about it for months afterwards. Tonight at the rehearsal, I saw what impressed her so. Watching your illusions, I never felt so connected to the beauty of sight, sound and movement. And the others in the room felt it, too." She pinned him with a long, silent scrutiny and though he wanted to look away, Adrian found he couldn't. She was mesmerizing him with her sexy, husky contralto. "You've been blessed, Adrian, though you can't see it. And you're luckier than most. Some people never find anyone to love or anyone to love them. You've been loved by a sea captain, a wife, and an adoring public." Adrian felt her open his palm and drop the compass into its center. He looked down at the fingers curling his own over the plastic and took comfort from the warmth. "You're a nice man, Adrian Magus," she murmured, "and all your barbed insults can't ever make me dislike you again."

She removed her fingers, leaving him to stare at the compass in his palm. He felt a strange wetness forming behind his eyes and willed it away.

"You're one hell of a counselor, Doctor." He closed his fist and cleared his throat. "You'd make one hell of a lap dog."

She gave a bright laugh and Adrian swung about, depositing the compass on the floor in front of them.

"Now," he grinned boyishly, "here comes my best trick yet."

Janice bent down, wrapping her arms around her knees, her attention glued to the compass.

Adrian raised his hands confidently, feeding off her excitement. Abruptly, the compass vanished, replaced by a small book. Adrian's fingers froze in place.

"What the hell? . . . "

"That's amazing, Adrian!" Janice exclaimed with a clap of her hands.

He cut her off with a growl.

"I didn't do that. I can't manipulate matter."

She panicked at once, inching closer to him with a gasp and quickly scanning the air around them.

"Who did it then?"

The question needed no answer. They both knew who had done it. Adrian reached out and picked up the book. Absently, he flipped through the pages.

"What is it?" Janice asked, peering over his arm curiously.

"Lisette's diary."

She snatched the book from his fingers and Adrian suppressed a desire to snatch it back. What was this new trick sent their way? Janice began flipping pages, scanning the passages.

"The answer is here, Adrian," she declared. "Why else would Lisette transfer the book to us here?"

"We don't know it was Lisette."

"I know," Janice stated. "Like Muriel said before, when we are slow to act, the ghosts push us along."

Adrian wrenched the book from Janice's fingers.

"I tell you there's nothing here." He flipped through the pages with annoyance. "It's a typical diary, filled with romantic, fairytale notions about Prince Charming." Adrian sent Janice a side-ways squint. "In this case, call Prince Charming the Baron Dumas."

She yanked the book from his fingers once more.

"We just haven't seen the clue, that's all."

Adrian swiped the book back.

"I tell you there's nothing here. Just a lot of female gibberish about living happily ever after. Lisette was a typical ditz." His gaze scanned the last pages of the journal, studying the sporadic passages of writing. "At least we can be grateful that once the ship docked Lisette didn't have time to write more of that romantic hogwash."

"What did you say?!"

Once again, the diary was ripped from his fingers and Adrian fought down an urge to box Janice's ears. She was being a royal pain in the ass with her insistent grappling of the journal. He watched as she eagerly bent over the dog-eared pages. What the hell was she looking for?

"Of course!" she exclaimed, a moment later. She smacked the pages and flashed the book at Adrian. "Right there all the time—beneath our noses."

Irked, Adrian peered over at the scrawled, faded handwriting. "What's there?"

With a hiss, Janice bolted to her feet and spun around.

"It's so clear, I don't know why I didn't think of it before. Lisette never left the ship. Those last entries aren't hers!"

"Don't be absurd!"

She bounced back down, slapping the pages of the book in emphasis.

"I'm right, Adrian. I feel it to the depths of my being. Lisette was murdered on the ship." Her hand swept the air. "The crawlspace isn't in this house. It's on the ship. Lisette never made it off the ship."

Adrian frowned, digesting her words. Could she be right? He inspected the scrawled writing closer. It was similar but he couldn't swear it was the same. And she had a point. The whole tone of the diary did seem to change at the end.

"I'm right, Adrian, you know I'm right," she insisted. "You hit it on the head before.

"Lisette was filled with romantic notions, the diary's full of it—except at the end. Trust me, Adrian, an eighteen-year-old girl is not going to stop fantasizing in her diary just because a ship has docked. If anything, with a wedding day approaching, she is going to be even more of an airhead . . . what's that smell?"

Janice's fingers brushed her nose. Simultaneously, Adrian's own nostrils filled with a sickly stench that cut off his breath and sent a series of sharp pains rippling across his forehead. The pain was so acute and unexpected he almost slipped from the steps. Holy Vegas, someone was trying to invade his mind. He dug his heels into the floor, throwing up a mental barricade. Beside him, he heard a stuttered cough and caught sight of Janice now holding her sweater to her nose in an attempt to keep from breathing the noxious odor.

Adrian knew it was useless. The spirit had finally found a weapon to use against them. Damn, there was that probing pain again in his head. Someone was seeking entrance, hammering at him with a muted strumming.

"I'm going to pass out, Adrian," Janice mumbled through the folds of material.

"Oh, no you don't." Adrian cautioned, leaping to his feet. Snatching her wrist, he dragged her up from the steps and toward the sacristy door. As they fled, the stained glass windows over the mounted crucifix began to rattle in their frames and behind them, a strangled groan wheezed.

Passing under the crucifix, Adrian felt a second sharp sizzle across his forehead. The probing was more insistent now, getting harder to keep out. He clutched Janice's wrist tighter and rushed them both through the sacristy door in two seconds, into the small room and out into a deserted atrium beyond.

The fresh air hit Adrian at once and he began to gulp in streams of it. Janice did the same, collapsing against the wall and bracing herself against it.

"I can't make it, Adrian," she murmured between a stuttered gulp. "I think I'm going down first."

Adrian opened his mouth to deny her words but the probing pain sliced off his breath. Clutching his head, he doubled-over.

"Adrian!" He heard Janice's call but it became distorted in his head. He willed the probing to stop, pleaded with it. It didn't. He felt fingers digging into his arm. "For God's sake, Adrian. Tell me what's happening to you. Let me help you."

"You can't," he groaned, "it's a mind meld." Another wave of pain shot across his temple and Adrian slumped, shoving Janice away from him. "Get away. Stand back."

She took a hasty step back but went no further.

"I'm not leaving you, Adrian. You can't make me."

Her words caused another stabbing pain to rip along his scalp. It was coming for him. Sweet Jesus, why him first? His question was lost in the hiss of static that bounced off the atrium walls and slammed him back hard against the cement piling and away from where Janice stood. The sharp wrench gutted his shoulder blades and collarbone and seared his lungs. Shit, but the spirit was as strong as Hercules. He struggled to gain his footing, ignoring the rousing pain emanating in his right shoulder.

In the next instance, a sparkle of multicolored lights appeared out of thin air before him. Stupidly, he reached out to ward it off and felt an immediate connection. The pain in his head subsided completely as the lights swallowed his fist. Fascinated, Adrian stared at the lights tripping up his arms to his shoulders, across his neck and rippling down his left side to his pants and on to the tips of his toes. He was going down, he could feel it. He was going to leave Janice at the mercy of the baron.

Swinging his head, he sought Janice through the scrim of light. His eyes lit on her frozen figure. She stood in stark terror, staring at the sprinkle of lights encasing him. Immediately he knew she thought he was being possessed by Lisette's murderer. If only he could find his voice, tell her not to worry. If only he could tell her he was in no pain. If only he could beg her forgiveness for what the baron was about to make him do.

A caressing urge bade him close his eyes and he did so, finally giving into the pull of the feathery caress on his brow. Ahead was darkness, a resting place. He felt his knees buckle and knew he was falling. He hit something hard, but couldn't name what it was. He was only aware of a deep voice calling softly in his head.

"I will do you no harm." The words were oddly comforting and Adrian felt his pulse rate begin to descend downward into a slow crawl. Willingly, he surrendered his mind to the lullaby in his head. "Dormez. Sleep. I will do you no harm."

Chapter 23

SATURDAY—5:15 AM

Janice felt as if whole sections of her body were torn away. A harrowing headache pounded her forehead and the heaviness in her energy felt like a millstone. Emotionally, she was spent, spiraling downward into a deep chasm. This couldn't be happening, she reasoned. Someone was trying to invade her mind. It was if she stood in the middle of a burning lake of herself, unable to escape. What did the invader want? She tried to think it out, but only found her thoughts murky and muddled. Save. Save someone. But who? Adrian! The word was a whisper of terror running through her mind.

Her gaze fluttered left, to the floor, to the body encased in swirling lights. Beneath the core of sparkles, Adrian's body was motionless and Janice's heart plummeted. Adrian was past helping. If the evil cloud hadn't spun his mind around and killed him, the resounding crack of his head against the atrium floor surely must have.

Janice felt her eyes watering and then a glaze seemed to come down around her brimming eyes. Now someone was probing her very soul, the invasion arousing fear and uncertainty. She felt a sudden nervousness slip back to grip her. Something disturbing was about to happen, but what?

A sharp pain ripped across her forehead and her knees buckled under the assault. Unable to catch herself, she hit the floor with a wrenching crack to her knees and right wrist. A sizzling fire shot up her right forearm. Broken! The word echoed and re-echoed in her mind, but for some reason Janice couldn't place it, connect it to any other word she knew. What was broken? She should know. Why didn't she know? Why wouldn't the probing go away? She'd will it away.

Throwing her head back, Janice tossed her hair across her shoulder in a gesture of defiance. The action brought doubled pain and instant understanding. Her left hand flew to her right, cradling it gently. She had broken her wrist. Sucking in her lower lip, she braced herself against the throbbing pain. *Get out! Get help!* The words reverberated over and over, taunting her mind. *Get out! Get help!*

Janice twisted her head, searching for the nearest exit. Get help? But from where? And from whom? She couldn't see a door and didn't know where to look. Distressed, she choked back a frustrated cry and tried to concentrate. There had to be a doorway out of this nightmare. Oh, why couldn't she think straight? Or see the room clearly? Why were the walls shimmering as if they were alive?

Suddenly, it struck her. They were alive. She wasn't hallucinating. The atrium walls were beginning to crinkle and fold in on themselves. What a wonderful illusion. She knew a man once who did illusions, didn't she? Who was he? Oh, why couldn't she remember his name!

Mesmerized, she continued to contemplate the receding walls. They were dimming, growing smaller, leaving behind a current of air that tickled her nose and fanned the ends of her hair. She was moving, but not moving. How wonderful. The atrium walls receded to a tiny pinpoint, finally replaced by an orange glow, then a purple, then a green and then back to the band of bright orange again.

Watching the colorful pinwheel, Janice suddenly felt a burning sensation in her chest, as if her lungs were being snatched from their cavity. She attempted to raise a hand to the area in self-defense but found her brain and arms malfunctioning. She was slipping away—stalked by a sparkle of lights that had appeared inches away from her knees. Dizzy. The colored lights were spinning toward her, making her dizzy. Time slip! She was time slipping. But to where?

The air around her colored to a cobalt blue and Janice felt her mind reel in confusion as jumbled phrases and thoughts tumbled through her head. She was going back in time. Sarah! She was going to see Sarah. Happiness. Joy. No, Anna. She was going to see Anna. Sadness. Despair. No, Aubert. She was going to see Aubert. Elation. Relief.

Janice tried to stop swimming through the haze of feelings and desires, tormented by the conflicting emotions pummeling her senses. Why was her own loneliness clawing at the back of her throat to get out? Silence. She waited. No sound emerged, just a well of tears that spilled over, moistening her eyelashes and staining her cheeks.

And then the pinwheel started again. One hundred years. Two hundred years. She was dying. Janice felt a wretchedness of mind she'd never known before. She was going to die. Like Lisette before her. Like Anna. Like Mama. Death was stalking her, like a black plague devoid of hope. The thought so depressed her, she flung out her hands pleading for mercy. This time her arms responded, galvanized by a suddenly functioning brain.

"Don't do this to me!"

At her plea, the color wheel ceased and the air around her stabilized. Pungent sea air invaded Janice's nose and she felt her mind connect to another's. Her pain subsided at once and its disappearance scared her almost as much as the darkness she was now kneeling in. No, correction, not total darkness.

Janice lifted her head, Lisette's head, and peeped through the square holes of an iron grate to a blazing blue cobalt sky. In the distance, white cloth flapped in the breeze, blocking out the sunlight. Janice heard a ship's bell toll off to her left. Now, Janice felt—Lisette felt—the rocking motion of the ship. She had been time slipped three hundred years by Lisette. She could feel her presence. Feel her emotions of fright.

Janice focused her mind closer to Lisette's and was startled at how easily the merge was accomplished. In a flickering, their minds collided and held. Janice saw what she saw, knew what she knew, felt the strange wetness around her knees.

Janice glanced down. Tidewater was seeping into the crawlspace.

She was below deck, a long expanse of bulkhead only inches from the top of her head. The space was small and cramped, barely room for one. Yet there were two heartbeats pounding in her ear. Hers and Lisette's? No. Janice's pulse skittered in alarm. Off to her left side, she could hear a muffled boyish moan. Chase? Janice refused to look over, confirm her fears. Instead, she reached up Lisette's hand and felt the brittle crack of weathered wood. And then she heard the soft, snapping sounds of the white sails in the breeze and looked out the grated iron holes again.

Two human shapes stood peering down the holes at her, at Lisette. The woman was vividly beautiful, dark and voluptuous, dressed in a rich, scanty evening dress. A wealth of jet black hair flowed up and back from a center part. In the glare of the dazzling sunlight, the woman broadcasted a regal certainty and flair.

The man beside her was magnificent, on the tall side of six feet. Janice could see the glimmer of gold buttons along the front of his uniform. Lieutenant Arthur, the first mate. His adjutant posture and bushy mustache bespoke a rakish nature. For the moment, he was relaxed, fingering a loose tendril of hair on the woman's cheek. What was her name again?

To Janice's astonishment, to Lisette's astonishment, the man wrapped his fingers around the dark fabric of the woman's sleeve and then slipped his fingers beneath the shoulder strap. The material slipped away at once, exposing one full, rounded breast. Gently, the man's palm caressed and circled the dusky nipple, teasing it to a pebble hardness. The woman remained impassive, ignoring the lightly stroking fingers. She looked past the man's head to meet Janice's stare head-on. Janice recognized the dangerous, crazed glitter as the woman murmured harshly.

"You'll never be a baroness, Izzy. I'll see to that. You'll never know the fire of Aubert's touch. You'll never hear the ragged whimpers of sheer need escape his lips." A soft gasp of her own departed the woman's lips as a tousled head buried itself against her breast.

Janice looked away instantly, wishing she could flee. She shouldn't be watching, didn't want to watch. Lisette called her mind back and Janice found herself staring out the grated holes once more into sneering eyes.

"Aubert should've been mine, Izzy. You know that. My blood is bluer than yours. You'll never feel the sensual heat of his naked skin. Never feel the eager tremors of ecstasy with him." Abruptly, she gripped the tousled head at her breast and ran her fingers through dark locks. Janice felt herself reaching up.

"Save the boy, Simone. If you must kill me, *me tuer*. But save the boy."

Janice's hand snaked to her left and collided with cold flesh. A muttered groan responded to the touch. Adrian? Janice ripped her mind away. No, not Adrian, Chase. The baron's younger brother, Chase. Janice peered up again through Lisette's eyes, out at Simone Villashay, her once best friend.

"Aubert will never marry you, Simone." Janice heard herself murmuring. "He gave his pledge to the king. Only the king can sever the betrothal."

Simone stiffened at the words and tossed the man suckling her breast away. She bent down giving a snarl, forgetting her half-dressed state. Janice drew back, frightened by the vehement glitter in her eyes. The iron grate above her rattled on it hinges as Simone shook it fiercely.

"I was going to kill you fast, Izzy. But now I think I'll do it trés lentement. Very, *very* slowly."

Janice heard the murderous edge to Simone's voice as she stood up and signaled to her companion. A knot of sheer terror ripped through Janice. Lisette knew what was coming, while, she Janice, was living through it for the first time. She looked beyond the holes to the bright sky. *Mother of Mercy, if there is a God, please help me. I don't want to die.* Janice's eyes found Simone again. She was hauling her evening dress up, hiding her nakedness. Once more, Janice saw her signal to the man beside her.

"Seal the grate. Slide the trapdoor."

Janice's body went rigid and for a moment she thought she had stopped breathing. Above her head, the trapdoor clanged shut and a cold darkness enveloped the space. The air stilled and a wave of grayness washed over Janice, over Lisette. Death was coming. Janice threw back her head, her own scream echoing Lisette's guttural cry of terror.

As if cued, Janice felt the roaring of blood in her ears and thousands of electric jolts jagged through her. She was slipping again. One day, two days. Janice felt herself coughing. Her thoughts tumbled over themselves, jumbled, nonsensical. Hungry, so hungry. Three days. Four days. Somebody please find me! Five days. Empty limbs, cold numbness, smell of low tide and crawling things. Oh, God, please stop the smell of crawling things!

Janice's prayer mingled with Lisette's. *Please release my mind. I can't die like this. Please don't let me die like this.* Dying was glorious peace. Anna said so. No pain, no fear. Give up. No use. Janice felt her mind connect again to Lisette's despair. No use. Janice's eyes flickered upward. Trapdoor sealed.

Her eyes fluttered down again. Her mind began to float and drift aimlessly. Is this all there is to dying? Janice wondered. It is a great ache, an ache that crosses great distances but finds no relief. Is there no merciful God to take pity?

A loud click sounded and the trapdoor over Janice's head lifted. Janice's eyes shot open. The iron bars were gone, a dazzling white light spiraling outward in its place. Janice dragged a weary hand to shade her eyes from the overpowering glare.

"Give me your hand, Izzy. I am here." The voice was deep, caring. It called softly again. "Je suis ici."

Janice dropped her hands and stared into the white light. She saw it more clearly without a glare. It had a vague, male human shape, a vague human hand reaching out. Janice reached out for the hand and felt her mind pulled back at once. In her head, a voice urged pleasantly.

"Non, Janice Kelly. You cannot travel this path with me. You must stay behind. And sleep. Fear not, your sleep will be an instant, no more."

Janice felt her whole body engulfed in tides of weariness and tried to arouse herself from the numbness weighing her down. She wanted to touch Lisette, ask her questions, see Aubert. Janice's eyes fluttered down, then up. A second white light floated beyond the crawlspace, a vague feminine shape alongside its companion.

"Merci. I thank you, Janice, for thy compassion."

Janice felt a curious wetness stinging her eyes at the pronouncement. Lisette was going away, leaving her without a glimpse of her face for the first and only time.

"Our souls will meet once more beyond." The shape shimmered as if gesturing. "I shall call you friend and you will know me. Now, sleep and fret not, your body will come to no harm. I will use it a brief instant and be gone."

"And Adrian?" Janice felt as hollow as her voice sounded.

"Like you, he is safe. Now, sleep."

Janice felt her eyelids flutter downward as if touched by feathery wings. Unable to argue, she let her mind go. Sleep came in a waft of sweet raspberry perfume.

Chapter 24

TIME SLIP

"Why are you crying, mon amie? Are you in pain?"

"Non. I cry in joy for I thought never to see you through human eyes again."

"Nor I you. For three centuries, I hungered to feel the breathless wonder of your kiss. Two lifetimes on the earth plane I sought you out. I called for you, but you did not respond."

"I heard you, but could not respond. The darkness held me imprisoned, but now there is only light. There is passion in your kiss, mon ami, and our tongues dance together in silent melody."

"The man's face pleases you?"

"Certainment. On the earth plane, he is trés handsome. Is the woman's face pleasing to you?"

"Oui. She bears a striking resemblance to you, when you were human."

"She gives herself to the man with sweet abandon."

"Oui. The man's body does fit her well. Even now, fire bolts of desire arc through him."

"Yet he fought against you taking him."

"His will is strong. He worries the woman will not catch fire from his flame."

"Yet she welcomes him into her body gladly."

"The man loves the woman. If he did not, nothing would have compelled me to answer your summons. But fret not, he will remember nothing."

"You will cloud his dreams?"

"He will have no pain except for that which his own mind makes."

"Trés bien. And now, we must away. The woman's body is stressed.

She cannot longer endure the two of us as one. I must away."

"I do miss you already, Izzy."

"Your pain will be only for a moment, mon cher. Fear not, you will see me again on some distant plateau."

"Oui. And I will take your hand again. Your heart will be my heart."

"It has always been so. So it shall be again."

"May the Supreme Light guide you to a safe haven, Izzy. Though you do not see me, I will always be beside you. Now, come kiss me. One final kiss to last perhaps an eternity."

"I love you, Aubert. Skin to skin, we are one."

Chapter 25

SATURDAY—5:30 AM

Janice heard a drumbeat throbbing loudly in her ears. Why didn't Bibi turn down the stereo? She couldn't sleep with that steady racket going on. No one could. The sound grew louder and Janice gave an exasperated sigh. She'd have to turn down the volume herself or she'd be deaf before morning. She forced her eyelids up, then sighed as they closed again. Good heavens, she felt drained and hollow and lifeless. And her back ached between her shoulder blades. She had to throw off this lethargy. Her eyelids flickered again and this time stayed up. The drumbeat was still hammering unbelievably loud. What the hell was that noise?

Suddenly, it hit her. She was hearing a heartbeat. Was she lying on someone's chest? She blinked her eyes rapidly and felt a light tickle of hair along her eyelashes. Tiny tufts of black hair swam into her vision. Adrian! She was lying on Adrian's naked chest! She craned her head and studied the stubbled chin inches from her face. He was sleeping, dead to the world—more handsome in sleep than when awake. She gave his face and forehead a once over, spotting a knotted lump along his right temple. She winced uncomfortably. If Adrian thought he had a headache before, wait till he woke with this one. Absently, she made a move to brush the swollen area and cried out as a white-hot pain seared up her forearm.

Rolling over on her back with a jerk, Janice clutched her right wrist, giving another yelp as the pain doubled its intensity. She tore her fingers away and brought her arm up in front of her face, choking back a gasp when she spied the mottled flesh. Good heavens, her wrist was three times its normal size. Broken! How had that happened? Understanding dawned at once and she swung her gaze to Adrian's forehead. She broke her wrist in the fall the way Adrian's knotted lump had appeared from the crack of his head against the atrium floor. But they weren't in the atrium garden any longer.

Janice looked up, trying to get her bearings. They were in a bed with white sails. White sails! The words sent an unexpected, icy chill slicing down her spine. Now, why should thinking of sails bother her? Lifting her head, she studied her surroundings more closely. Draperies, a table edged in a red glow, a small musical birdcage. Her brain skidded to a halt. How in the hell had they gotten from the atrium garden into the solarium and onto the bed that was part of Adrian's set pieces?

Janice thrust the question away. She didn't want to know. The thought was too disturbing since all she could envision at the moment was herself and Adrian transformed into some flesh-eating zombies roaming the chateau with no will of their own. She brought her glance back to her throbbing wrist and cupped it gently. Her wrist needed attention. But how to get it? she wondered.

Her gaze sailed away to the solarium windows still drenched in red. Nope, scrap that option. A doctor's help was out. They were still prisoners. She'd have to make do, tolerate the pain. That is if she could stop shivering long enough to think coherently. Why was she so blasted cold? She glanced down at her chest and gasped. She was stark naked, her breasts and stomach caked in goose bumps. Where in the hell were her clothes? Had Adrian taken them?

Her head whipped around, catching sight of lean muscled buttocks and thighs and she choked back a groan. They had made love, she was sure of it. Why else would their clothes be missing and her skin still tingling as if thoroughly caressed?

Shaken, Janice slid to the edge of the bed, peered over it and spotted a speck of blue peeping from the hem of the silken sheets. With a hasty swipe, she gathered it up with her good hand then searched the floor for her missing bra.

"Great." she muttered, a second later. Her bra was nowhere in sight. Swinging upright, Janice tossed the sweater over her head. She needed to get warm fast. Her teeth were beginning to chatter from the chill hanging in the room. Carefully, she babied her sore wrist through one sleeve. This was unbelievable. She had just made love to a man and couldn't remember one second of doing it. Her good hand slipped through the remaining sleeve easily and she pulled the fluffy material down and around her torso. How had she sunk so low? How could she have let Adrian make love to her when she knew he was adamantly against it? How could she have let him touch her in the most intimate of ways?

A sputtered moan broke her reverie and Janice felt the bed jiggle beneath her buttocks. Swiftly, she sprang from the bed and swung about. Adrian was stirring, finally coming out of his imposed exile. The thought of him waking and spotting her hovering over his nude body sent a wave of panic through her. He would say something spiteful, she knew. He might even make a cruel joke about what had happened between them. She couldn't bear that. Not when she didn't know what kind of lover he had been or how responsive she had been to him. She had to get out of the solarium before he wakened fully. Where in the hell were her slacks and underpants? God, why wouldn't her wrist stop aching?

Diving around the edge of the bed, Janice searched the floor, relieved when she spotted another flash of blue. From the top of the bed, a second muttered groan shattered the air. Diving for her slacks, she scooped them up and returned to the empty side of the bed. She had to find her underpants. Her gaze raked the sheets, finally spotting a flash of white lace peeping from beneath Adrian's stomach. Could she extricate her panties without his feeling it? No, not without the use of both her hands. She'd have to abandon the panties.

Grimacing, she looked out over the set pieces, her glance falling on the tiny, musical birdcage. It had once made beautiful music, but now sat idle and silent. Suddenly, she felt like the small stuffed creature perched inside. Janice cradled her wrist gently and dropped back on the bed. How long had they been unconscious? Her jumbled thoughts currently held no memory of time. She did have a vague recollection of a handsome face looking down at her, but whether the image belonged to the Baron or Adrian, she couldn't be sure. Perhaps, when her brain found its natural rhythm again, it would supply the answer to that question. *If* her arm stopped aching long enough, that is.

*

The portrait continued its metamorphosis. With each passing second, new images stained the canvas. Watching the transformation, Jasper realized he'd never again doubt the existence of mind over matter—the ability to control substance and its density. It was truly remarkable to stand and watch the marriage of time and space, see how easily the symbiosis could occur. Something out of nothingness. If ever he had doubted the power of the human soul to survive beyond the grave, here was the proof there was life beyond. No living, human entity was projecting the images seeping onto the canvas. The only question left was who was directing the matter? Lisette or the baron?

Jasper was sure the wailing spirit next to him knew. Otherwise, her keening wail would've subsided. It hadn't. As each feature became sharper, more recognizable, the spirit's wail became more tormented. He switched his thoughts abruptly. Why did he keep referring to her as "the spirit" when he now knew her human name? Simone Villashay. The name had sliced across his mind the moment the first spots of color saturated the painting in front of them, miraculously restoring his precognition powers in the process. He was himself again and it felt good.

Concentrating on the portrait, Jasper understood the spirit's devastation. The striking red-headed woman etched in oil only a few moments ago had vanished completely. In her place stood, not one figure, but two. Jasper had no doubt he was seeing the images of the baron and Lisette as they had once appeared in earthly, human form. The woman coming into view had vivid red hair, too, the only similarity to the image that had vanished. However, the face depicted now was heart-shaped and daintily pointed instead of curved and regal. The body type showcased slender limbs, petite and flower-like, rather than a statuesque figure. Studying the dainty features, Jasper agreed with the baron's choice. He, too, would have preferred Lisette's delicate looks to Simone's sultry, wild demeanor.

The fusion of color began to subside as quickly as it had come. In seconds, the portrait finished its metamorphosis. With its ending, Jasper's ears popped under the forceful impact of the spirit's sudden wrath. The keening wail lost its shrillness, rumbling into a deep gargle as it shifted rapidly from torment to anger. Deep and ferocious anger.

Immediately, Jasper took a hasty step away from the portrait to avoid what was coming. Over his head, the air stirred and beneath his feet the wooden flooring began to vibrate. He slanted a quick peek at the circle of lights. Once more, the cloud resembled a whirling cyclone, showering the room with crackling static. Muriel's body was lost to his view through the scrim of lights, and Jasper felt his heart plummet. Every minute Muriel was forced to endure the spirit's presence, her life force moved further away from his.

The vibration beneath Jasper's feet intensified and a lone portrait toppled from the wall. He felt an urgent tug on his forearm and balked, not wanting to leave Muriel so defenseless. In his ear, he heard an urgent growl, a fiercer tug on his arm.

"Come away, man. You can't help her. Not at the moment."

Jasper's heart took another nosedive, realizing the truth of Lloyd's words. To make any hostile gesture toward the cyclone at the moment would surely get Muriel killed. A figurine exploded on the north wall of the room and sprayed the floorboards. A second figurine shattered in its wake. And then a third.

The circle of lights moved then, startling both men with its agility. Jasper backed up, his senses shifting into high gear. As before, he felt his mind collide with the spirit's. Only this time, she forced the contact. Once more, Jasper felt a searing fire bolt rip along his forehead. He severed the mind link and took a second step back. As he did so, the chandelier above his head began to shimmy, clank, and jerk. He shied away, his senses now fully alert. She was coming for him, her rage escalating from simmer to a full-blown boil. But why was she striking out at him? It made no sense. He posed no threat to her, not as long as she held Muriel prisoner.

As she swirled across the floorboards, each small object within her wake came alive, magnetized by her growing energy level. The air filled with flying debris, piano keys, vases, and urns. Like missiles on a specified trajectory path, the objects hurled at Jasper. He ducked, shielding his head, had to duck again and again as the sheared fragments found new life within the whirling cyclone and struck out at him.

A hurled candlestick struck Lloyd full force and the other man stumbled back under the impact. A howling wind from deep within the cloud's central core began and Jasper covered his ears in self-defense. The howling inched to a powerful screech.

Reaching the center of the gallery room, the spirit stopped its advancement as if now that she had gotten their attention she intended to speak. Still, Jasper didn't lower his defenses or move a muscle. They weren't out of danger. The spirit's agitated state was merely a prelude of what was about to happen, and Jasper knew with certainty the spirit had every intention of venting her rage wherever she could. She would use every portion of the room, every nook and cranny as a weapon against them. At last, through the howling wind, she spoke and Jasper's nose twitched under the familiar odious stench.

"Do you seek to confuse me?" Her voice was no longer one but many—male, female, hideous in pitch. "I know the woman will not succumb to the man. I see your treachery. I have seen the magician transform matter. He creates what is not there. His illusion is strong but he shall pay for his treachery. And you shall see the woman I hold die before your eyes."

Jasper knew the last words were meant for him—to tear his heart still beating from his chest. For a moment, he thought about surrendering, giving into the spirit's domination and then in the next second, bright images of Muriel's face flashed across his mind's eye. One stark, clear word followed. *Survive.* Intense astonishment touched Jasper's face. Deep within the circle of lights, some part of Muriel was still alive. Some part begging him to stand firm, no matter the pain.

Rejuvenated, Jasper faced the circle of lights squarely. She sensed his defiance at once and as if to prove her superiority and intent, she let a sprinkle of lights ripple. From the base of the cloud, a small stream of fire shot across the floor toward the base of the east wall. Striking the baseboard, the wall casing exploded outward, showering the main floorboards with white plaster. Jasper ducked but not before spying the gaping hole left in the center of the wall.

A blood-curdling scream pierced the roaring din and Jasper swung around. Around him, one by one, the family of portraits began to topple from the wall with a thunderous clang.

Chapter 26

SATURDAY—5:50 AM

Adrian rolled over with a snarl.

"Who took the sledgehammer to my head? Was it you?"

The confirmation reply was swift and Adrian heard the strained curtness.

"No. You hit your head when you blacked out."

Adrian attempted to sit up and the movement made his stomach roll and pitch. He fell back in self-defense. Sweet Jesus, what had happened to him?

"I'm going to throw up," he stated loudly. He forced his eyes open and then swiftly threw his arms up to cover them from the blinding glare of light. Holy Vegas, he felt like a hibernating bear, finally awake from months asleep in a darkened cave. He dropped his hands, his eyes finally adjusting to the light, which he realized wasn't all that bright. It was just that his mind was choosing to creep back to reality at a snail's pace while his body was screaming to get on with it.

Raising his head quickly, he was sorry a second later that he had. Throbbing pain ignited along his temple and he reached up and brushed his forehead gently with his fingertips. His fingers collided with a knotted lump. Well, Janice was right. He had smacked his head against the atrium floor while trying to ward off the sprinkle of lights. Had he given himself a mild concussion? He lifted his head again, and this time, the ache was not so acute. Better. No concussion. His vision was clearing.

His gaze strayed to Janice's frozen form at the lower edge of the bed and sailed away again. Where in the hell were they? His gaze landed on a familiar set piece. He was in the solarium. In bed with

Janice. He rolled to his side and studied the rumpled sheets. They had made love. And not so very long ago. Her fruity perfume still lingered on the pillow and his naked body. He'd recognize her smell anywhere.

Adrian let his gaze rake Janice's profile and noticed the tight lines of her posture. She was tense, biting her lower lip. And she was clinging to her slacks as if they were a lifeline. Was she scared of him touching her again? Why? Had he hurt her? The thought made him sit up rapidly and had Janice tossing her slacks across her naked thighs and scooting down the sheets away from him. Why was she so jumpy? She couldn't be blaming him for what occurred between them, could she? It was no one's fault. She scooted over again, to the very edge of the bed and Adrian found himself barking sharply.

"Relax. I'm only looking for my clothes."

True to his words, Adrian looked down the length of the bed in search of his trousers. Nothing. Twisting around, he began to search the bed, his hand arcing across the silken sheets. A second later, his fingers collided with bits of white lace stuffed beneath his buttocks. He pulled out the offending fabric and found himself suppressing a chuckle. Well, these weren't his. He hadn't come to wearing bra and panties yet, had he? He tossed the undergarments across the bed.

"Get dressed."

She didn't move or comply with his command and Adrian wondered for a moment if she had gone deaf. Had she been hurt in the mind swap with Lisette? A grim thought sliced through that one. Had he forced himself on her? He had to know.

Scrambling to the edge of the bed, he started up, teetered precariously and clutched the edge of the bed to keep his knees from buckling. So much for doing that. Firmly, he willed the room to stop spinning. When it did, the stage floor swam into view and he spotted his missing shirt and trousers.

Quickly, he snatched up the pants and slid them on. Behind him, Janice remained poised like a statue on the bed, ignoring his movements. She was giving him the silent treatment on purpose. And it was starting to piss him off. Did she think to make him pay for what they had done by freezing him out? Well, let her. Though how in the hell she could be blaming him for what was neither of their faults, he couldn't fathom.

"Get dressed!" He ripped the words out impatiently, defying her to cross him this time. When she didn't move a muscle, Adrian twisted across the bed, grabbing her arm. "I said get dressed!"

Her scream was ear-splitting and Adrian reeled back in astonished confusion. What the hell had he done now? His eyes followed her hands as she cupped her arm gently. Sweet Jesus, her wrist was twice its normal size. No wonder she had been sitting like a zombie. She was in excruciating pain and keeping it from him.

Adrian's throat constricted suddenly. My God, had he broken her bones? In a flash, he was around the bed and dropping to his haunches in front of her. She gave him a brief glance, sucking in her lower lip, and then rocked back and forth absently. Adrian studied her pale cheeks and the beads of perspiration coating her forehead. He didn't know how she was managing to keep her cries concealed. Her arm was a hideous purple color. The skin was already bloating, would soon resemble stretched rubber. Infection would set in next.

Unable to mask his inner torment, Adrian broke the silence between them.

"For God's sake, did I do that?"

She looked straight at him finally, gritting her teeth.

"I broke it when I blacked out, I think."

"You think?"

Adrian felt the corners of his mouth twist in disgust. She stopped rocking then and they stared at each other across a sudden ringing silence. Like him, she wasn't sure and he could see it in her eyes. Adrian's head swirled with doubts and his heart refused to believe what his mind was telling him. He *had* forced himself on her. She had fought against him making love to her and when she had, he had broken her wrist to keep her subdued. Sweet Jesus, he hadn't thought he could be such a bastard. To hurt a woman for not wanting him, refusing his advances? Had his subconscious wanted her that badly?

A muscle tic flickered along his jawbone as his gaze took in her white face and clamped lips. Should he beg her forgiveness? Explain he didn't remember hurting her? Would she believe him and accept his apology? Judging from the glassy tint to her eyes, she wouldn't. He wouldn't if he was in her place. If he were her, he would be compelled to seek revenge.

Hell, he'd apologize to her anyway. He owed her that. Reaching out, he laid a hand on her right knee.

"Janice, I'm . . . "

Her good hand came down on his rapidly.

"Don't," she begged, "don't say anything. I don't think I can bear it."

Hearing the trace of tears in her voice, Adrian snapped his mouth shut. He looked down at her swollen flesh.

"If you won't let me apologize for making love to you, at least let me apologize for having to help you get dressed."

She colored up furiously at his words and it took all Adrian's willpower not to sweep her into his arms and kiss her soundly. If she would just let him kiss her—give her one drugging kiss that would prove to her how crazy he was about her. Prove to her he loved her with a fierce, abiding devotion beyond the physical.

A piercing scream shattered the air, startling the pair.

"Did you hear that?" Janice asked, glancing up at him. An explosion of the wall next to the bed was her answer. She came up off the bed and into his arms so rapidly that they both shivered at the contact. Adrian was the first to move.

"We've got to get out of here."

He bent down and pulled Janice's leg through frilly lace. The scream doubled in pitch, redoubled again. Matching his motion,

Janice hauled the frilly lace up around her hips and into place. Just as swiftly, he had her slack legs in place and she was stepping into them. The scream switched to a heavy thrumming and to Adrian's ears, it seemed to be nearing the solarium doorway down the room from them.

Adrian gave a last upward tug and Janice's slacks fell into place. Hastily, he struggled with the zipper, barely getting it in to the top before a second explosion rocked the stage floor and blew a hole in the solarium wall that housed the fireplace. The pair staggered back, stunned by the fire bolt singeing the wall and the acrid smoke billowing through the gaping hole. Around their heads, the air stirred and both anticipated the hideous shrieks seconds before they began.

Thinking fast, Adrian captured Janice's good hand and pulled her down the proscenium steps. Hitting the main floor running, they just managed to stay ahead of the showering fire bolts popping along the baseboards at their feet. The hideous shrieks were another thing. They remained unfazed by the pair's rapid escape and took up the chase aggressively.

Rounding the doorway into the corridor, Adrian could only hope history wasn't about to repeat itself. If it did, this time he was sure he and Janice would not get through it alive. A moment later, Adrian was forced to slide to an abrupt halt with a heated curse. Janice careened into his back, almost toppling them both. Righting herself, she peered over his shoulder at the small puffs of smoke filtering through the baseboards, blocking their way.

"We haven't a chance," she stated a second later.

"We're not out yet," Adrian replied. Now, if he only believed it.

Chapter 27

SATURDAY—6:00 AM

The air shifted overhead and the shrieks became clotted jargon, inhuman screams that hung like strips of cloth above their heads. Adrian scanned the charred streak of black lining the corridor wall, wondering what they did now that they were boxed in perfectly. One forward step and the wall would blow. He felt a light tap on his shoulder.

"We've got to chance it, Adrian. The Grisombs need us."

Adrian nodded, tapping into the same sense of foreboding that she did. It was payback time and Lisette's murderer had summoned all the dominions of evil to her side. Survival was now the name of the game. Janice's fingers slipped into his palm in a gesture of encouragement and Adrian took heart from it. She didn't hate him, at least not totally. His gaze found hers.

"We go on three. Ready? One . . . two . . . three!"

Adrian took off, charging into the billowing smoke with Janice tightly in tow. To his amazement, the walls around them stayed intact, making their race through the scrim of smoke seem almost ludicrous. That is, until they reached the gallery doorway and the walls behind them blew out in a series of popping explosions.

Looking back at the showering plaster, Adrian realized nothing had been left to chance. They had been allowed to pass unharmed on purpose. And now, the gathering forces meant to box them in further. Force them into the gallery room to accept whatever fate awaited them.

Straightening his shoulders, Adrian took a deep breath. Beside him, Janice did the same. Together, they dove into the room. Adrian ducked immediately, barely dodging the flying debris soaring in the air above him. Across the way, he could hear the gutted strings of a harp as the catgut was rapaciously torn from its frame. Anger! Sheer, white, hot anger. An anger so consuming it was burning away the very room around them.

Adrian cast a glance to his left, searching for the cause of the angry tirade. His gaze settled on the swirl of dark lights. Like a tornado straight from the bowels of hell, the mass of darkness hooted and bawled. The shrieks above their head shot in to the cloud core, releasing a fetid stench that reached Adrian's nostrils and had him drawing back from the festering mass. His eyes scanned the space around the cloud.

He spotted Lloyd and Jasper at once, both dodging a hurled candelabra. Adrian grasped the situation immediately. Both men had obviously tried to oppose the dark cloud and their insolence was being neatly rewarded. But where was Muriel?

His mind connected with hers at once. From inside the avenging cloud she called to his mind. *Save Janice. It wants Janice.* Beside Adrian, a portrait skidded across the floor wreathed in flames. He side-stepped its path with a lumbering hop. Before his eyes, the dark swirl of lights turned opaque, revealing Muriel's dainty features and plump body.

Adrian heard a gasp from beside him and barely managed to hold onto Janice as she made to rush past him. She had every intention of helping Muriel and he couldn't let her. To do so meant instant death for her.

"Let me go," she hissed, struggling against his stranglehold. "I can save her. I know who holds her prisoner."

"You can't save her," Adrian growled, "she's beyond help."

"Not yet. I know who holds her and what she wants." To Adrian's amazement, Janice called out to the swirling transparency. "I'm here, Simone. It's me, Izzy."

Beside Adrian, another fiery portrait careened and skidded. Another harp string twanged from its confine. The dark cloud mushroomed outward and moved forward, bringing Muriel's captive form with it. It swirled toward Janice, and Adrian pitched himself in front of her. A reedy laugh burst from the central core of the cloud. Muriel's lips began to twitch.

"And still the man thinks to protect the woman from me. You cannot. She will sacrifice herself for the woman I hold prisoner. Do you not see that?"

Adrian did see that. He also saw clearly that Janice's sacrifice would be useless. If Muriel was not already dead, she was nearing it. Her body was nothing more than a puppet for the dark mass to threaten them with. Adrian scoffed openly.

"What I see is a spirit so cowardly, it preys on old women because it does not have the courage to drain the life from strong ones." He spoke contemptuously, hoping to gall the spirit's vanity. The spirit he was facing down had once been a beautiful woman consumed with jealousy. She had desired the baron for her own and Lisette had gotten in the way. Adrian felt a sudden spasm of relief wash over him at the knowledge. If, after all these years, she still clung to that jealousy, he could bring her down. Her vanity was the key.

A vase hurled itself from the side bar at Adrian's head. He and Janice both ducked, the porcelain whizzing past their heads and crashing to the floor with a huge splatter. It was clear by the misdirected impact the cloud was confused by his verbal attack. His mind connected again with Muriel's. Though barely alive, she was mixing his thoughts with the cloud's, infusing it with the disturbing, erotic image Adrian had seen once before across the rim of a shattered glass. Now, Adrian saw it in full, understood it in full. Legs intertwined, Janice's body vibrated with liquid fire under his steady thrusts of possession. With each deepening thrust, Lisette's soul was being set free. Adrian pulled his mind from the image, determined to show no sign of relenting.

"I wanted the woman and I took her," Adrian stated. "You are too late."

At his words, a keening wail spiraled from the cloud.

"You lie! The woman hates you. She would never submit to you."

"She had no choice. I forced her." Adrian swung about, seeking Janice's wrist. He prayed God would forgive him for what he was about to do. Grabbing her swollen arm, he held it up to the shimmering spirit, ignoring Janice's tortured outcry. "See for yourself. Her wrist broke in the struggle."

A mewling wail whimpered and Adrian knew the spirit was confused by the swollen proof.

"I will hear it from the woman's own lips."

Adrian stepped into Janice at once. He knew she was angry with him. He could sense the fury behind her tears of pain as she opened her mouth to seal his doom with the cloud. He edged closer, lowering his voice.

"You tell her the truth and you will have killed Muriel as surely as if you took a knife and plunged it through her heart."

His threat stung and Adrian saw Janice's mouth snap shut. Her gaze scoured his face.

"You've touched minds with her and the cloud. I can sense it." A frown saturated her brow. "Muriel's dying, isn't she?"

The question was frank and Adrian answered with a ring of finality. "Yes, I think so."

"You arrogant sod," Janice stated simply.

The air around their heads crackled and a last fiery portrait sledded by their toes, startling them both. Janice whirled, studying the transparent cloud. Adrian didn't think he would ever forget a single detail of her face as she cloaked her feelings and challenged the spirit with deceptive calm.

"I resisted. He broke my wrist and then he took me. You are too late. Lisette's soul is free."

A terrible, keening moan sprang from the cloud and Muriel's lips. Beneath their feet, the floor shook with the cloud's fury. Turning dark again, the cloud shielded Muriel from their sight.

Willfully, it began to spin once more, whirling like a tornado and sending an intense level of noise from its central core. Hateful words were hurled at the group, bouncing off the gallery walls and sounding like the desecration of a temple. Next to him, Janice covered her ears in self-defense.

Soon, the voice became many, hideous in pitch and suddenly there was only a single laugh and the laugh became a soft ghost thing in the distance. The swirling lights gave one last flash and then vanished abruptly, leaving Muriel to crumple like a tossed away rag doll.

The men dashed across the space in an attempt to catch her up. Jasper was there first, lowering her into the cradle of his arms. Janice fell to her knees, placing her good hand lightly on her chest.

"Muriel!" The call was urgent and Adrian felt his heart skip a beat as Muriel's eyelids flickered open at the call.

"Out of danger?" she asked, breathlessly. Her eyes transferred from Janice to Jasper. "Out of danger?"

Before he could respond, her eyelids flickered down again and Adrian knew she was fighting with her very last breath to stay alive long enough to hear his answer. Jasper reached out and stroked her cheek.

"Out of danger, Muree," he answered.

Her nod was barely discernible and Adrian swallowed a rising lump in his throat.

"Fight, Muriel," Janice pleaded, tapping her chest. "Fight to stay with us."

Muriel's eyes flickered open again and settled on Janice's face.

"It's no use, dear," she murmured. "My lungs . . . are gone, and I feel . . . a great pull. There is somewhere . . . I must go."

Janice shook her head vigorously, refusing to let her give up.

"I know you can fight through it if you just try. Please try!"

A hand covered hers rapidly and Adrian heard a smothered sob escape Janice's lips.

"No tears," Muriel urged. She lost her breath and then gathered it again. "I anticipate . . . . it will be a great adventure where I'm going." Her gaze drifted left, found Jasper's bright stare.

Taking a deep breath, she gathered the last of her energy. "I love you . . . Jasper. Have I told you that . . . today?"

He took hold of her hand and squeezed it firmly.

"It was said in every glance you gave me, Muree."

"I'll wait for you . . . Jasper."

"I'll find you," he stated earnestly. Bending his head, he planted a light kiss on her lips. A light wheeze trickled from between her lips.

"Your kiss always could . . . take my . . . breath away." Her lids slipped down over her eyes and, giving a small pleasant sigh, she stopped breathing. In his mind, Adrian felt a brief piercing and knew Muriel's spirit was wishing them all a last farewell. Beside him, Janice broke down sobbing. Lloyd's arm came around her, sharing her pain and offering her comfort.

Feeling her anguish, Adrian felt his own gaze cloud with tears. Swiftly, he forced himself to look away, too moved by Jasper's careful gathering of the still figure into his arms.

Searching the balcony window across the way, Adrian saw that the red, dazzling glow had fled. In its place, a dark cowl of blackness again. He gave a choked, nearly hysterical laugh as he caught sight of the rounded moon. It seemed bent on scurrying from one dark cloud to another. The darkness pressed down on him and he gave another desperate laugh. History did indeed repeat itself. A life for a life. Lisette was free and so were they, but at what cost?

Adrian closed his eyes, listening to Janice's soft weeping and knew that cost. In each of their chests, there was a hole where their hearts used to be. And as always, as in the past, death had come to surround him. He would have to be moving on again. It was a bitter pillow to swallow and he didn't know how he was going to make it go down.

A hand descended on his shoulder, cutting into his dour thoughts. Glancing up, he found Lloyd feebly gesturing. Turning to the window, Adrian spotted Janice's slender figure perched on the window sill, her gaze studying the night skyline.

Adrian clambered to his feet, responding to Lloyd's unspoken request at once. Six steps later, he was at the window, leaning against the opposite frame and studying the tiny black streaks of mascara staining Janice's cheeks. She ignored him purposely for a moment and then her gaze drifted to his face.

"Stay together, isn't that what you said, Adrian? Stay together and we'll all get out alive? Well, you were right all along. We should've stayed together rather than opening the door on a lot of old, black memories that should've stay buried."

Adrian folded his arms across his chest, his gaze sweeping her face.

"We can't go back and do it differently. So why agonize over it?"

She shot him a withering glance.

"Why? Because there were other options. Other choices!"

"None that mattered."

"God! I hate when you do that! You argue out of spite. I say black, you say white! Well, do me a favor, get out of my face! I can't stand the sight of you!"

Her gaze swiveled back to the skyline beyond the window and with deliberate coolness, she ignored him again. Chilled by her hostility, Adrian hoisted himself from the frame, drawing a step nearer.

"If it's any comfort to you, I can't stand the sight of myself either."

Turning on his heel, he strode away, sidestepping the mangled scraps of debris littering the gallery floor. Hearing his name, he ignored the summons and continued his trek to the door. Escaping into the hollowed-out corridor, he bent and began the arduous task of digging a pathway through the pile of rubble.

Chapter 28

SATURDAY—11:00 AM

Ignoring the noise and bustle of the milling work hands, Janice stood at the edge of the pier studying the gray, green gloom of water slapping against the wood pilings of the loading dock. Just beneath the rim of the surface, she could see a school of minnows darting to and fro, scooping up nourishing bits of algae hanging from the barnacles littering the posts. Watching their frenetic swish, she gave a sigh. She was as hungry for food as they seemed to be. However, she knew her stomach would balk if she put anything in it. Eating in her present mood was useless, as impossible as growing wings on her back and flying home to Aspen.

Sighing a second time, she let her gaze arc up leisurely, following the blinding dazzle of the sun's path on the churning sea, across to the web of inland coves. For a moment, she was content to let her mind scale the smooth shoreline, blocking out the distant crashing of waves against the craggy cliffs about her. She was going home and high time. Her nerves were shot.

Forcing herself to relax, she took a deep breath, inhaling the bitter sea air. The icy breeze kicking up was invigorating, chasing away the long hours of imprisonment. All that was left to do now was to board the ferry standing dockside. The sustained whine of idling engines droned through Janice's consciousness and she spun on her heels.

Hastily, she tuned into the hive of activity before her. The ANNIE B's departure was only moments away, the raucous laughter forgotten as the engrossed dockhands now struggled through the last stages of hauling in the mammoth towline. Had it been only yesterday she had stepped onto this pier for the first time? Yesterday, she had promised Captain Bowers she wouldn't spook any ghosts. Well, she had kept her word. She hadn't spooked them; they had spooked her.

As if pulled by a magnet, Janice found her gaze drifting upward to the roof top turrets barely visible above the surrounding seawall. Witchwood had beckoned her to cross an ocean and solve a three hundred year old mystery. Why had she been chosen? Her gaze slid to the prism of light cascading through the stained glass alongside the turrets. That answer would remain a mystery to her, at least in this lifetime.

Someone sharply called out her name, and Janice swung to see the figure striding the timbers toward her with a brief wave. In seconds, she found herself buried in Jasper's warm embrace. Laying her head on his chest, she remained silent, content to listen to the steady, strong beat of his heart through his overcoat. How was he able to maintain such a stalwart front with Muriel gone? He was a veritable fortress and she was a total wreck. His embrace became an affectionate bear hug and Janice heard his voice raise a notch to be heard over the din of work hands.

"You mustn't blame yourself, Janice," he soothed. "Simone took Muriel within seconds. Even I couldn't break the meld, though I tried."

"We should've stayed together," Janice mumbled, swallowing the growing lump in her throat. "Muriel would be alive if we had."

He pushed her from him and studied her face.

"Are you so vain as to think you were the only one in that house willing to sacrifice yourself for the others?"

Janice detected the subtle censure in his question. A contrite apology quickly formed on her lips.

"Jasper, I didn't mean . . ."

He cut her off with a tight squeeze.

"We were all faced with choices. You chose your path. Muree chose hers."

Janice buried her face once more into Jasper's chest, feeling the sting of tears caressing her lashes. Did he mean there was some good in Muriel's death?

"One wonderful soul reached out across time to us," he mused. "That soul asked for nothing more from us than compassion. We answered that summons, each in our own way. We connect so rarely with each other here on this earth, but for one brief instance, when it really mattered, we proved that all who have passed on still live and there is hope in the life beyond, for even the most sinful . . . little child, big soul," he finished confidently.

Janice reflected on his words, her throat tightening. The truth was so eloquently simple that she had missed it. Jasper was right. Last night had been horrendous but it had also affirmed life after death. It had been the beginning of a new identity. Giving a warm smile, she patted the front of Jasper's overcoat.

"Little child, big soul," she repeated.

"They're ready for you, Janice," Lloyd's voice cut through the space and Janice peered around Jasper's imposing form. "Your suitcase is on board and Dr. Graves has the hospital on standby for you."

"You're not coming with me, Lloyd?"

He shook his head slowly.

"No. The police aren't finished up at the house yet. Besides, my goodbye would only consist of begging your forgiveness." His quick look at her bandaged wrist had Janice murmuring softly.

"It's not anyone's fault, Lloyd. You know that."

"Yes, well, that doesn't make it any easier," he replied. He cleared his throat and signaled her again. "Captain Bowers doesn't like to be kept waiting."

Janice nodded and then held her hand out to Jasper.

"Will I see you in Aspen, Jasper?"

He clasped her fingers.

"In the summer. I'll bring the twins. We'll picnic at Hollow Lake."

"It's a deal," Janice replied. With a last toss of her head, she started down the walkway toward the gangplank. As she walked, she steeled herself against the one final goodbye she was dreading.

Adrian. Silently she prayed he was already on board—as eager to ignore her as she was to ignore him. She couldn't face a formal goodbye. If she did, she knew she'd break down, perhaps even blurt out she hadn't meant the hateful words she had hurled at him in the gallery. And that she couldn't stand. She had to break clean from the weekend. No matter what.

Glancing ahead, a suffocating sensation twisted her lungs. She wasn't going to be lucky. Adrian stood at the entrance ramp, Ginger by his side. They were awaiting her arrival, and for a moment, Janice slowed her steps. Then realizing how foolish she must appear, she picked up her gait again.

Rubbing her bandaged wrist nervously, Janice sensed the air of isolation that hung about Adrian's slouched shoulders. His black hair gleamed in the dazzling sunlight and she wondered if she would forever be haunted by his good looks. Haunted. She gave a shiver. Not the best word to use in the situation. Three steps from the ramp, Janice cast another prayer heavenward, asking for strength and pleading for Adrian to stay silent.

Toes touching the gangplank, Janice knew God didn't intend to make their parting easy. Adrian stepped forward, touching her coat sleeve tentatively.

"Janice, I . . . "

She didn't let him start. She cut him off in mid-word.

"Get away from me, Adrian. The sight of you makes me sick."

The words jarred him and, though he managed to pretend indifference, Janice knew she had wounded him to the quick. Gathering his dignity gallantly around him, he touched his forehead to her in a mock salute. In a flash, he had vaulted from the pier to the deck of the ferry, ignoring the small walkway. He disappeared quickly among the stacks of crates and packages and bodies and Janice felt a stab of guilt bury itself deep within her chest. That had been a mean thing to say. He hadn't deserved it. She hadn't realized she harbored such a cruel streak when it came to him. She wanted to hurt him thoroughly and she had. Janice felt no surprise when Ginger's thoughts echoed her own.

"Why didn't you just plunge a knife through his heart? It would've been kinder." Janice's gaze pierced the small distance between them. Ginger was angry with her, deeply angry. It showed in the purse of her lips. "That was *too* cruel," she emphasized when Janice remained simply staring at her.

"I know," Janice finally admitted, "but it had to be done."

For a moment, Janice thought Ginger would understand her reasoning but her next words were far from sympathetic.

"He cried over you, you know. Cold-hearted Adrian who never gives a damn about anybody but himself. He didn't think I saw him but I did. He loves you desperately but he doesn't know how to tell you."

Janice looked away. Dear God, how much more could she bear?

"He'll forget and go on," was all she could manage to mutter. Ginger moved away at once, stepping onto the ramp, and then as if having an afterthought, she turned back again.

"It shouldn't be so easy for people to throw love away."

Their eyes caught and held for a brief instant and then Ginger whirled, leaving Janice to climb the ramp alone. Alone. The word echoed in her mind and sternly mocked her. She'd have a lifetime of alone thanks to her runaway tongue.

Unexpected tears blocked her vision and Janice felt her toes hit the edge of the gangplank. Whoa, she cautioned herself. If she weren't careful, she'd be having more than her wrist fixed at the hospital. Slipping her toes back onto solid board, she hopped the last yards onto the lower promenade. Immediately, she crossed to the stairwell and wound her way to the second level promenade, coming to rest when she reached the aft guardrail. Seconds later, the lurching vibration of revving engines rattled the flooring beneath her feet and she knew the ANNIE B's departure was underway. A short horn blast confirmed the fact and with a stuttered creak, the ANNIE B scratched the wood pilings and began to backwater away from the mooring.

Leaning over the railing, Janice spotted Lloyd and Jasper, who exchanged a brief wave with her and then left the dock, striding from the pier to the cliff stairwell. Following their path, Janice's gaze shot ahead to the house at the top of the cliff wall. In time, she would heal and so would Adrian. Hadn't her father always said not to worry, that time was the wind that blew down the corridor slamming all the doors? Yes, but life had taught her that, once slammed, the door could never be reopened. Ginger was right. It shouldn't be so easy to throw love away.

Clinging to the rail, Janice closed her eyes. She had seen too much in the last twenty four hours, experienced too many painful scenes. And now she was going to face a lightless future without Adrian. Or try to. Suddenly, Janice realized she was beyond pain and caring. From here on out, she would simply hang onto survival.

Chapter 29

SIX MONTHS LATER—MACEDONIA, MAINE

Lloyd studied the portrait before him. How many more nights would he find himself leaving the solace of his bedroom to stand before the canvas? For six months, the painting had haunted him. For six months, he had awakened from deep sleep only to seek out the portrait. He didn't think it had anything special to impart to him. No, all that needed to be said was etched in the lines of the loving couple portrayed. Lisette had found freedom at last—in the arms of her true love. It was there in the excited light of her eyes and the shared embrace. Lloyd could almost feel the baron's uneven breathing on Lisette's cheek as he held her close. He could almost feel the tangible bond between them. The invisible heat of attraction they shared.

A creak on the floor board signaled a new visitor to the room.

"Have I disturbed you again, Dora?" he asked, swinging his gaze to find the woman in question plowing across the room toward him. Her sniff was dutiful as she reached him and a glass was shoved into his hand proving it.

"Warm milk. It will make you sleep," she stated tartly.

Lloyd hid a smile at the matronly cosseting. He took a quick sip of the liquid.

"You're a prig, Dora. Have I ever told you that?"

"At least six times a day. Don't make no matter to me. You don't mean it. It's just your way."

Lloyd swatted the thin line of white coating his upper lip.

"Yes, it's my way."

Dora scanned the portrait before them.

"You never did tell me which room you found this beautiful, old portrait in," she commented.

"Don't remember," Lloyd evaded.

Her tell-tale sniff boomed again and Lloyd suddenly grinned as her ample bosom twisted toward him.

"You're too young to have bats in your belfry, Lloyd Marks! Of course you remember. You just don't choose to tell me."

Lloyd let out a boyish laugh and then drained the remaining swirl of milk. He loved nothing better than making Dora squirm with curiosity. Flinging out his free arm, he tossed it carelessly across her shoulders and spun them both around.

"I have told you the truth, Dora, plenty of times. The portrait was left by a ghost."

She wrenched away from him, throwing her head back and placing her hand on her hips in defiance.

"Still standing by that story, are you? Well, you may have fooled everyone else around here with that mumbo-jumbo, but I'm not fooled. You found that painting in the old wing. Plain as the nose on my face! Ghosts that leave pictures indeed! Fairy tale mush!"

Lloyd laughed again, scooping her fingers from her hips and depositing the empty glass into her palm. Quickly, he placed his hands on the small of her back and nudged her forward.

"I never could fool you one bit, could I, Dora? You're absolutely right. I found the painting in the old wing attic."

"Just so," she commented, sailing out the door in front of him.

Stopping at the light switch, Lloyd cast a backward glance at the portrait. "Boy meets girl. Boy loses girl. Boy gets girl back. The very best of fairy tale endings, eh, Dora?"

Her fractured snort said it all.

"Bats in the belfry, that's what!"

Lloyd flicked the light switch, giving a wry smile. No, not bats, ghosts. Ghosts in the belfry.

Chapter 30

SIX MONTHS LATER—MADSEN, OHIO

The rectory door clanged shut on its hinges and Jasper gave a small sigh of relief. The last of the congregation had finally dispersed and he had the rest of his Sunday all to himself. What to do first? Easy. He'd call the twins and finalize their travel plans to Aspen. Decide which of them would pick up and pay for the tickets.

For some inexplicable reason, Jasper felt an unexpected surge of excitement at the prospect of seeing Janice Kelly again. He didn't know why he should. It wasn't as if they hadn't talked. They had talked incessantly over the last six months, each swapping stories of their childrens' busy lives. He was lucky, he knew. Lucky to have her for a friend. Her frequent calls to the rectory had sustained him in his first, lonely months without Muriel.

Adrian had called at first, too, offered support, but over the last two months, the calls had dwindled and finally stopped. Had Adrian's world taken a further downward spiral? He thought so. Should he invade Adrian's time-line and check on his health? No, that would be an invasion, an intrusion of his soul. Better to offer up a prayer of encouragement instead.

Strolling up the aisle, he did so, and then selfishly he added a second prayer, one of matchmaking. Janice and Adrian belonged together, like he and Muriel—he'd stake his collar on it. There had to be a way to bring them together. He'd think on it. He'd pray on it. And in a moment of quiet thought, he'd slip his mind away and ask Muriel's opinion on it. Muree! Funny, how effortlessly his thoughts flew to her these days. And funny, how he had always thought death would part them forever. It hadn't. She was still here, sharing parts of his everyday life.

Jasper's eye caught the cross etched in the stained glass window above the altar mantle. For a moment, he studied the bank of rainbow prisms. She hadn't left him, not his Muree. She was always there, just around the corners of his mind. And she listened. And she believed in him. She always would.

Making a hasty sign of the cross and a half-genuflect, he started up the altar steps to the sacristy, disrobing as he went. Passing beneath the stained glass etching, he sent up a small hello to Muriel. A moment later, the air stirred above his head and Jasper smiled knowingly. That was his Muree. She never could let him have the last word on anything.

Chapter 31

SIX MONTHS LATER—LAS VEGAS, NEVADA

"God damn it, Adrian, how can you live like this?"

The question was edged with apparent disgust and Adrian winced as the overhead light snapped on, interrupting his melancholy brooding. The glaring light filled the room and instantly set up his hackles. He wished Todd would go to hell. And if he didn't know how to get there, he'd damn well tell him how. Was it daybreak already?

Eyeballs smarting from lack of sleep, Adrian shaded his lids, but he knew the motion was more a reflex action to keep Todd from seeing the haggard, desolate light in his eyes. He heard approaching footsteps on the carpet and then caught sight of familiar patent and leather shoe tips. A second later, Todd's snarl rolled contemptuously over him.

"Jesus, Adrian! You look frigging anorexic!"

"And a gracious good morning to you, too." Adrian cajoled sweetly. He thought his cool response disguised his simmering rage adequately.

"As if it were morning!" Todd snorted. The shoe tips disappeared from view and Adrian lifted his head, following Todd's path to the dining room table. Once there, his friend deposited an assortment of letters and a small package on the tabletop. "It's ten o'clock at night, if that means anything to you," he stated, sarcastically.

Tucking himself deeper into the chair, Adrian ignored the barb and went back to his brooding. Or tried to. Todd's repeated oaths as he snatched up discarded clothing from the floor kept Adrian from fully concentrating on his melancholy. Soon, the shoe tips appeared in his line of vision again.

"Jesus, Adrian, why don't you just blow your brains out and be done with it?"

"Go away, Todd," Adrian snarled, nastily.

When the shoe tips remained, Adrian lifted his head. A second later, he was glad that he had. If he hadn't, the circle of keys heading for his face might've done some major damage to his right eye. He dodged the attack, deflecting the keys away with a swat. They ricocheted off the back of the chair and dropped to the carpet with barely a sound.

"You'd like that, wouldn't you?" Todd growled at him. "You'd like to be left alone to rot." Adrian offered no comment, trying to keep a lid on his simmering temper. "How long since you ate anything?" The question was so unexpected and asked with such real concern, Adrian tried to answer it. He couldn't remember how long, so he hedged.

"A couple of days."

"You want something now?"

"No." The syllable was more swallowed than spoken.

"Jesus, Adrian, if you're this crazy in love with the woman, go tell her. If she's all the things Ginger says she is, she won't turn you away."

"Screw Ginger!"

A chiding growl reverberated around his head and Adrian knew he was straining his friendship with Todd to the max.

"That's nice talk," Todd replied. "Did you learn that from the baron?"

"Fuck you!"

"Ah, that's better. Now, will you call the woman and ask her to marry you or shall I?" Adrian made no comment, choosing to let a cold silence become his answer. "She lives in Aspen, right?"

Todd moved away, striding toward the desk phone. Adrian was out of his chair in a flash, barreling after his receding back. He'd tear the son of bitch's heart out. See if he didn't.

He wasn't quite fast enough though, or else Todd sensed his

coming, but Adrian found himself plowing into Todd's chest and bouncing off it as he whirled about. Feet planted firmly, fists clenched, they stood glaring at one another, each silently daring the other. Suddenly, Todd's face split into a lopsided grin.

"My God, you fucker, you're scared! You're afraid she'll turn you down." He snorted out a laugh and Adrian knew the snort was one of pure glee. He fought down an impulse to ram his fist through the nearest object.

"Of course, she'll turn me down," he snapped. "She should. I broke her wrist, raped her!"

Todd's grin died instantly.

"Neither of you knows that for sure. You were both caught up in some damn fugue. Why are you putting yourself through this hell?"

Why? He couldn't do anything else, Adrian knew.

"You'll never understand, Todd," he quipped, suddenly deflating. Just as suddenly, he realized how sick in mind and body he had become. He drifted to the window and opened the shades. A glittering array of marquee lights lit the night skyline. He stared at the crowd of passers-by walking the strip. Todd thought he felt guilty. He didn't. No, the pain stemmed from his inability to remember what making love to Janice had been like. He had had one shot at loving her and he didn't remember it and the knowledge gnawed at him like a cancer. He hoped he had been a giving lover, riding the currents of desire clear to the top, finally exploding in simultaneous fulfillment? He hoped her face had glowed in the aftermath of climax and she had whispered she loved him. He hoped . . . *that's an awful lot of hopes, Adrian, old buddy.*

Adrian felt a light touch on his shoulder but didn't turn.

"I do understand, Adrian. And for what it's worth, I believe that making love was a mutual consent—for both of you. Forget your damn pride. Fly to Aspen and talk to Janice. Get down on your knees if you have to and beg her to marry you. Better yet, camp on her doorstep till she says yes."

"It's not that easy, Todd. She's got a daughter."

"For Christ's sake! You're a frigging magician! Kids are crazy about magicians. Everyone knows that."

For the first time in months, Adrian found himself grinning. Todd was a sappy son of a bitch—a true closet romantic. Hiding his grin, Adrian turned from the window and gave Todd a brief nod.

"I'll think on it."

"And that's all you'll ever do on it," Todd replied in disgust. He spun on his heel and strode back to the table. Snatching up a banded stack of papers, he began to riffle through them one by one. "Jesus! How long since you answered mail or paid any bills?"

"Two . . . three months."

Todd gave a soulful sigh.

"More like four or five. You better come take a look at these and tell me what needs paying. I'm assuming you're not ready to work again?"

"No!" Adrian's snarl was loud and emphatic.

"Okay, okay. Simmer down. I'll call Jilly and tell her to turn down the Stardust offer."

Adrian grunted, whirling from the window and joining Todd at the table. Flipping through a second banded stack, his heart plummeted. There was an appalling number of e-mails. Was he that popular with audiences? Did they miss his performances that much?

Resigned to the fact that perhaps they did, Adrian sat down and glanced at the first e-mail. He read a few words and then pitched it. A second followed the first, then a third. Perusing the fourth, his scowl became fierce. Damn teeny boppers. Nothing but stage door groupies and star wannabes writing him. Were they the only ones enamored of him? Didn't anyone his own age enjoy his performances? He picked up another sheet, read a few lines, and pitched it.

"Well, I'll be fucked!"

Adrian glanced up, surprised by Todd's vehement curse. He

found Todd staring at him, a curious light in his eyes.

"This one's from Aspen," he announced. He raised a small envelope and Adrian saw him take a quick sniff of the edges. "Definitely feminine."

Adrian's heart began a wild foot race with his stomach and he chided himself for reacting like a lovesick fool. Janice wouldn't write him. She hated him with a passion. No, there were loads of people living in Aspen who considered themselves his fans. This letter was from one of them.

"Guess we can toss this one," Todd said briskly. He pitched the envelope into the garbage can alongside the table.

Adrian came out of his chair with a fevered curse.

"God dammit, Todd, what the fuck do you think you're doing?"

"Oh, did you want to read that one?" he remarked casually. Adrian bolted around the table and fished the envelope from the trash. "Sorry, thought any correspondence from Aspen was garbage."

"You've shit for brains," Adrian mumbled. He studied the handwriting and return address. What had prompted her to write to him after all these months? Hadn't everything been said that day on the pier? Was she having second thoughts about that day? Sending him an apology? No, he couldn't be that lucky. The stars would fall out of the sky before an apology would be issued from her lips. She hated him. He sank back in his chair, ignoring Todd's piercing stare. Slashing the envelope open, he read the colorful missive enclosed once, then reread it a second time.

"Sweet Jesus!"

Todd leaned in, closing the gap between them.

"What is it, Adrian?"

Adrian passed the card to Todd, not at all surprised to hear an astonished whistle leave his lips a second later. The card fluttered to the table in front of him and Adrian plucked at it absently. What did he do now? Beside him, Todd leaned back in his chair, blowing through his cheeks.

"Jesus, Adrian, I'm sorry."

"Are you?"

Stunned by the question, Todd shot upright in the chair. He exchanged a quick glance with Adrian and then, all of a sudden, both began to laugh uproariously.

Chapter 32

SIX MONTHS LATER—ASPEN, COLORADO

The sound of doorbells chiming filtered through Janice's consciousness and she stopped painting. Beyond the doorway, she heard the patter of tiny footsteps on the hall carpet. She lifted her head in expectation, her eyes glued to the doorway. As she thought, a flash of blue jeans streaked by at a reckless pace, heading for the staircase. Janice's mouth tilted upward as she listened to the tiny thumps on the carpeted steps. Sarah was off to answer the front door again, the little minx. She supposed she should stop her. Over the last several months, she had grown impossible about answering the door. When the chimes sounded, she responded. If she was upstairs, she ran down. If she was outside, she ran in.

Janice frowned suddenly. Should she be worried about her behavior? Her actions were amusing, and so far she had chalked the behavior up to just that. But now her habit seemed off-kilter. Was Sarah's preoccupation with answering the front door a delayed reaction to Jimmy's non-presence?

Looking back at the recent months in her mind's eye, it dawned on Janice that Sarah was answering the door as if she was expecting someone. Why hadn't she seen it before? Sarah was obviously sure someone was coming to visit. But whom? Janice tossed her paintbrush into the fresh jar of water beside her easel, grimacing at the resulting blue-green tint. Sarah couldn't be expecting her father. She had said as much.

"Are you still painting?"

Janice jumped, startled by the question. Her glance slid to the doorway once more. Seeing her sister's plump form, she hid a smile. Nine months pregnant and all stomach, she surmised. If

245

Bibi didn't have the baby soon, they'd have to take to calling her the Pillsbury Dough Boy. Janice's smile snaked its way out.

"All finished." She dropped her palette onto the makeshift worktable by the easel and sighed. "It's finally done. Come see."

Bibi sped to the easel, her eagerness showing in her hurried waddle. Coming to a halt in front of the finished portrait, she drew in a sharp breath.

"It's the best thing you've ever done, Jan," she said sincerely.

Janice's gaze traveled to the finished colors. Yes, she thought so, too. It was the best thing she had ever painted. But then, she thought, why shouldn't it be? The painting had come from the depths of her soul.

"Jasper will love it," Bibi said quietly.

Janice studied the faces and figures depicted.

"I'm going to call it *Across Time*. What do you think?"

Bibi cocked her head left, then right.

"Yes, I see that." She turned from the painting and gave Janice a knowing smile. "You're not quite over that experience yet, are you?"

Janice hid a smile. You're not quite over Adrian yet, are you? That's what her sister really meant. Grinning suddenly, Janice stroked her protruding stomach.

"Ask me that again after the baby's born."

Bibi gave a stuttered groan and sought a resting place along the edge of the bed.

"Honestly, Jan, I hate you. I'm as big as a house. And you're simply rounded."

Janice caressed her protruding stomach.

"He may be small, but he's an active little thing. For the last two days, he's done nothing but kick at me. I think he wants out."

Bibi tossed her a reassuring smile.

"You're sure he's a he?"

Janice chewed on that thought for a moment. Yes, she was sure. She had had a brief flash in the early days. Not enough to see clearly. But she had sensed that the life growing within her was definitely a male child. She grimaced at the direction of her thoughts. What was wrong with her? She had the urge to blame Adrian for wishing a boy on her, when she would've liked her next child to be a carbon copy of Sarah. As always, Adrian had had the last joke on her. If he wasn't going to be around to provoke her, he was going to annoy the hell out of her with a Mini Me of himself. A perfect mirror image that she would have to look at every day. Year in and year out.

Pulling her thoughts back sharply, Janice realized she was being stupid. Adrian didn't even know about the baby, much less determine its gender. Meeting Bibi's curious stare, she realized her sister was still waiting for an answer.

"He's a he," she stressed confidently.

Her sister grinned.

"Boys are nice."

Janice started to agree, but lost her train of thought as Sarah raced into the room, screeching her name.

"Mama! Look! I knew it would come. I knew it wasn't lost forever."

"What is it, sweetie? What's come?"

Sarah barreled into her knees, stretching her tiny hand up to Janice.

"See, Mama, your compass."

Staring at the plastic circle cupped in the tiny palm, Janice's heart did a rapid flip-flop and the air in her lungs seemed to evaporate as if sucked out through a straw. Her compass! Reluctantly, she took the round circle from Sarah's proffered hand, trying to keep her voice steady as she did so.

"Sarah, sweetie, where did you find this?"

"The magician found it." She began a light hopscotch from one foot to the other and Janice's pulse skittered in alarm. Her hand flew to her throat and for a second she thought she was going to pass out. She studied Sarah's nimble hopping and then found herself stuttering stupidly.

"Magician? Here?!"

"Uh-huh. He's downstairs with Uncle Roddy. He's very handsome, Mama."

Janice's hands flew to her mouth. Adrian here! But how and why? A flash of white began to move across her line of vision and spinning, Sarah spotted Bibi edging her way to the door, a notorious crimson flush staining her cheeks.

"Don't you dare move another step!" she commanded. Quickly, she returned her attention to Sarah and lightened her tone. "Sarah, sweetie, you know how when guests come to our house we're good hosts? How we offer them something to drink?"

"Uh-huh."

"Well, I need you to be a good hostess right now and offer the magician some of your lemonade."

She didn't wait for Janice to finish the sentence. She exploded into a clumsy pirouette and bolted from the room, hollering for Peter as she ran. Sighing heavily, Janice gathered her strength and spun to confront Bibi. Her words were heated.

"You sent for him? After I expressly forbid you to?"

Bibi gave a mock shrug.

"I didn't send for him," she hedged, "I promised you I wouldn't."

"Well, then, why is he here? He wouldn't come without a reason." That there was a reason was clear by Bibi's awkward rocking. "You called him?" Janice asked in disbelief.

"No. I didn't call him."

Janice's eyes narrowed suspiciously.

"Just what did you do, Bibi?"

This time her sister had the good sense to cringe and Janice was glad she did because otherwise she was sure she would have launched her entire set of paintbrushes at her.

"I sent him an invitation to the baby shower," Bibi murmured softly.

Janice let out an astonished screech, surprising herself as much as startling Bibi, who shied away quickly.

"You told him about the baby! After I said you were not to?!"

"He has a right to know he's going to be a father."

"I was going to tell him," Janice snapped, "but in my own way."

"When? When the kid's going off to college?"

"That's a rotten thing to say and you know it! I had every intention of telling Adrian about the baby."

"Is this a private fight or can anyone join?"

"Adrian!"

The words were stuttered in panic as Janice swung about. His tall figure lounged against the doorframe and Janice found herself magnetized by the sight of him. Lord, he was gorgeous.

Thin, but still gorgeous. With the lift of his eyebrow, he scanned her stricken features. Immediately, Janice felt a rush of color to her cheeks.

"Well, at least saying my name no longer makes you sick," he said quietly. "I would hate to think I made a pregnant woman nauseous." Janice flushed again, stung by his sarcasm. What a memory he had. He was throwing her last words to him up in her face. "You look good, Janice. Very good." Janice felt herself coloring up even more furiously. He wasn't going to make this reunion easy. His gaze darted quickly left and Janice saw him study her sister intently. "You must be Bibi. I gather I have you to thank for the invitation?" She didn't reply or nod, speechless by the turn of events. If the whole situation weren't so preposterous, Janice thought she would laugh. She regretted the thought in the next instant as Adrian signaled to Bibi politely. "I'm sure there's something you want to do downstairs." Janice heard the emphasis on "downstairs" and knew the words weren't a request.

A flash of relief crossed Bibi's face at the edict and, seizing the opportunity, she bustled forward. As she reached the doorway, Adrian stepped aside, giving way to her stoutness. His lips curled up derisively as she sped out onto the landing.

Her departure left a void of silence behind that neither seemed to know how to fill. Flustered, Janice tried to think of something appropriate to say besides the obvious Hello. In the next second, Adrian had saved her the trouble and worry.

"Aren't you going to ask me how I am?"

Though his caustic reminder shook her up, Janice managed to look him directly in the eye.

"How are you, Adrian? You look thin."

"I've been sick," was his instant answer and Janice immediately regretted the question. He made it sound as if his illness was her fault. Was that true? Janice began to twist her fingers nervously. The gesture made her even more self-conscious.

"Are you getting better?" she managed to ask, then wondered how she could be firing off such inane questions when her only urge was to fling herself into his arms and beg his forgiveness. He made no comment, just stared.

Biting her lower lip to keep it from quivering, Janice wondered how she had ever thought she would forget him so easily. Even for all his thinness, he was devastatingly handsome. The sight of him was slowly draining the air from her lungs and causing her heart to flutter nervously in her breast. And now he was lifting an eyebrow curiously at her. Was that nervousness she sensed? His next words confirmed it.

"My health depends on you, Janice." She didn't like the sound of that. "Rather, it depends on whether I can convince you in the next minute to let me kiss you."

Janice's mouth dropped open in surprise. God, he wasn't going to start this foolishness all over again about kissing, was he? She couldn't bear it if he did. She had to distract his mind. But how? Out of the corner of her eye, she spied the standing easel and spun toward it. She knew instantly she had guessed right. He sprang from the doorframe and followed close on her heels.

Halting before the painting, Janice could only hope that the beauty of the portrait and its subjects would catch his fancy. It did.

He came to a halt beside her, his gaze riveted to the figures depicted.

"Do you like it?" she asked hesitantly. She stole a peek at him, realizing his answer meant the difference between pain and pleasure.

"Very much," he replied, no trace of sarcasm lacing his voice. Janice breathed a sigh of relief. "Are you planning on selling it?" The question was so unexpected, it overwhelmed Janice. Was he thinking of buying it?

"No, it's a present for Jasper. He's coming to visit next month with the twins."

At her pronouncement, Adrian's head snapped around and studied her face, as if memorizing it. For one thrilling moment, Janice felt her heart stop. He was going to kiss her and she was going to let him. He knew it and she knew it. Disturbed by the smoldering desire rising in his eyes, Janice found herself spinning around. Dear God, she couldn't kiss Adrian. If she did it would be all over. She'd end up married to him.

The feel of warm arms encircling her waist from behind startled her, but she didn't pull away. Instead, she looked down at the long slim fingers lightly resting on the top of her stomach. A warm breath tickled her ear as he muttered hoarsely.

"Don't send me away, Janice. I can't eat. I can't sleep. I can't work. I can't even concentrate. Your image haunts me more than it ever did when I was a boy. Please tell me you didn't mind what happened between us. Tell me you'll love this baby because I'm its father." He paused to catch his breath and Janice took a moment to interrupt.

"Adrian . . ."

He cut her off immediately.

"No, don't say it. Don't say it can't work out. It can. I know it can. If it's Sarah, I'll win her over. I'm not so hard to take, am I? No, don't answer that . . ." He must've realized he might get an answer he didn't want to hear because he released Janice's waist and spun her around so fast she had to clutch onto his shoulders to keep from falling. Again, their gazes met and held. This time

Janice saw him grin sheepishly. "At least, let me kiss you. I know if you let me kiss you, I can prove to you how crazy I am about you. I have great lips."

Janice's lips twitched with a will of their own at his arrogant bragging. He was being boyishly charming, and a charming Adrian was a deadly Adrian. She shook her head.

"Every time you kiss me, Adrian, some part of my anatomy seems to swell up."

He caught the sly reference at once, and chuckling, hauled her into his arms. His lips swooped down and devoured hers swiftly. It was a long, drugging kiss and the assault sent a shockwave clear to the tips of Janice's toes. Her knees suddenly gave way, turning to jelly, and she found herself collapsing into his chest. He absorbed her weight easily with his own and all lucid thought fled from her brain as his tongue swept the roof of her mouth. And then, just as if it seemed the kiss would never end, he let go her mouth. Janice managed a breathless choke. He raised her chin upward and then his fingers found their way to her mouth. Suggestively, he outlined the curve of her moist lower lip.

"Told you I could prove it," he whispered arrogantly.

Before she could object, his mouth covered hers again hungrily. Swept away, Janice's arms automatically wound around his neck. He was right, damn him. He did have great lips.

A sudden screech split the air.

"Aunt Bibi! Come look! Mama's kissing the magician!"

Adrian twisted free of Janice's lips and turned toward the door. A flash of blue jean streaked from the room at a breakneck pace.

"She's a lively chatterbox."

Janice dropped her forehead onto Adrian's chest, sighing pleasurably.

"She's a notorious tattletale. We'll have no secrets." She lifted her chin and nuzzled into his throat. His knuckles found the side of her cheekbone and caressed it affectionately. Her sigh resembled a delighted purr and Adrian chuckled again, taking hold of her chin. With a ragged breath, he planted a kiss on each side of her lips and then along her cheekbones.

"I have dreamed this moment a thousand times in my head. How I would kiss you . . . make love to you . . . " His lips found her earlobe. "Say you forgive me, Janice. I'd give everything I own to go back and relive that night. Change things. Keep Muriel alive. You've got to believe me."

Janice pulled away, meeting his tortured gaze. Did he still think she blamed him for Muriel's death? Standing on tiptoe, she brushed her lips lightly across his.

"None of that matters now, Adrian. Honestly."

He tugged on her waist, drawing her back into his embrace.

"You smell heavenly. Come kiss me."

She responded to his words, melding her body into his. A secret smile softened her lips.

"Je suis ici, mon ami."

He gave her a lop-sided grin and dipped his head.

"Vous parle Français trés bien, mademoiselle."

Inhaling sharply, Janice pulled back again. A curious glint entered her eyes.

"A gift from the baron," he replied, quickly.

Grabbing the back of his head, she pulled his face toward her.

"C'mere. Let me show you a little something the baron taught me."

Adrian grinned boyishly.

"I've a better idea. Let me show you a little something the baron showed Lisette."

A minute later, Janice knew what it was to be thoroughly kissed.

About the Author

Rachel James is a lifelong reader of romance and has been writing romance since the age of thirteen. She spent many decades in theater and film (both off-stage and on) and holds an Associate Arts Degree in Music. Besides being a prolific writer, she is a Spiritual Guidance Counselor who coaches clients via the Metaphysical Arts. She currently resides in South Florida.

In the mood for more Crimson Romance? Check out *The Luminary* by Elle J Rossi at *CrimsonRomance.com*.

www.ingramcontent.com/pod-product-compliance
Lightning Source LLC
Chambersburg PA
CBHW010634100726
47900CB00011B/2829